PRAISE FOR T[illegible] DUOLOGY

A convoluted plot, excellent worldbuilding, and relentless suspense. . . . This is a stunner.

— THE PRAIRIES REVIEW

Engrossing and atmospheric.

— READERS' FAVORITE (AWARD WINNER)

An admirable heroine and a chilling premise.

— KIRKUS REVIEWS

An irresistible story.

— BLUEINK REVIEW (STARRED REVIEW)

A dynamic sci-fi thriller.

— BOOKLIFE REVIEWS

Stellar writing and thrilling plot twists.

— JORDAN ROSENTHAL, AUTHOR OF *HOW TO WRITE A PAGE TURNER*

I live in Medford Lakes. There are four books in this series — with Book 5 on the way. This is Book 2. If you don't see Book 1 "They Will Be Coming For Us" in this little library, please check the others — I'll leave several around town. Please leave a review on Goodreads or Amazon if you enjoy this book! Thank you ♡

JOVIAN SON

KIM CATANZARITE

forster publishing
A LUCY H SOCIETY BOOK

This is a work of fiction. Names, characters, organizations, places, events, and incidents are either products of the author's imagination or used fictitiously. Any resemblance to actual persons, living or dead, or actual events is purely coincidental.

ISBN 978-1-7359522-3-9 (paperback)

ISBN 978-1-7359522-2-2 (ebook)

Printed in the United States of America

1 3 5 7 9 10 8 6 4 2

Published by Lucy H Society Books, an imprint of Forster Publishing, United States of America. Distributed by Ingram Book Group, www.ingramcontent.com.

Editor: Tricia LaRochelle

Cover Design: Damonza

❀ Created with Vellum

For my family

“There is no time to wait for Darwinian evolution to make us more intelligent and better natured.”

— STEPHEN HAWKING

JOVIAN SON

1

If they only knew. These Russian girls who flit around my son with stars in their eyes, with their straight-legged jeans and belted suede coats, their thoughts of sex and dating and maybe even marital bliss written all over their optimistic faces. Poor, naïve adolescents with their lips painted purple or pomegranate, wishing they were older, more experienced, prettier—or whatever it is young women these days wish for when in the company of attractive young men.

I can't blame them for showing interest. There's no doubt Evander is special. He's not your usual eighteen- or twenty-year-old, and not only because we moved here from America. He's tall, for one. He has a nice face with the kind eyes of my late husband and a calm, unwavering disposition. He laughs easily, as if there is nothing to worry about, as if we've never had anything to worry about. He's sweet and smart and funny, and I don't say these things just because I am his mother.

I'm standing on the sidewalk next to a busy park stretched wide in the center of Metka. It's the usual

December cold, but that doesn't stop Russians from coming out. People of all ages play here after school, gather with friends, stroll the path that parallels its perimeter.

The nearby town of Tula, where Evander and I live, is too small for a park of this size. Tula is poor by most standards. Even by Russian standards. Evander is big, as I've said. Far too big for Tula. He needs to stretch his legs, which is why he enjoys a walk to Metka on most days. It's "better," he says. There are neighborhoods here, some of them quite nice, and apartments, shops, schools. People he can talk to. *Girls* he can talk to. Today he has met three: the one who makes him smile and her two friends.

To find him surrounded by three girls is not surprising.

Evander can't go anywhere without drawing attention to himself. He collects wayward glances the way the pied piper collects children—not only from girls but from women. Probably even some men. People of all ages take an interest in him. He is what one calls "charismatic." In Russian, it's "*kharizmatichnyy*."

My Evander has a muscular build that's broad shouldered and lean, much like my husband, Andrew, would have been if he had been an athlete instead of a normal person with a nine-to-five job. I use the word *normal* loosely. Not much is normal when it comes to my husband's family, the Jovians. Evander is exceptional—or, as the Jovians liked to say, "marvelous." And that's why these girls hover around him in their high-heeled boots and long straightened hair. From the looks of their fashion and their book bags, they're secondary school students, probably "seniors," as we called them in America.

I pull out my cell phone and pretend to check email, moving my finger up and down as if scrolling. It's not a working phone. We can't afford real phones. The FBI froze my bank account when they escorted us out of America on the premise that we have connections to the Russian government—we don't actually have any connections, though it's true that my biological parents, long dead now, were KGB. They died on a mission when I was four years old.

For now, I am merely the mother of a son, standing a short distance from a bench at the park, upon which my boy, like many boys across the country of Russia, enjoys the company of a few lonely, laughing girls.

If things were different, this scene that plays out before me might be amusing. But things are what they are, and there is no way to change them even if changing them is what I long for.

The pretty girl with light-brown hair and a couple of blue streaks that highlight her large eyes sits beside Evander on the bench. She's the one he pays the most attention to while the others continue to stand. Evander plays it cool—cool comes naturally to him—answering questions, responding with an air of genuine interest, genuine kindness.

Though he doesn't face my direction, he knows I'm here. When I first arrived, he glanced over his shoulder, and as soon as he saw me, it was like the click of a magnet between us. He showed no surprise, no anger, no annoyance. He's a good son. He understands.

Some might assume I am overprotective, and about that, they are right. But I'm *not* the only parent lingering around this park. Plenty of young mothers watch their children climb trees, play tag, gather in clusters. I don't stick out like a sore thumb, to use another saying I learned when I lived in Pennsylvania. Evander's friends aren't aware of our mother-son connection. I am not here to embarrass or harass him.

I'm here to observe. I'm here to make sure he makes good choices.

The girl he pays most attention to says, "Come back after dinner. I'll be waiting."

I shake my head in amusement. *This* is why I have to linger around, hidden in plain sight as I am. Because the one he's interested in is always interested in him. He hates that I keep an eye on him, that I tell him he's too young for girlfriends, but I have good reason.

Evander is not just some American who happened to move to Russia.

I can only imagine how many girls have asked him to meet them in the dark of night. I'm not always there, standing under the tree, and he doesn't tell me everything. I know this.

"Tonight?" he says as if considering the offer. "Maybe." He has the calm of an astronaut.

The girl is cute with her carefree smile and eyes that say, "pretty please." She's a pixie compared to my giant of a son. Too sweet for my liking.

"If not tonight, then you must come back tomorrow," she says.

It's a moment before he says, "I have to go," and rises to his feet.

Still seated on the bench, the girl offers her hand to him. He takes it and holds it for a moment. His expression seems more intense than usual. There's a seriousness that shines through the placidness in his eyes, a determination that worries me.

He *likes* her.

And that is a problem.

He smiles and says, "*dosvidaniya*," which means *goodbye*.

I start walking before their hands release. I walk for two blocks before Evander's footsteps catch up to mine, far enough from the park where no one will see us. He's filled with the giddy energy people exude when they flirt, happiness rolling off him in falling-in-love waves.

This is not normal for him.

"I'm glad you're happy," I say, "but you won't come back tonight." I'm still not used to this tall version of my son and the way I have to tilt back my head in order to read his face.

Staring straight ahead as we continue down the road, he says, "I knew you would say that."

"And you also know why."

"Because you must always ruin my fun?" He has turned sideways to face me, and his grin says he's not picking a fight, yet I sense a layer of discontent roiling below the surface, one that's tired of me—of life like this. I can't say I blame him.

"I don't *always* ruin it. Do I?" I'm fighting myself because I wish he could have a girlfriend the way young adults do. Just not yet. It's too soon. He knows it's too soon.

"You do, actually." He faces forward again. Stepping more heavily now that his happy moment has peeled away like a layer of dead skin, he strides ahead of me. He's so even, so unfazed. Sometimes it's jarring. I find myself wanting him to express his anger, to shout at me, have a fit, throw something the way human beings do.

But he never does.

"I'm sorry. I can tell that you like her," I say. "And you know why it can't be."

"Yes, I know."

"So, you'll stay home tonight. We can do something fun. Watch a movie, play cards, maybe." I sound overly excited about this. Like I am selling a lie.

His cheeks fall flat, and his voice brims with sarcasm when he says, "And we'll have popcorn. I know how these nights go, Mom. You're holding me captive for my own good."

The word *captive* forms a knot in my brain. The Jovians held me against *my* will, so this doesn't sit well with me.

"You're my son, and I'm raising you safely. You're free to go wherever you like."

He rakes his fingers through rich brown hair, shiny like mine was before I felt it was important to dye it. "That's true," he says. "I'm free to go wherever I like as long as you're nearby to spy on me." He jams his hands into his pockets and slouches until his back stoops. This is more emotion than he usually displays.

"I promise it's not forever. Just until I figure out—"

"That everything is temporary?" The arch of his brow makes me wonder whether he's mocking me. Uncle Jimmy said the same thing. Is Evander quoting Uncle Jimmy, or—he can't be. He was only a baby when Jimmy returned to Mintaka.

"The important thing is that I have managed to keep you away from them," I say, expecting, I suppose, a pat on the back. Some gratitude, maybe, or just a vote of confidence.

"You have done that much, but at what cost?" he says.

It seems the question has been melting on his tongue for some time. But he doesn't gloat; there's nothing harsh in his tone.

"We live in Russia," he says, "and you never wanted to come back here."

It's true. I loved America. I had planned to stay there for the rest of my life. Then again, I made many plans when I was young. I married Andrew, and we *planned* to have a family with two, three, however many children we wanted. I was going to be a teacher.

Now I have just one plan. For me and my son to stay together. For the Jovians to keep their hands off him. And if living with him in a remote village in Russia with my non-blood-related sister and her family is the only way we can do that, then so be it.

"Yes, well, parents sacrifice for their children," I say.

"I know you're doing what you think is best."

His saying so pricks a thorny nerve with me. Until today, I had assumed we were in agreement when it came to living in Tula, when it came to hiding out. As annoyed as he was becoming, I thought we were in this together.

"I'm grateful to Aunt Helena for taking us in, for sharing her home with us," he says with an air of wisdom beyond his years. "I understand that we don't have choices of where to live, but more and more I feel like I'm searching for the freedom within my confinement."

Uncle Jimmy said I should give into it—the Jovians and our future with them—he said I would "find the freedom within my confinement," but that was not something I could accept, so I found a way out. Now I suppose I've become the one who confines. Now that he's grown up, does Evander want to find a way out, too?

He continues to walk, his long legs taking him several paces ahead of me. I know he's right, that I've kept him too close and interfered in his life whenever I've deemed it necessary. But what else can I do?

Evander is only ten years old.

He has the body and intellect of a person twice his age.

He is human, and he is Jovian.

And very soon now, his relatives will be coming for us.

2

The next morning, Evander and I join my sister, Helena, at the breakfast table, and a buzz of vibration settles in my ears. This buzz that runs like an undercurrent through my mind is nothing new. Sometimes it's a gentle hum, and other times it's an unignorable storm. Today it's as if a fly flew into my ear and became trapped in the cage of my skull. It began the day Andrew's younger cousin, David, showed me his true extraterrestrial self and tried to take Evander from me. I held on even as a bolt of energy passed through my body, and ever since that moment, I've suffered these strange headaches, this near-constant hum. I'm pretty sure that whatever David did to me welded me to the Jovian family psyche—their intellectual oneness—if only in a vague, foggy way. Sometimes I wonder if I'm thinking what the family is thinking.

I have, for instance, strange daydreams that often come to me as I stare out the window or wash the dishes in the kitchen sink. It's like I'm traveling through an abyss of space that I occupy only in my mind. I have to believe it's the Jovians' influence. I've spent hours in these daydreams, floating through vast swaths of emptiness before I come to a place where the green glow of a nebula takes my breath away or a sparkling cluster of sister stars draws my eye. They are, I imagine, the stuff of undiscovered solar systems, the sort Jovians come upon with their high-powered telescopes made in their Starbright factories. I've visited all sorts of heavenly bodies in my mind. Sometimes I'll skim past a black hole that pulls me close as if I were a wayward ship, its utter blackness threatening to take me in and never let me—

"Sveta? Sveta, my God, have you gone completely deaf?"

I raise my head from the coffee cup I've been staring into and meet my sister's eyes.

Helena beams frustration, her brows quivering with impatient exasperation. "Uh," I say. "What is it you were—"

"Is there vodka in your coffee this morning? Or do you have one of your headaches again? Where *are* you?"

Evander reaches across the table and squeezes my hand.

I'm grateful for his support. He knows of the undercurrent in my mind, of the constant hum in my ears.

He turns his head toward his aunt and says, "She's fine."

Helena's annoyance appears in the way she forces the words out of her mouth: "Okay, so you'll be there then? You'll go to the school for me?"

I have no idea what she's talking about. *Why would I go to the school?*

Evander leans toward me. "It's Aunt Helena's volunteer day at the library. Last week, you said you could cover—"

"Ohhhhh. *Da.*" I say with an overzealous nod. "*Da, da, da.*" My son's words have rung a distant bell beyond the drone in my head. Helena works the farm with her husband, Ivan, and like every good parent, she also volunteers at the elementary school from time to time. I probably would, too, except that Evander takes his classes at home, most of them college level.

"Yes. I'll go. Of course. It will be my pleasure." I raise my brows and shift my eyes back and forth in a humorous way.

Evander chuckles and shakes his head. He calls me the equivalent of a goof, in Russian. The word is *shootnicha.*

Helena sits back now that I have agreed. "Don't be late. It's from nine o'clock until noon." Her condescending look grazes over the length of my body. "And wear something else."

I drop my chin and observe my clothes. My favorite flannel pajamas, worn at the edges, are a faded blue that matches my eyes, which are also worn around the edges. "Are you saying pajamas are not appropriate for the school library?" I smile, but my lightheartedness is a transparent veil. Helena knows me well, and therefore she knows this bit of cheerfulness is fake. "And how much will they pay me for this grueling work that I am to do, dear sister?"

She frowns as she stands and pulls her purse strap from the back of her chair. "I'm going to make you see Dr. Popov if you keep zoning out like this. It's getting worse."

"She's just tired," Evander says with a casualness that's convincing. "You worry too much. Stop being a *worrywart.*"

We all speak Russian to each other in this house, but Evander has said *worrywart* in English.

"I don't know what that is," Helena says, adjusting the strap of her purse over her shoulder. "Sounds ugly."

"And yet it's accurate," he says, passing me a subtle grin.

I can't help but see my husband, Andrew, whenever I look into my son's blue-green eyes. Years of longing ball up my throat when I think of how he died before his time—how the night before he died, he'd told me he loved me so much that he felt as though he would split at the seams.

"I'm tired," I say in Helena's direction. I might be speaking too loudly. The buzzing in my brain has reached a low roar at this point. "You would be tired, too, if you were my age."

I sip my coffee and try to appear normal.

"I *am* your age," Helena reminds me as she walks away. "You're six months older, and I'm only thirty-five. So maybe you should try this thing called sleeping."

Her ten-year-old daughter, Alexandria, arrives at the end of the short hall in what would be the foyer if this house were big enough to have one. She wears her red school outfit and snow boots. "Where's Daddy?"

"On the farm," Helena says. "At work."

"Can Evander come to school with me today?"

She often asks this question.

"You know he studies at home," Helena says, while she fusses with Alexandria's thick, blonde hair. "Did you even brush this before you braided it?"

"But he *should* be in my class. Then Sergei wouldn't make fun of me so much."

"You tell Sergei that Evander would like to speak with him after school. Okay, Evander? You'll talk to Sergei for us?"

"It will be my pleasure," he says, his face taut with seriousness as he lands a pretend punch in the opposite palm. A second later, though, his shoulders bob as he laughs. My son, the gentle giant. His physique may be of the sort that frightens small children, but he has never hurt anyone in his life.

Alexandria skips over to where Evander sits at the kitchen table and embraces what she can of him with her small arms.

He hugs her back.

They are adorable.

Then she walks back to Helena and says, "Why is Evander so big?" not exactly in a whisper.

"Why are you so big, Evander?" Helena shouts.

Evander passes me a glance before answering. "Just good genes, I guess."

I stifle a laugh. Everything funny in this world has some truth to it.

"That's not why," Helena tells Alexandria. "The truth is that the baby food your aunt fed Evander in America is filled with growth hormones. All of their sports competitors are raised on it so that they have a chance at winning gold in the Olympics. But we Russians usually beat them anyway."

"Is Evander training for the Olympics?" Alexandria asks in awe.

"Who knows? Come now, or we'll be late." Over her shoulder, she says, "Don't forget the library, Sveta, or I swear I'll make you see that doctor."

The door opens and closes, and I breathe a sigh of relief.

Evander stands, takes the dishes that are shiny with melted butter and leftover jam, and piles them in the sink. He proceeds to wash them. He's as easygoing as they come. A well-behaved young man. Adoring son. Everyone in Tula loves him. Too many young ladies dote on him. He's too attractive for his own good.

I worry about the many ways I may one day lose him: pretty girl, tremendous job opportunity, alien abduction.

I enter my room and find something presentable to wear—jeans, a bulky woolen sweater—then I make my bed and toss the dirty clothing I'd left on the floor into the laundry basket in the corner. It's cold in the bedroom. That's why Evander does his studies in the kitchen, near the woodburning stove. It's cold in all of the bedrooms, as cold as it was at the orphanage in Petranko. I realize it's strange for a mother and grown son (even if he has been alive for only ten years) to share a room, but there's no other option. Helena's house has two-and-a-half bedrooms. The "half" would make a decent closet in America; Alexandria sleeps in there on a tiny mattress on the floor with a few stuffed animals.

When we first arrived in Tula, Helena had recently given birth, and she and Ivan had moved into this house that Ivan inherited from his father. It sits on a plot of land once used to grow rye. The farm has been subdivided for the four brothers, and while it is no longer viable for commercial growing, they produce a good share of vegetables, much of which Helena cans each summer.

The buzz in my head has not let up, not settled back as it usually does, and that worries me. Something may be going on in the Jovian world, something that involves me and Evander. I dread the day David decides Evander and I have been free for too long, that it's time for us to go back to the family. I wish he would forget all about us, but the chance of that is probably zero.

I grab a hairbrush from the top of the crate I use to stow my clothes and then peer into the hazy hand mirror hung on the wall as I attempt to smooth my hair. My dark roots are showing. I'll need to buy more highlighter the next time we go into town. I hate my dry, lightened hair, cut to my shoulders in a bob similar to the way my mother-in-law, Caroline, always cut hers, but since we returned to Russia, I feel safer looking different than I used to. And the blonde blends with the few silver streaks that turned up the day David used his strange and unearthly powers to try to convince me to give up Evander.

"Evander, come here, please," I say.

The chair legs grate over the kitchen's wooden floor, and his footsteps approach.

"Yes," he says, leaning a shoulder into the doorway.

I'm pretty sure he already knows what I'm going to say.

I pat the corner of his mattress. "Sit. What are you reading this morning?"

"American history," he says as he lowers onto the bed across from me.

This is a surprise.

"I thought you weren't going to take that class."

"Changed my mind. Last minute."

"American history interests you?"

"The Constitution does, yes."

An annoyed sort of skepticism makes me squint. The Jovians would be thrilled to know he's studying American history, and I wonder if I'm not the only one in this house who has a foggy sense of what the family is doing and thinking. Is it possible the Jovians have imparted their desire for him to learn about American government? Years ago, when Evander was a baby, Uncle Jimmy told me the family intends for its descendants to grow up and take leadership positions in the community, and eventually the world. So this may be Evander's natural curiosity, or it may be the Jovians' influence. But right now I have more important concerns.

"I wanted to talk about the girl," I say.

Evander wears a blank stare that's jarring to take in. He has Jovian DNA, and the emotionless gaze is their signature look.

He says, "I didn't meet her last night."

"Yes, I know, but you wanted to."

He turns his head away as a coy smile takes over his face. "Yes, I wanted to."

"What's her name?"

"Nadia," he says. It's obvious to me that he's trying very hard to keep down the happy gleam that's determined to shine from his eyes.

So I was right: he likes her.

"Okay," I say in my in-control voice. "Well, I'm going to have to ask you to stop growing up so fast. I really need you to be more child-like."

He tilts his head and scrunches his brow, conveying his confusion. The stubble on his chin reminds me he learned how to shave a couple of years ago. Then I start laughing, and he joins me.

"I think it's a little late for this conversation," he says.

His physical size and obvious maturity are not what I'm talking about. I need him to remain young in the overall sense, though I know there's absolutely nothing I can do about his quick rise to adulthood.

"But you know why your growing up so fast upsets me," I ask.

"Yes, I know. Because when I'm ready to start a family, David will be coming for us."

I thought we'd have more time before Evander grew into an adult's body and mind. When he was a baby, he not only walked but ran after just one month. He spoke many words, too. I suppose fully grown at ten makes sense for him. And yet I would do anything to change that. I would do anything to travel back to a simpler time when he was still a baby, and I, a young mother.

"I'm not sure it will be David. Maybe one of the others, or several of them, will come. Do you doubt me when I say so?"

"I never doubt you. You're my mother, and I trust you completely." He looks up at me with a transparency that's pure. "The Jovians want me for their own reasons. I know that."

"We can't go with them, whoever it is that comes. I have to protect you."

"Because I'm different from most people. I'm *unique*," he says in a joking tone that sounds so much like Andrew it makes me shake my head.

"You are," I say. "And look at you. You're not a ... You've become ..." I can't speak the words out loud because I'm afraid the Jovians might hear everything I say, that they may be thousands of miles away but still have a direct line into my head. David was right when he said, "Earth is not so large." The distance between Russia and Kirksberg, Pennsylvania, or wherever they may be, has never felt large enough.

I sit on the edge of my bed and lean toward Evander with an I-mean-business expression. "We have to be careful. I can't let you go out alone anymore. You know I'm not trying to punish you."

He shrugs a little like it's no big deal, then takes a deep breath and stares at the wall in front of him. I'm sure he's wishing the conversation would end. If he were a normal young adult, he'd most likely be swearing at me right now. He'd be stomping out of the room, slamming the door, promising to leave and never come back.

"You can't go out with Nadia. I'm sorry because I can tell that you like her. It's just better that you don't, uh, you know, fall in love." The phrase makes me cringe.

He laughs in a mocking way that lets me know I'm getting far ahead of myself. "I just met her," he says. "I'm not in love."

"But you could be, if you were to get to know her better."

"Well, then I won't get to know her better, all right?"

The "all right" bothers me because it signals a certain amount of dissatisfaction brewing. But I can't worry about that because I'm already sweating at the thought of seeing the Jovians again. Caroline and her cold perfection, Aunt Constant and her deceptively kind ways, David with his sharp-as-a-blade eyes and mysterious power. I'm no match for them. My only hope is they don't know Evander is fully grown. Because once they find out, we're doomed. The best plan I have consists of running. And I know how ridiculous that is. I've prepared a backpack and stowed it under my bed. It contains Helena's passport (the FBI confiscated mine ten years ago), some cash Andrew's best friend, Fran Vasquez, gave me when we left the US, and spare toothbrushes for

Evander and me. I'd carry a knife or some other weapon but that would get us stopped at the airport. If we are to flee, we'll be able to take only as many supplies as we can carry, and I'll need to gather them quickly, which is why I wear Andrew's wedding band on a gold chain around my neck. I can't risk leaving it behind.

Evander stirs. "Are we done? Because I have work to do." He gestures into the kitchen.

"They'll take you if they think you're ready," I say, my voice quivering. "They'll take you and get you married and make you start a family."

He reaches his hand out to me and holds my clenched fist.

"No one is here," he says. "No one has seen me. No one knows where we live. You were sure they were coming a year ago, and they didn't. They still haven't come. We're fine. Nothing has changed."

"I know," I say softly, though I'm unconvinced. I'm well aware that I have one of these meltdowns every few months, and I hope this one passes without incident. But it won't if Evander starts dating, falling in love, doing the things adults do. Not if the Jovians are, as I suspect, a collective brain that dreams the same dreams and thinks the same thoughts. I'm not clever enough to camouflage what I think 100 percent of the time.

He stands, takes a step away from me. "Okay?"

I nod. If I speak, I may cry, and I don't want him to think I'm breaking down.

"You have to get to the library," he says.

He's right. Helena will be livid if she finds out I was late. *She* thinks I'm having a breakdown.

As I gather my things to leave, Evander returns to the table where his text on American history awaits.

"I still don't know why you're taking American history this semester," I say.

"You wanted me to take art history, and I didn't want to. It's my choice since I'm the one taking the class, correct?"

I stand there, trying to remember the discussion concerning this choice. Maybe it occurred during one of my more vigorous brain fogs. "Of course it is," I say. I've already told him he can't fall in love. Who am I to stop him from learning about the Constitution?

He goes back to reading. "So you better get to the library, then."

I grab my sheepskin coat from the hook on the back of the bedroom door. I bought it at a thrift store in Moscow during our first winter back, and it's the warmest thing I own.

"I'll be home in time for lunch," I say. Then I leave out the front door, and lock it behind me.

3

That night during dinner, there's a knock at the front door. Little Alexandria jumps from her chair and runs. No one tries to stop her. A moment later, she yells in singsong: "Evander, you have a visitor. It's a gir-rl!"

All of us—Helena, Ivan, Evander, and I—look up from our dinner plates and stare at each other with questions behind our eyes.

I pass Evander a "this is bad" face, which he ignores as he rises and steps away.

Ivan mutters the Russian equivalent of, "Good for you, kid," and a torrent of worried feelings descend upon me.

Those of us who are still seated at the table continue to eat, or not eat in my case. I hear Evander's whispers, but not the actual words.

Alexandria has returned with happy energy. "She's so pretty."

"Okay," Ivan tells her. "Eat your dinner."

Ivan is a nice man of few words. I like him because when we first came to Russia, he didn't ask questions, and also because he has never complained about me and Evander living here.

"You eat your dinner, too." Helena juts her chin in my direction, and I bite my lip and squelch the urge to join my son and the pretty girl at the front door. I feel they need chaperoning.

A moment later, the two of them appear in the kitchen entry.

"This is Nadia," Evander tells us with a reserved kind of smile that lets me know he and I are doomed.

The girl lifts one hand displaying a glove with the fingers cut off and waves with a humbleness I had not detected yesterday when I saw her at the park. She gazes in my direction, but after only a second, her eyes seek out the floor. I appreciate her timidity. Her cheeks are a naive shade of rose.

Evander proceeds to introduce each one of us, starting with me.

I do my best to smile, though my lips rebel and the best I can do is curl them into a crooked scowl. "Hello," I say, in English, which is dumb because we live in Russia.

After the introductions are through, Helena asks Nadia to have some dinner. A bit of the potato I've been chewing flies out of my mouth when I say, "No."

Helena and Ivan turn to me with wide eyes, as if I have committed an unforgivable sin.

"Thank you, but I have already eaten," Nadia says, ignoring me, probably because that's what Evander has instructed her to do. "And I'm sorry for the interruption." Her voice is attractive.

"I've finished eating," Evander says before dropping his chin in Nadia's direction. "Let's take a walk, maybe go for hot chocolate?"

"Sure," she says.

Then he turns to me. "If that's all right?"

He knows the answer. He knows it's not all right. We just spoke of this a few hours ago. But what can I do? I can't act like a lunatic in front of my family, in front of this girl. They won't understand why I fear letting my (seemingly) eighteen- to twenty-year-old moose of a son go for a walk in the early evening with this petite teenager. It's not like Nadia might mug him or make him do something he doesn't want to do.

So I cough for a second, buying time, and when I accept that there's no way out, I say as sanely as I can, "Come right back," my face quivering and my insides out of control because I'm about to lose everything in this world that I've fought so hard to keep.

Evander holds my gaze, then says, "Okay," and they turn and step away. They're through the hall now, at the front door. The urge to beg him not to go wrestles the understanding part of me that says, *Just this once let him have his fun.* The front door thuds closed.

I stare at my dinner plate, the buzz inside my head rising up like a sudden thunderstorm. I grasp Andrew's wedding ring and zip it back and forth along my neckline.

"He'll be fine," Helena says. "We've talked about this. If he's more of an adult than a child—and we all know that he is—you need to give him a longer leash. It's only natural."

My fears spin like a cyclone that whisks her advice away as soon as the words hit my brain.

"Please, Sveta, you have to stop being so damned overprotective," she says.

The air makes a sound as it passes through my constricted throat. I try to nod, but I can't. I can't move or I'll lose control.

And then she says, for the one hundredth time, "If you don't stop acting so strangely, I will make you see Dr. Popov."

My dead husband joins me in a dream. We're at the house in Ashbury Falls, North Carolina, halfway up the mountain in our spacious ranch, sighting constellations and planets on the back deck the way we always did when he was alive. His warm breath enters my ear as I rest upon him as if he were a cushion. "Are you happy you married me," he asks.

The question has a whiff of the familiar.

I say, "I'm never happier than when I'm with you."

He wraps his warm arms around me like a ribbon on a gift box and squeezes me close. His five o'clock shadow gently whisks my cheek. "That's good to know."

"Why do you ask?" I say, shivering as the hair on the back of my neck rises.

"Because I need you to wake up."

His tone is suddenly dire, but I can't lift my head. His lap rocks like a raft over choppy water, and when I finally manage to get upright, a beetle flies straight for me and becomes twisted in my hair. I pull it out, wings and legs crumbling in my hand. Another flies at me from the right, then one from the left.

"What's happening?" I yell.

"Wake up," he shouts. "You have to wake up."

The panic from the dream follows me into the conscious world. My head is still buzzing as I turn over and swipe the hair from my sweaty face. The clock says 10 p.m., and Evander's bed is empty. I stand too fast, swooning with dizziness.

After Evander went out and Helena and I had cleaned up dinner, she followed me into the bedroom and insisted we drink a couple of shots—to settle "our" nerves. I could hardly stand to be awake without knowing where Evander was and what he was doing, so I grabbed the bottle from her and took a long, spiteful swill. It was a mistake I regretted only ten minutes later when I became drowsy listening to her blather on about how Evander was perfectly fine, that it was normal and right for him to want to spend time with a girl, and that I needed to loosen my grip.

And now that I'm awake, I realize I'm still in my shoes, fully dressed in my jeans and turtleneck. It's dark, Helena must have turned off my light. I'm off-balance, and I've crashed into the bedroom door. My shoulder smarts as I move through the hall toward the kitchen, the nightlight from Alexandria's tiny closet of a room guiding me.

Where is Evander?

How could I have been so stupid to fall asleep? I flick on the ceiling light in the kitchen. On a chair in the corner, Evander's American history book catches my eye. He wasn't supposed to take American history this year. Now I remember: he was supposed to take art history, and he even looked forward to it—or so he'd told me at the time. Did he lie to me? Did the Jovians contact him and set him on a different path?

I stride back down the hall, unlock the front door, pull it open, and step outside. Like a charging bull, the frigid night air moves straight through my clothes, chasing away the warmth of the house. I wrap my arms around myself as I stare across the empty yard through cold, watery eyes. My pounding heart sends a flush of heat through my neck to the tips of my ears.

I drop my head, wishing the damn buzz away. "Wake up," Andrew told me. "You have to wake up."

Why don't you just come down here and help me? I think.

I scan the sky for Orion's belt and Uncle Jimmy's home of Mintaka. This time of year, we also have a clear view of Jupiter. It shines like a star, one of the brightest celestial bodies out there. Tonight, it's also red.

Behind me, the door to the house makes that dragging sound as it opens. I turn. It's Helena in her robe, her face pinched with worry. "What happened? Where's your coat?"

"Evander is gone."

"He didn't come home?"

"No," I say as I approach her.

"He's probably at Nadia's, or maybe one of her friends has a car and they—"

"*They've* taken him," I say, as intensely as I know how.

"Who?"

"The Jovians."

"How can you know?" Her fear of my poor mental health shows in all the tense places of her face, the arches of each brow and the line that sinks in between them.

"Come back inside," she says. "He went out with a girl. That's all. It's normal."

I frown at her in an ugly way. "Do you really think there is anything normal about Evander?"

"Calm down," she tells me.

I can't calm down because they've taken him. And because there's an unmistakable buzzing in my head and if it doesn't stop soon, I'll need that doctor she keeps threatening to call.

"You don't believe anything I've told you about America and the Jovians," I say, "but it's all true. Everything I told you the night we arrived is true."

"Of course I believe you. Your ten-year-old is a giant who has grown at unbelievable speed, but there are some things I don't want to accept, and your Jovians are one of them."

Finally, she admits it.

"It's been ten years," she says. "Why would they come back now?"

"They *need* him. I thought they'd come for the both of us, but they really only need him." Saying it out loud makes it true, and my stomach swells with a wave of sick, green fear. "How could I let this happen? How could I have been so stupid?"

Helena puts her hands out to me, as if she might be able to stop my spiral downward. She's too late. The spiraling has begun.

"You did nothing wrong," she says. "He likes this girl, and you let him go out. That's what any mother would do."

I close my eyes and squelch the urge to tell her she's wrong. Because I'm not any mother: my son is both human and Jovian. "I knew better," I say. "I shouldn't have let him."

Then I push past her into the house.

She trails after me in her scuffing slippers. "What are you going to do?"

"I have to find him. I can't let them do what they want to do."

"But it's only been a few hours. He could be asleep in Nadia's living room."

"He wouldn't do that. If he were able to get home, he would be here. He knows how I am, how much I worry."

"He *is* responsible," Helena says with loud enthusiasm. "That's why I'm sure he'll be back soon."

I grab the backpack with the money and Helena's passport from under my bed and throw it on top. *What do I need?* It's hard to think with the rumbling in my brain obscuring my thoughts. I go to the crate where I keep my clean clothes and toss a few things at the backpack—my other pair of jeans, two pairs of socks, a sweater, two tees, underwear—before pressing it all inside. My ears have begun to ring, and I'm breathing like a runner. I whisk my one photograph of Evander from my dresser. It's a passport photo from last year, though I never had his passport made because I have no paperwork for him. No birth certificate. No proof of his American citizenship. Still, I had hoped I could make it happen somehow, and now I realize that was naïve of me, just like hoping the Jovians wouldn't come tonight was.

I slide the photo into an outer pocket on my backpack and zip it closed.

I have to get out of here. I need to book a flight, I need to —throw up. I run the few steps to the bathroom, then hover over the toilet. Nothing happens as the ringing in my ears circles like a siren. I take a step sideways to the sink and splash cold water on my face. I don't have time for this, but I hesitate to gaze at myself in the mirror. The face staring back at me reflects the hard lines of someone under attack, with dark notches below my blue eyes and hair too pale for her colorless cheeks.

I grab the sunglasses from the top vanity drawer, then lipstick and an eye pencil. I'll need these things to convince the Jovians I'm still young, that I can still be useful to them, that I could make them another marvelous grandchild even though I'm no longer of prime child-rearing age. Maybe they'll believe it. If not, I'm afraid they'll toss me away without a thought.

"What will you do for money?"

I'd forgotten Helena was there, watching me.

"I have a little," I say as I pass her on the way back to my room.

I throw the glasses and makeup into the backpack and zip it closed, then pull my sheepskin coat from the hook.

When I reach the front door and open it, Helena pulls me back. "Please don't do this. What if he returns?" She sounds more desperate than I'm used to. "How will I reach you?"

I don't want to leave like this, but I have to. They've already taken him. He could be halfway across the world by now. The buzz in my head reaches a crescendo as I sink into Helena's embrace. I squeeze my eyes closed, fearful I'll collapse, weak from the sensory overwhelm.

Just when I think I can't stand another second, I'm plunged into an earth-shattering silence.

The buzzing stops, and it's like being released from the barb of a hook. I fall forward and struggle to catch my breath. "Thank you," I whisper.

Helena shakes her head. "For what?"

Some movement in the front yard catches my eye.

Standing beside the tree at the end of the drive is the tall, lean silhouette of a figure poised in our direction. I didn't hold out much hope that I was wrong about the Jovians having Evander, but any I did have just sank into the ground like water.

"He won't come home," I whisper.

Helena stretches up on her toes so she can see past me. "Who is that?"

"It's Edmund. My father-in-law."

4

Helena tells me to come back inside, to stay away from "that creepy man," but I can't. I have to go. I have to find Evander before it's too late, before he's too far out of my grasp. So I tell her it's okay, that I'll be okay.

"They won't hurt me," I say, though I have no idea what they'll do with me. "Close this door and lock it."

Then I say "I love you," and walk away sensing Helena's reluctance to shut the door behind me.

As I approach Edmund, I realize he's not wearing a coat. So much for trying to look normal. He has the same brown-gray hair that I remember, the same straight-as-a-board elitist air like he should be smoking a cigar and holding a meeting with all of the members of the board. And yet, he's different. Younger instead of older. Or maybe I'm just older, and he has stayed the same.

A sleek limousine of the sort I have not seen in a decade thrums in the shadows just beyond a row of trees that mark the edge of the yard. I stop in front of him but keep some distance between us, maybe five, six feet.

"Good to see you," he says.

I maintain eye contact as a familiar rush of energy climbs my spine and rides the curve of my head before dissipating into the night air. It's a mere shadow of the zap of electricity that once raised the hair on my scalp when I first met Andrew's relatives.

"I'd hoped never to see you again," I say.

The insult hovers in the air between us.

"How is your sister, Helena?" he says.

I'm not sure whether I should take that as a threat. The Jovians are strange. Sometimes they sound intimidating when they're actually trying to be civil.

I glance away with a sigh. "Where is Evander? Is he in the car over there?"

"No, he's not."

Edmund's lack of emotion brings it all back. The Jovian evenness. Their impenetrable calm. Uncle Jimmy was the only one of my in-laws who reacted with genuine emotion, became flustered in front of me, showed real love for me and Andrew. I wish he were here now.

"Then why are you here," I ask.

"It was time we had a visit. And a conversation."

I blow on my cold hands, remembering that I've been dreading this day for the past ten years. I should have better prepared for this moment, for the possibility that they would take Evander and leave me behind. I should have made Evander stay home. Why did I let him go out with that girl?

Edmund brings his hands together palm to palm, which makes him appear empathetic. Some Jovians are good at playing the game of being human. He's mediocre. When he speaks it's with a tone of authority. "It's time for Evander to move on."

"I'm the only one who can decide that," I say with restraint. "Evander is only ten years old."

I have no doubt Edmund knows what Evander looks like at this point, knows he's a fully grown specimen of a human. But I don't have much else to work with; reminding him of Evander's age is my strongest argument.

"We both know he's mentally and physically mature," he says. "You've done a wonderful job raising him, Svetlana, and I mean that. But you can't keep him here any longer."

"I know him better than anyone else. I'm his mother, and he's still a child." My insides have slumped toward my feet. I'm losing. I always knew I would lose this battle, but it still hurts. "Edmund, please, he's only ten."

"Russia was temporary," he says as if my words mean nothing. "You knew we would come."

The frustration I've lived with for so long simmers in my chest, and I thrust my hands into my coat pockets. "Right, of course. Everything is temporary. Are the Jovians temporary, or will they be around for millennia? Maybe they already have." I frown wickedly. "I won't be alive that long, that's for sure, and I want to spend as much time with my son as I can."

"I understand completely," Edmund says with pretend earnestness that I easily see through. "We want you to come back to Kirksberg, to live in the house you and Andrew remodeled when you first married. We want you to be a part of the family again."

At that, my calm façade goes by the wayside. I'm exasperated as I say, "The family still lives in Kirksberg?"

"We never left."

Fran kept an eye on the situation after Evander and I were forced out of America. At that time, none of the Jovians could be found: not in their homes in Kirksberg, not in Ashbury Falls, not even at the Chateau L'Origine. He also said their company, Starbright International, continued to run, but that the FBI was denied entrance due to Starbright's association with NASA.

Could the Jovians have evaded authorities for this long? David had transformed into the supreme being and basically caused the sky to fall, so how could the FBI have ignored that? I'd assumed the family went into hiding somewhere—some other state in America. And maybe they did, and now they had returned. I've been out of touch with Fran for more than three years, and a lot could have happened in that time.

"Evander will be at the house in Kirksberg?" I say. "We'll live there together?"

Edmund's face gives nothing away. "He's not there yet. He'll be there soon."

I groan. "When is *soon*? *Soon* means one thing to me and another to you."

"Yes, time is relative to the individual."

A disgusted sound rattles my throat. He's giving me the Jovian speak, and I'm in no mood for it.

"He'll be there," he says. "He has something to do first."

"So if I go to Kirksberg, he'll join me there *eventually*, which means in a few weeks or months?"

"Yes, yes, a few weeks or months."

"You're just borrowing him, then? You're going to give him back?" I allow myself a half smile, which Edmund does not return.

"Your son has important work to do. He won't return to Russia."

I kick a rock with the toe of my boot, and it rolls onto the road. "We'll see about that," I say under my breath.

He checks his watch. "There are no secrets between Jovians. You're quite aware by now."

I know David reads minds, but I'm pretty sure the rest of them receive vague messages and thoughts the same way I daydream about outer space. Then again, David may simply tell the others what they need to know. Either way, I doubt their collective thinking provides a clear line of communication.

Edmund has been observing me in silence. "Do you think Andrew would want you to keep his son from us?" he says.

The answer is yes, he would. I know that for sure. But Edmund probably won't believe me if I tell him that Andrew has spoken to me, that he warned me about his arrival that very night—that even ten years after he died, I have to believe there's still a connection between us.

"I don't know what he would think," I lie.

"Should we continue this conversation in the car? You'll be more comfortable," he says, gesturing toward the limo.

The engine purrs and clicks in wait of Edmond's return.

I'm cold, he's right about that. And I want to get a move on. "Is Caroline in there?"

"No one is in there."

"Where is Evander right now?"

"He's no longer in Russia. I don't know where he is exactly."

"And what are you going to do with me?"

"I'm not going to do anything with you."

"Nothing," I say. I was right. They don't need me. They don't care what I do as long as I go along with their plans for Evander, and that's what I'm not willing to do. The family always finds a way to make me feel worthless.

"I see you've packed a bag," he says. "You seem to be going somewhere, and I'll give you a ride, if you'd like."

"I guess I'm going to Moscow, to the airport," I say. "And I need money."

"I'll help you any way I can," he says.

The limo's interior reminds me of a booth at a fancy nightclub.

Edmund sits facing me with his long legs crossed, his feet outfitted in shiny black shoes. The Jovian wealth comes through in the potent scent of leather, a bar with sparkling glasses and full bottles of alcohol, tinted windows for that exclusiveness rich people exude, and classical music playing at a tasteful volume. I look down at my well-worn coat, dull with a layer of everyday grime, my scuffed black boots, anything but delicate with chunky plastic treads and fake leather uppers that are both scarred and wrinkled. Even *I* am well worn, with my two-toned hair, bed-headed unkempt, and jeans with holes of the sort that take years of wear before they show up.

I'm surprised Edmund recognizes me.

"I figured you would have traveled by spaceship," I say. "Why do it the old-fashioned way?"

He's been gazing out the window, but now turns his head in my direction. "You've always had an interesting way of communicating."

"I could say the same about you—and your entire family." Boldness comes easy at the moment. I've heard that happens to people when they live in fear for too long: they learn not to give a crap, as Americans say.

Edmund reaches into a space near the bottom of the car door and pulls out a black cardboard envelope. He opens it and removes a small pile of things: one of them is a credit card, which he hands to me. It has the name Helena Peterman on it. Helena's adopted name.

"It matches your passport," Edmund says.

He knows I'm posing as my sister. Surely he knows that the FBI put Svetlana Peterman Jovian on America's "do not enter" list when they escorted us out ten years ago.

"Do you also have a cell phone for me?"

I don't thank him as he pulls one from the console beside the bar and passes it to me. I'm sure the Jovians want me to have a phone so they can track me, but I'll turn off the GPS as soon as we reach the airport.

"I want to talk to Evander," I say in a casual tone. "Please tell me the number."

"You can't reach him now."

"When will I be able to?"

He stares blankly. "I can't say for sure."

"Your answers are so much like Caroline's. When she kept me in the tower at Chateau L'Origine she told me nothing. How is she? Are you two still pretend married?"

"When you reach Kirksberg," he says, riding over my words, "we'll give you the keys to the house and a car. My phone number is in the contacts. Call me when you arrive."

I never said I was going to the house in Kirksberg, but if he wants to think I am, that's fine. I'll try to find Evander before then, and if I do, I'll take him someplace safe away from them. Iceland, maybe. Or a crowded city like New York or Beijing. I mustn't think about it because David could be listening in on my plans as I think them.

"How does that sound?" Edmund says.

"Fine," I tell him.

"Or, you could just stay here, in Tula, with your sister. The choice is yours."

The Jovians have a very strange idea of what constitutes a choice. They force you to do what they want and then they expect you to be happy about it. I have no intention of living in my old house (which the Jovians own), no intention of ending up in the center of their vast, sticky web. I have another plan, but I'm blocking it from my mind because that is what I have to do. Mind control is the only way I might actually get ahead.

"I can't stay here and do nothing when my son has been kidnapped," I say.

"He hasn't been kidnapped."

"Only because Jovians don't understand the word *kidnapped*."

Another silence follows. Edmund is so still I'm not sure he's breathing. Maybe he doesn't need to breathe. Maybe he only breathes for show.

"Can you at least tell me where he is? You know I'm worried."

"You're a good mother," he says without a modicum of feeling. "And Evander is fulfilling his role as a Jovian. You will see him again, so there's no reason to worry."

No reason to worry?

That is a joke. One I don't care to explain to him. I ease back in the seat, close my eyes, and let my frustration simmer. I know only too well that arguing with Edmund will get me nowhere.

5

With a violin quartet drifting through its speakers, Edmund's limousine takes me to Moscow, a three-hour ride. I'm surprised when he drops me at the airport instead of offering to fly me to Kirksberg on the private jet that's no doubt waiting to whisk him away. Then he could keep an eye on me. Or, maybe I'm right, and the family doesn't care where I go.

They're probably hoping I get stopped trying to leave the country.

The sun hasn't yet risen, but the airport bustles like it's the middle of the day. I join a line behind twenty or so other travelers, which is good. It will give me time to make a plan. I don't want to think too much in case David is listening to my thoughts, but something tells me I don't have to worry about that anymore. The strange buzz in my head has disappeared, and I'm not feeling "attached," not feeling that head-humming outer-space connection anymore. All of it came to a crashing halt when Edmund arrived.

Maybe now that they have Evander, they don't feel the need to eavesdrop.

I don't know, but the truth is I don't have a choice whether to think or not to think right now. I have to settle on a destination, and I don't have many choices. They took Evander yesterday evening, which means they've had a half-day head start. I don't know if they put him on a plane, train, or rocket. For all I know they could have teleported him to Kirksberg. He also could be in Ashbury Falls or anywhere else in the US—or the world.

And that makes me sweat.

I need to keep a cool head and think this through. It may be some time before I find Evander, and I have to accept that. Unless I want the Jovians to control my every move, I'll need to find a place to live.

I don't know many people in America. Fran and his wife, Lisa, Andrew's and my best friends, live in Washington, DC, as far as I know (at least they did three years ago when I last spoke to Fran), but he's in the FBI, and if he realizes I've come back, he might decide it's his duty to return me to Helena and the farm. I would hope he wouldn't send me away once he hears what has happened to Evander, but he's pretty loyal to his job, so I can't trust him to be on my side. I wish I could.

Other than Fran, I could search for my adoptive parents, Dana and John Peterman, and hope to catch them in between humanitarian missions. They travel all over the world, and I have no idea if they'll be home—or even whether they live in Kirksberg or upstate New York at this point. We haven't spoken in ten years, and that's a thought I can't dwell on without getting sick with guilt, so I'll push it away for now. I'm fairly certain that no matter how they're feeling about our estrangement, they'll give me a chance to explain myself if I reach out to them. We were close, and I just don't think they'll shut me out. They're not that kind of people.

Now that I have a cell phone, I could try to track them

down, but I can't do it right now because the Jovians may have a way to tap into the activity on my phone—they monitored and manipulated my computer back when I lived in Kirksberg and Ashbury Falls—and if they know I want to reach my parents, they may do something to prevent that from happening. So I have to be patient. I need to get on the plane without one of them trying to stop me. Edmund could have stopped me if that's what the Jovians wanted to do, but that doesn't mean I'm free yet, so I'm going to be careful.

I'll fly to Kirksberg because I think Edmund was telling the truth about bringing Evander there. But I'm going on my own terms. If I can track down my parents, I'll stay with them while I investigate what the Jovians have been up to for a decade and where they've taken my son.

I really hope they're not reading my mind right now. Maybe I should make up another plan just to throw them off.

I'm in row twelve, the window seat. The seat next to mine is empty so far, but when I look up from my magazine, a woman bustling down the aisle seems to focus on me, so it may be hers. She's fifty-ish, wearing a fuzzy woolen hat and a scarf bubbling like lava from the collar of her bulky full-body coat. Her personal item, a taupe-colored leather shopping-style bag weighs down one side of her body; it's stuffed to fatness with her laptop peering out the top. Behind her, a piece of carry-on luggage trails like a baby elephant. She stops in front of me, smiles as I catch her eye, and drops the personal bag into the seat. Her laptop tempts me like a warm loaf of bread waved under my nose. She turns around and lifts the carry-on into the bin above with a lot of clunking and scraping sounds.

"That looks heavy," I say, so she'll know I speak English.

"Oh, I assumed you were Russian," she says, giving her luggage one last shove. "All Russian women are beautiful."

I'm unable to camouflage my surprise because I feel even more weathered than usual. "I speak English, but I'm both American and Russian," I say.

"Uh-huh." She lifts the leather tote with the computer sticking out, holding it the way one would a toddler, and lowers into the chair, her coat and scarf overflowing into my space along with her flowery perfume. She pushes the tote to the floor and uses the toe of her foot to nudge it under the seat in front of us. A magazine and some candies in a tin spill out. The computer remains put.

"I was supposed to be in first class, but my assistant screwed up again," she says, bobbing the thumbs-down gesture a couple of times. "He's definitely not batting a thousand."

"Oh, yes," I say, as if I know what it's like to have an inadequate assistant. "You have business in Philadelphia?"

"I live there. I just travel to Russia on occasion for work. You?"

"I'm going to visit family. I've been away for very long time." I turn up the severity of my Slavic accent. Something about an accent makes people seem more innocent—or so others have told me—and I want to seem innocent.

"Well, good for you," she says. "I make this trip once a year, and no offense to you Russians, but I don't look forward to it at all. I'm not a great flyer." Her hands are clasped together but her fingers keep fiddling as if too nervous to remain seated. She takes a dramatic breath in and out, then struggles to bend forward and reach the computer on the floor.

"I'm the same way," I say, wishing the laptop were mine, wishing I could ask her if I could borrow it. But I can't. Not yet. Not without drawing suspicion. "I'm Svetlana." I reach for her hand.

She takes it and says, "Maryanne."

"Well, Maryanne, maybe we should calm our nerves together with a few of those little airplane bottles. That's what my sister always does, and she sleeps the whole way."

"That sounds good. I have some work to do first, but I'll take you up on it later."

She boots up the computer and tells me how she never has enough time during the regular workweek to get everything done and how she really loves her job, so she doesn't mind the overtime. I'm not listening as intently as I seem to be. Instead, I am watching her fingers as she types in her password. She's lucky I'm not a thief.

Two hours later, we're giggling as we drink her favorite cocktail: cosmopolitans. She tells me about her "much-younger" boyfriend and how she hates his dog. They're going to fire her boss soon, she says, and promote her in his place. She talks a lot, which is great because I don't have to say a thing. After she has sucked down two drinks to my half of one (I ordered a soda so I can deposit the alcohol in the can), she excuses herself to the bathroom.

I wave down the flight attendant and order two vodkas.

Maryanne returns, flopping back into her seat.

"Just in time," I say as the flight attendant delivers the bottles.

"Oh," Maryanne says, with a weary chuckle.

"It's vodka, *my* favorite." All Americans assume vodka is every Russian's favorite, but that's not true. I actually prefer wine spritzers.

A slow-blinking numbness crosses Maryanne's puffier-than-before face. "Well, I don't need it at this point, but, I mean, what the hell?"

We pretend-clink plastic cups.

She tosses hers back and arranges her coat on top of her like a blanket, piling up her scarf like a pillow. It's only minutes before raspy snores begin, and I reach for her computer.

I'm googling to my heart's content: "Peterman, Dana and John, New York. Albany. Saratoga. Glens Falls." Nothing. Not one viable listing in upstate New York, though I'm pretty sure they moved there. I try "Peterman, Dana and John, Kirksberg," and our home address comes up. The house Helena and I lived in when my parents were there and when they weren't. After that, I come across a listing on New Moon Real Estate. For sale. Ten years ago. I click on it. A full listing reveals the details of the house. The real estate record at the bottom says it was under contract, but then there's a blank space where the names of the new owners should be. The last named owners are Dana and John Peterman. The tax record shows amounts paid for the past ten years. As far as I can see, Dana and John still own it. Could they have moved back? Maybe the sale fell through? They may have been forced to move back if the sale fell through. That would explain why I'm not finding an address in New York.

No matter what, this might be very good news for me.

I clear the laptop's recent history and press restart. It would be nice to keep Maryanne's computer, considering she can easily afford a new one, but the idea of becoming a thief doesn't appeal to me. I close it up and slide it back into the bag at her feet.

As the pilot lands the plane, a nervous excitement fumbles around my stomach. I finger-comb my hair, wishing I could magically make it smooth and presentable, more like Helena's in her passport photo. I get my big sunglasses out, praying the disguise will be enough to take me safely through the checkpoint in customs. Svetlana Peterman Jovian is not welcome in the USA, but hopefully Helena still is. I don't know what I'll do if her passport doesn't get me through.

Maryanne complains of a headache as we head up the jet bridge. Her hair is matted in the back, clothing rumpled, laptop threatening to jump ship. As we near the top of the bridge, I wish her well and head in the opposite direction. It's the middle of the night in Russia, so I don't want to call Helena right now, but I do want to make sure she hears from me. Instead, I call Alexandria's school and leave a message asking the office assistant to please tell my sister I've arrived in America safely. She's a nice woman, and I know she'll deliver the message.

A crowd of passengers cluster as I near passport-checking lanes. My palms sweat as I take my place in line behind a young couple and dip into my backpack to retrieve my sister's passport. I fiddle with my hair, putting it up in a messy bun. I'll keep the sunglasses on until I reach the front of the line.

"Next." It's the lane with the old man with fluffy gray batches of hair around the sides of his balding head.

I smile as kindly as I can and hand him the passport, then push the glasses up like a head band—and try to look confident.

He stares me down like a detective would, and I flick my eyes away, convinced I'm caught.

"You look like someone," he says, gruffly, and I laugh as casually as a person who's clenching her jaw can.

"People are always saying that," I say.

"Hm." He eyes the passport photo again, then flicks back to me. "Are you on that TV show with the brothers who hunt for demons and what-not? Angels, ghosts, you know the one, popular with the kids."

Relief washes over me, spreading its pleasantness across my face. "Unfortunately I am not an actress."

"Well, you could be."

With this hair? With these bags under my eyes? Americans are nicer than I remember.

"What are you doing here?" His voice has taken a sudden business-like tone.

"I'm sorry?"

"You haven't visited in some time. Ten years, to be exact. What's the reason for your visit?"

"Oh, yes, family. I'm here to see my parents. Long overdue." I puff out my cheeks. "Quarrels, you know."

He thumps a stamp in Helena's book. "Good luck with that. Enjoy your stay."

I swipe the passport from the counter and continue down the cordoned-off lane, past yet another TSA agent who stands with arms crossed at its end. My heart is pushing the blood so forcefully through my veins that I'm afraid one of them will rupture. But I've made it back into America without the help of the Jovians, and this is cause for celebration. Now that I'm through, I'm pretty sure Edmund hoped the authorities would detain me.

I open yet another door and meet with a mob of travelers passing like cars on a highway. Several planes must have disembarked at the same time. As I wait to squeeze into the flow, my backpack, much fatter than I'm used to, becomes ensnared by the metal door frame and causes me to spin out. I'm very close to face planting on the floor, but it doesn't quite happen. The river of rushing people bumps out around me, and I struggle backward to get out of the way. With my backpack mashed against the wall, I straighten the straps so it sits right again.

I glance up, and one of the people passing catches my eye. I only see him from the back. It's a young man in a group of five or six girls, and from where I stand, he looks like Evander. He has the same tall, lanky swimmer frame and deep-brown hair. He even walks the way Evander does, without hunching at all in spite of his height. I know it can't be him—it's doubtful those girls are Jovian—but I can't stop myself from shouting "Evander!"

A few heads turn vaguely in my direction, but not the one I want. I cut into oncoming traffic, upsetting an older lady who grumbles at my back. Through the swiftly moving crowd I remain fixated on what I can see of him. He's wearing colors Evander doesn't wear: rusty brown corduroys and a striped green-and-white top, not at all like Evander's plain jeans and long-sleeved black T-shirt or hoody. It can't be him unless the Jovians forced him on a plane and made him wear new clothes, which they might have, I realize. And I can't be sure unless I see his face.

I try not to knock anyone over as I slip through the spaces in between travelers, hoping to make up ground. But groups of people keep merging into the foot traffic, and soon enough I'm pushed back by a slow-moving family with five lumbering children. At the end of the corridor, I reach an intersection and check both left and right, but there's no sign of him either way.

He's gone.

Evander would never wear brown corduroys, anyway.

And what are the odds that I would arrive in America and find him at the airport? That would be far too easy.

6

In the taxi on the way to Kirksberg, I prepare to dial my parents' phone number, which I remember from when I lived there. It's a landline, and if they still have the house, they may still have the number. But I'm nervous for this phone call. The more I think about it, the more I worry that Dana and John may not have appreciated the way I disappeared from their lives. Then again, I didn't exactly do that. The year I became pregnant and Andrew died, I tried to reach them in the Middle East. They were on a humanitarian health campaign at the time, and who knows what the Jovians might have done to prevent them from receiving my messages. I don't blame my parents for our failure to communicate, and I hope they don't blame me. The Jovians wanted to isolate me—they wanted me to have no one to turn to—and Dana and John don't know anything about that. I hope I can explain it to them.

These thoughts first bring a lump to my throat, and then just make me want to throw something glass out the window and watch it smash to pieces. But the only thing I have to throw is this cell phone, and that will not be happening.

I make the call. After the phone rings four times, I'm pretty sure no one is going to pick up. Before I left America, I was so used to trying and failing to reach my parents that I'm worried I may never speak to them again. But then, a miracle: Dana's familiar, energetic *hello* practically stops my heart. "Oh my God, Dana, it's Svetlana." I laugh so loudly that the driver checks the rearview. I put my hand up in a gesture of apology.

"Svetlana! Is it really you?" She sounds as emotional as I feel.

"How are you?" I shout. "How is John? It's so good to finally hear your voice. You have no idea how long I've wanted to speak to you."

"Oh, sweetheart, where are you? Are you okay?"

"You're not going to believe this, but I'm in the US. I'm in a taxi."

"Well, that is … Wow, that's wonderful." Her voice muffles a bit as she shouts, "John, where are you? It's Svetlana, she's in the US. … Yes, on the phone. … Well, I don't know if Helena's with her. Is Helena with you, Svetlana? And Evander? Is my grandson with you?"

"I'm alone," I say, "but I'm heading to your house right now, and I'll explain."

"This is too good to be true," Dana shouts. "Did you know we arrived home from Kenya just last week?"

"I didn't. But I'm so glad you're home."

"What great timing you have. When will you get here?"

"In about …" I check out the window to see where we are. "Half an hour or so."

"I'll be waiting outside," Dana shouts. "I'll be there with bells on."

With bells on. Dana has always been one for American sayings, and I've always enjoyed the way she uses them.

"I can't wait to see you," I tell her, and we hang up.

The driver pulls to the curb in front of the colonial-style home that Helena and I lived in for seven years. With shaking hands, I pay him and struggle out of the back seat, my backpack following after me like a swollen turtle shell. I run across the front lawn, my breath visible in the cold air.

Dana's there, by the front door as promised, and so is John. He's about a foot taller than she is, and Dana still wears her brown, wavy hair short. John has his big glasses with rectangular lenses and an approachable way about him. A navy-blue puffer coat zips up to Dana's chin, and John has the same one in dark green. They both wear jeans. They look pretty much just as I remember them, and that brings me great comfort.

"Look at you," Dana says, her brown eyes crinkly with delight. "You're all grown up. Your hair . . . "

I run to them and open my arms wide to hug them both in. They can't know how relieved I am to find them home, to reconnect with my family. A few hot, reluctant tears squeeze from my eyes, though I don't want Dana and John to know how much it means for me to be with family right now, how desperate I am to climb back into their lives.

When the hug ends, Dana pats my head and says, "It's okay, you're home now. You're home." And that only creates more devastating cracks in my armor. I'm fighting a terrible urge to bawl.

Dana says, "I wish Evander and Helena could have come."

"Let's get inside, you two," John says, as he nudges us toward the door. "It's freezing out here."

We enter the house, which feels as warm and inviting as it did when I lived here. That indescribable scent one can only call "home" chases the sadness from my body. Little has changed from what I can see. Dana leads me into the living room, sits me down on the same khaki-colored couch I remember paired with the same glass coffee table with the chip Helena made in the top when she dropped a glass bottle of soda on it. Dana sits beside me as she asks how the flight was and tells me what a wonderful surprise this is and how much they've missed me.

John unzips his coat and sits in the armchair a few feet away, rubbing the cold from his hands.

I let Dana talk while I settle myself, remembering that this is the house where, after knowing each other for only a week, Andrew and I fell into a serious conversation that ended with him saying, "If you're sure about what you want, then you should quit your job, finish grad school, and agree to marry me."

Dana and John never even met Andrew, but I know they would have loved him.

"Is everything all right?" Dana says. "You seem to have disappeared for a second."

I snap out of my bittersweet thoughts of Andrew and temper the urge to divulge everything about the Jovians and what's happening now: what they've done to me, what they want to do to the rest of the world. But I can't do that yet.

"It's just so nice to be back," I say. "I'm literally overwhelmed."

"I bet," John says. "It's great to see you, kiddo."

"So, first things first," Dana says, and her hands make a clapping sound upon her thighs. "Helena's still in Russia?"

"Yes, she's married to a nice man named Ivan, and they have a daughter, Alexandria, ten years old."

"Oh, that's great." Dana's eyes soften as if this news warms her heart. "I figured she would have her own family by now. And how is your son? Is he in Russia, too, or here in the States somewhere?"

I've thought about how I will answer this question, how

I'll tell them the truth about the Jovians with some missing details because I don't want to frighten them or make them worry that I'm unhinged. "Evander's not here yet, but he will be soon. He's with my in-laws doing some sightseeing, and I'm not sure when they'll reach Kirksberg—"

Dana clasps her hands together and brings them up to her smiling lips. "We'll finally get to meet him. We were so sorry we weren't in the country when he was born and before you all left for Russia."

Left for Russia. That's so Dana. Forever careful with her words, even when I know it probably broke her heart that both of her daughters left the country without saying good-bye. The truth is, Helena and I won the proverbial lottery when they adopted us as teenagers. It's rare for children over the age of five to end up finding parents. It's also true that the older we grew, the more Dana and John traveled for their humanitarian efforts, and I know their being away for extended periods of time bothered Helena. But they cared about us so much, and that meant everything to me. I never would have avoided them if I'd had my way.

But Dana and John don't know that.

"I'm very sorry we had to leave," I say. "It's a long story."

"No worries." Dana's eyes brighten with anticipation. "So, Evander will be here soon? What is he now, about ten years old?"

"Yes, but, um . . . " I pause and release a bit of nervous laughter. I have to do something to prepare my parents for the sight of ten-year-old Evander. They need to be aware that he doesn't look like a child.

"You'd be surprised how big he is," I say.

Dana shares a glance with John before saying, "That's great. A big, healthy boy."

"Yes, but what I mean is that if you didn't know him, you would think he was a teenager, not a ten-year-old. Even his face is, well, pretty grown up. He's not at all your typical child." It sounds awkward but I don't know what else to say.

"I guess you and Andrew provided some good genes," says John, joining the conversation. He has always taken a backseat to Dana's chattiness.

I can't tell them the truth about Jovian DNA, so I say, "Yes, I guess that's it."

"Do you have a picture?" John asks.

"I have just one picture, believe it or not, and it's a passport photo, very formal, so you'll see what I mean about looking old for his age."

There's so much they don't know. They don't know that Evander has always been homeschooled due to his advanced growth and maturity, which is why we don't have school photos. Not to mention we don't own a camera or a cell phone that works. I don't even own a wallet to keep a photo in. Which is sad, considering I have no record of Evander's growth—no record of our life together. If I told my parents all of this, they would worry about me, so I keep it to myself.

"Please get it now," Dana says. "I'm beside myself with curiosity."

I've never seen her so eager about anything, but I understand: Evander is her grandchild.

I reach for my backpack and unzip the pocket with the photo, then pull it out, gaze at it for a moment before I hand it to her. I miss him so much already.

Dana holds it far from her face, muttering something about needing her readers, while John gets up behind her so he can see as well. "Boy, you weren't kidding," Dana says, squinting at the picture. "Isn't that amazing? He looks to be at least fifteen."

"Yes," I say, stifling the urge to tell them he easily passes for twenty. "It's funny when all the high school girls stare at him as he walks by. I want to shout, 'Look away, please. He's just a baby.'"

"He resembles you quite a bit, or at least when you had your brown hair," John says.

"Ugh, I know." My fingers get caught on a knot as I rake them through my off-color strands. "I hope to return to my natural brown soon."

"Will you be staying with the Jovians?" Dana asks.

"Oh, no. They only wanted to spend time with Evander. They picked him up, and I took a later flight." I pause to corral the consternation that rises when I hear these words spoken. I clear my throat. "Which is fine because I want to spend some time with you two. Would you mind if I stay here?"

"Of course you can stay," Dana says loudly. "I'm so glad you want to. I was afraid we'd have just a short visit before you'd say you had to go."

"I wish I could have called and given you some notice," I say, "instead of inviting myself like I have."

"Don't be ridiculous. This is your home. You're welcome anytime."

"I'm so glad to see you both."

Dana rises from the couch. "Why don't I show you to your room? Sometimes I sleep in there when John snores."

"She's kidding," he tells me.

Dana moves toward the kitchen. "You know you've taken to snoring in your older-middle age, John."

"So you claim." He winks in my direction. "Is this all you have? Just one small bag? Did the airlines lose your luggage?"

I swing the backpack over my shoulder. "I prefer to travel light."

"I'll say. Maybe you could give your mother a few tips."

Dana takes me to my bedroom, which they've redecorated in a simple gray hue with white trim. Apparently, they put my clothes and other things in boxes and stowed them in the attic. Dana and I talk for a couple of minutes, but now that my adrenaline levels are back to normal, I can't stop yawning from the jet lag.

"You look tired," she says. "Better rest for a bit."

Jet lag is one of those terrible things in life you can't do much about, and as soon as she leaves, I pass out.

It's two hours later and I feel like my head is filled with helium. I would have slept longer, but the sounds coming from the kitchen paired with the tantalizing scent of roast chicken have pulled me out of a dream of Evander. He was a baby, and I was running scared through the park with him in my arms just before the dream dispersed.

I head into the kitchen where Dana, John, and I pick the chicken clean. The plates are scraped and placed in the dishwasher the same way we used to share the task of cleanup when I was a teenager. We have resumed our places at the table for after-dinner tea or decaf coffee the way we used to as well. Helena would leave us at this point, preferring to spend the time alone in her room, but I always stayed with Dana and John to discuss things like plans for the future and whatever part of the world they would be visiting next.

With my stomach full for the first time in a long time and the house so warm and clean, and a feeling of love and security coming from my parents, I'm ready to tell them more about my life.

"There's a lot about me you don't know," I say at a break in the conversation. "And I don't mean that in a mysterious way. It's just that, after I married Andrew, so much happened that you weren't here for."

Dana and John pass each other guilty-looking glances

before Dana sets her teacup down and says, "We regret not being here for you when Andrew passed. We're very sorry we received your messages so long after the fact."

I put on a sincere face, void of animosity. "I know you would have come if you were able. It's no one's fault. I don't blame you."

"We should have been here after he died," John says smoothing his napkin. "It was bad luck all around. The draught in the Middle East was the worst it's been in, well, I think ever. Every day was harder than the last. There was no water. We were literally doing whatever we could to drum up as much aid and as many bottles and cases of water as possible, and then personally transporting them to remote villages. We didn't stay in the same place for more than a day at a time."

Dana's on the edge of her seat. "We were out of our heads with worry when he heard Andrew had died. And mind you, we didn't hear until a month or so after it had happened. But please tell us, where did you go, what did you do?"

"Andrew and I lived in Ashbury Falls at the time, in North Carolina."

"Oh, wow, we've been to Ashbury Falls before," John says. "Isn't that where we took a tour of the castle, what's-its-name?"

"L'Origine," I say with my heart in my throat. "I know the castle well." I swallow as the reminder of the castle's tower takes me back to a stone room overseen by my mother-in-law, Caroline, a time in my life that was filled with hopelessness and anger. This is going to be harder than I thought. "What I have to say isn't going to be easy for you to hear." My voice quivers as the air I breathe catches on what feels like little barbs in my throat.

Dana reaches out and takes my hand. "You can tell us anything. You know that."

I close my eyes and will myself to remain calm. "I was pregnant when Andrew died, and when it was time for me to give birth, the Jovians, they, um, took me. They drugged me. I have no memory of the birth. Afterward, they kept Evander and me against my will—in a tower at L'Origine."

Dana's jaw has gone slack. *"Drugged you and kept you?"* Her voice reaches a noticeably higher octave. "Why would they do that? For how long?"

"We lived there for several weeks."

Blinking rapidly, my mother sits back in her chair, her hand resting on her chest. "For weeks?" She reaches for her phone as if thinking of dialing the police.

John leans toward me, the skin around his eyes wrinkles as he squints. "Are you saying that they—"

"They kidnapped us. Brought us food. Let us outdoors only at night. No one knew we were there."

"Those bastards." Dana makes a fist of her hand and bangs it with a thud onto the wooden tabletop. The lid of the sugar bowl jumps as if startled. "I can't believe this. What the hell for?"

"Because they are strange, to put it mildly." I try to smile but don't quite get there. I look up at the ceiling, take a breath, and sigh. "It's okay. They treated us well. They—"

"That's more than strange," John says, with a frown that makes him look mean. "That can't be the only reason they did it."

"It wasn't," I say. "They said it was because Evander is, or was, a special baby. They thought he required special care."

"In what way?" Dana says.

"In every way, I suppose," I say. "They were also hosting an event at the chateau with the extended Jovian family, though I didn't know it at the time. Jovians came from every part of the world. It was a celebration, their way of introducing Evander to the family."

"Couldn't they have just asked you to go along instead of taking you?" John said.

"You would think so." I shrug and rake my hand through my hair. "I didn't know what they were really like when Andrew was alive, and honestly, I don't think he did, either."

"Honey, oh my goodness, I'm so sorry." Dana shakes her head as she reaches her hand out to me again.

"That's why I had to go back to Russia. It wasn't because Helena left or because you were away. I didn't want to leave. This was my home, and I loved it here. I especially didn't want to leave without talking to you first. I had to go because it was the only way for me and Evander to be free of them."

John drops his head and slumps in his chair. "I don't know what to say," he says. "I wish we'd been here for you. I've wished that for years."

Revealing why I had left and what had gone on for so long lifts the guilty weight from my shoulders. I feel lighter, a bit dizzy, like I'm no longer alone in this fight against the Jovians. I have my parents on my side, and maybe with them I'll have a chance at getting Evander back.

Dana gets up. "I'm going to make tea," she says. "Anybody want some?"

John and I decline.

"I always heard the Jovians could be difficult businesspeople to work with, but kidnappers?" John says, staring into the kitchen table. "No one would believe it."

"Oh, I know," I say, as I chew my bottom lip.

Dana fills the teapot with water. "Well, don't you worry about that. *We* believe you. One hundred percent, don't we, John?"

"Of course we do. It's sad to think that everyone around here treats the Jovians like celebrities."

"The Kirksberg community assumes they're good people," I say. "They're wealthy. They employ hundreds at Starbright."

"And all this time . . . " Dana stares into the distance. "How did you get away?"

"A friend of ours who works for the FBI helped—Andrew went to college with him. He's a great guy."

I can't tell them what happened in the park that day. How Fran met me there, how he tried to stop David from using his supreme powers. That would be too much too soon.

The stove makes that bright and snappy sound as a flame sparks to life. The stove in Russia was ancient and always required matches, so it's a sound I haven't heard in years.

"Thank God for him," Dana says. "He must be the one who called us a couple of times when we were still in the Middle East. Fran Valasquez, or something like that?"

"Vasquez," I say. "He was a good friend."

"So, Fran got you out," John says, "and ten years later, Evander is vacationing with the Jovians."

I stare at the wall in front of me and consider where Evander might be. "They're not actually vacationing. I told you that because I didn't want you to worry. The Jovians came to Russia and took him from me. For ten years I've watched my child like a hawk, but they still managed to—" My voice breaks, and I stop there.

Dana, by the stove, has jammed her hands on her hips. "Again? They took him again!" She gazes past me now, at John, as if to say, "We have to do something about this."

"Edmund, Andrew's father or . . . " Uncle Jimmy is really Andrew's father, but I don't need to go there now, ". . . Edmund came to tell me—"

John tilts his head in question. "He came to you in Russia?"

"Yes, and he said they were taking Evander somewhere before they get to Kirksberg."

Dana moves closer, puts her arms around me, and rocks a little side to side. "Please don't worry. He'll come back, or we'll get him back. We'll call one of our Amnesty lawyers if we have to. And in the meantime the Jovians are his family, so I'm sure he's safe with them."

The Jovians are his family, but that doesn't mean he's safe with them, though I won't say that out loud.

Instead, I say, "I do think they'll eventually come here, and Edmund did say they'll let me see him." In spite of what I say, the doubtful side of me has returned, and I'm on the other side of confident, fearful I may never see my son again. If David still has access to my thoughts, he might send someone to get me tonight or tomorrow. They might force me to go back to Russia, or send me back to L'Origine, or maybe they'll just load me into a rocket and launch me into another galaxy.

"I'll call the Amnesty lawyers in the morning," John says. "I'm sure Louis can suggest a course of action."

"But maybe the Jovians simply want to spend some time with their grandson," Dana says, letting me go and stepping away. "They haven't seen him in ten years, so it would make sense."

She's trying to lessen my worry, to cut the family some slack. But I know they don't deserve it.

The teakettle begins to whistle, and she returns to the stove.

John's brows rise as if suggesting that what Dana said is something to consider. "That's true. They probably miss him. They probably miss the both of you."

"Still, they shouldn't have taken him," I insist.

"Of course not. Of course not," John agrees. "The way they've gone about this is absolutely wrong. But maybe it's not as bad as you think. Maybe they'll take him to see a few sights and then you and Evander can go home together. Or stay here. We would love it if the two of you would stay with us when he arrives."

"Oh, I'd love that, too," I say. "But it all depends on *them* and whether they can leave us alone and let us live our lives."

John leans in with a stern expression that brings out the strength in his clear hazel eyes. "We're here now, and we won't let them bully you. Don't worry about that."

"Thank you," I say. "Believe me, I feel so much better now that you know what's been going on."

Even though they don't yet know enough.

"Just being here in this house with you brings me great relief," I say.

But will it make a difference?

"And we'll stay here in Kirksberg until you see this thing through," Dana says, bobbing her tea bag up and down in her cup.

"Oh, good," I say. "No trips planned for the near future?"

"No," she says, "we're taking a much-needed break."

7

I sleep late into the next morning. When I wake, I first become angry about Evander's unknown whereabouts, and then I remember that I'm with my parents and they're going to help me get through this.

I'm not alone anymore.

Last night, I realized something, too. The hum in my head has not returned, and I'm not sure what that means. I haven't had any visions of outer space, and my Jovian intuition isn't telling me a thing. Maybe Edmund really did switch off the connection between us. I hope so because I want to do some snooping around town and via computer to see if I can figure out what the Jovians have been up to for the past ten years—and what they plan to do with Evander now.

I take a shower and find some of my old clothes in a box in the attic. The jeans still fit, though more snugly than I remember, and I have always worn plain, classic tops and shoes, so I don't feel too out of date (aside from my bad hair).

I log onto Dana's computer and start my research. After about two minutes, I learn that there's not much for the public to see concerning the Jovians except for the Starbright

International website. A photograph of Edmund, CEO, in a sharp suit, looking wealthy for the camera, joins a photo of the four-story state-of-the-art facility with its shiny bump of a telescope sticking out like a metal head on top. Other photos show the telescope from inside, as well as the glassy foyer and its marble floors. A couple of pictures feature people in business dress and white lab coats, but it's no one I recognize.

Dana calls me to lunch. I hadn't realized it was already noon.

I'd also forgotten how good and plentiful the food in America was. Dana has made a green-and-purple salad along with tofu burgers and baked sweet potato fries. I'm on my second helping when the doorbell rings, and the hair on my arms stands straight up.

I spring from my seat, my napkin drops to the floor, and the chair makes a terrible screeching sound before clunking back and forth, threatening to fall.

I race to the back door, which is only a few steps away, but I can't get there fast enough. "Don't tell them I'm here," I whisper-shout.

"Who?" Dana says, jolting upright. "Oh my God, do you think it's *them?*"

"I don't know! I'm going out. I have to hide."

I push the door open and run without coat or shoes, not caring about the cold. At first I think I'll hide in the bushes, but then I continue to the garage. The side door is unlocked, and I open it and carefully close it behind me.

The damp smell of tires and engine oil hits me first. In front of me the old maroon-colored sedan brings back memories of going for ice cream and accompanying Dana to the grocery store—but the sight of a second car staggers me to a halt. I've seen this car before, but not here, not in Dana and John's garage. It's light green and compact, an electric car just like Uncle Jimmy's. The one I called "the grasshopper" due to its color. Through the back window I see one of Dana's sun hats, a pair of gardening gloves, a few hardcover books, and sneakers. It makes sense Dana would have an environmentally friendly car like this one, though my parents never had two cars. They always got along fine with just one because they were away from home so often. A moment passes before I remember that I'm out here because someone rang the bell at the front door.

I walk, careful not to step on anything sharp in my sock feet, to the other side of the grasshopper and squat to the ground.

Then I wonder whether it might be Evander who rang the doorbell. I stand and creep over to the garage door's rightmost windows, making sure I remain concealed. There's a car parked at the opposite end of the driveway, not fancy at all. Black with a rusty dent in its front bumper. It's not a Jovian vehicle, that's for sure, which means it's not Evander.

I stand there, as still as one of the rakes or shovels hung upon the wall behind me, for the next several minutes. Finally a man emerges from the direction of the house. He's widely built with overgrown hair that covers his eyes in front and stretches in wavy tendrils down his neck in back. Something seems to be wrong with his right side. He may have a limp, and his coat hangs in a strange manner. He unlocks the driver's side door and tosses a pad of paper into the passenger seat, then gets in himself, and closes the door.

He doesn't look in the direction of the garage.

It's weird because he resembles Fran, if Fran were to have a breakdown and let himself go to hell. But Fran would never do that. Then again, I'm sure Fran has noticed that "Helena Peterman" entered the country yesterday—someone at the FBI would have alerted him—or maybe not because Helena's only crime is being my non-blood-related sister.

Whoever this man is, his car grinds to life as if it's made with rusted parts. Then it slowly backs out and speeds away.

Seconds later, the side door of the garage swings open and John leans in. "Hey, you in here? He's gone." He narrows his eyes and scans the area.

"Who was it?" I say, drawing his attention with the sound of my voice.

"Mr. Vasquez, your old friend."

"What? That can't be."

"He said his name was Fran Vasquez, and that he was your friend."

What happened to him?

"I take it he's changed since you saw him last," John asks.

"He was built like a superhero when I knew him. And his face, too, he was closely shaved and . . . " I pause to think. "His hair was always so nicely cut. That man seemed, I don't know, crushed."

John leans into the doorway and crosses his arms. "Well, he said he was notified that Helena had entered the country, and figured she might come visit us. He gave your mother his phone number in case she shows up. He also said that if you happen to be with her that you don't have to be afraid to call him."

I look back to where Fran's car was parked. "But I'm not supposed to enter the US, and he knows that."

"Dana told him we haven't seen either of you in ten years. I couldn't tell whether he believed her or not."

"I can't call him. If Fran finds me, he'll probably make me go back to Russia. He's very loyal to his job."

"Do you know how he lost his arm?"

The words rattle my brain. "He lost his *arm?*"

"He has a prosthetic. I think it's his right arm."

"No, I didn't know. No wonder he looks so different."

"I guess he's been through a rough time," he says.

I can't believe it was Fran.

John gestures to the house. "You want to head inside?" He's not wearing a coat and neither am I, and I've begun to shiver. I walk through the garage, and he closes the door behind me.

"I was under the impression Edmund and the rest of the family already knew you were here," he says.

"Yes, but Edmund doesn't know I'm with you. He knows I flew into Philadelphia, that's all."

"Don't you think he'll assume?"

"The Jovians think you moved. *I* thought you moved. The house was for sale—"

"Oh, right," he says. "The sale fell through, so we came back."

"And when did you get that green car, by the way?"

"That's your mother's. She always wanted an electric one."

Later that afternoon, I borrow the grasshopper, which Dana says she bought at least eight years ago, though she can't remember exactly when—it was between her trips to Egypt and Somalia, she says—and she would have traded in their other car but the resale price was practically nothing, so they decided to keep it.

The grasshopper doesn't like hills too much, just like Uncle Jimmy's didn't. It's only a fifteen-minute drive to the top of the tallest hill in Kirksberg where the Jovians built their sprawling state-of-the-art facility, which gleams like a coin in the sun. It's almost quitting time for the office and other workers, and my plan is to park and observe who comes out the front entrance. I want to see if I recognize any Jovians.

I'll have to pass through the security gate first, and that

may be a problem, but I've already thought of what I'll say when the guard stops me.

As I near, the booth appears to be empty. I continue past slowly so as not to draw attention. There's a guard standing on the outgoing side. A thirty-ish Asian man, well built, turns and puts his hand up. I've already passed, so I stomp the brake—the car jolting—before he gives me a go-ahead wave as if he knows who I am.

Could he have recognized me? Even with my lightened hair and sunglasses? How is this possible?

My nerves quiver throughout my body as I continue to drive, unsure of why he has waved me through. I suppose it's possible he knows me as Andrew's wife. Maybe Edmund told the security staff that I'd probably make an appearance. I never told him I was coming to Kirksberg, but I'm sure he assumed I would do as he said. Or maybe this man has mistaken me for a Starbright employee. It could be any of these things.

As I drive down the incline into the parking lot, I descend into the dreary remembrance of the last time I entered a Starbright building. It was Ashbury Falls, and I'd come to see Andrew's body. The Jovians didn't allow the police to bring him to a morgue, because Andrew wasn't human. My husband, the test tube baby, was the most human the Jovians were capable of producing, though he never knew it. They made Andrew in the hope that he would meet a woman and make a child, and in doing so, start a hybrid generation, a new race that's both human and Jovian.

What was the chance I would be the woman to do it?

Plenty of open parking spaces reveal themselves in the far corner of the lot. I creep my way to a group of four or five, then slip the car into reverse and back in. The view allows clear access to the front entrance, though I'm farther away than I'll want to be if Evander exits the building. I doubt that will happen, and that's okay. I'm only here to observe.

I leave the car on, letting it purr with heat and defrost so the windows don't fog.

It's not long before men and women in suits begin to pass through the front doors. Some of them are alone, some in pairs. A lot of them are young; I can tell because they have the fit bodies of those in their twenties. The administrative assistants, no doubt. No young person wants to work past five o'clock on a—what day is it?—*Friday*. Can't be Saturday. When did I leave Tula? I'm not even sure. When I look up again, what I see draws me forward, and I bump my chin into the steering wheel. "That can't be Evander," I whisper.

I fumble the seatbelt, which I hadn't yet removed, then struggle to untangle myself from its shoulder strap. I grope the armrest in search of the correct button to unlock the doors and then remember that the car is still running. I grab for the keys, twisting them as I struggle to pull them out. I don't dare take my eyes off of this person, so I've done all of this while staring through the windshield.

The young man I'm looking at wears a long, gray business-style coat that's wide open, and he's passing in between two cars in the first row of the lot. I've stepped out of the car and tried to slam the door at the same time, successfully catching the heel of my boot, and now the top half of my body spills to the ground. I'm on hands and knees for a second before I struggle back up and regain balance. Then I run.

As I pass through a row of parked cars, I hear more than one or two engines starting. *No, no, no, no, no!* I shout, "Evander! Wait!"

I've made it midway through the lot when out of nowhere someone crashes into me. I'm tackled, literally, my shoulder taking the brunt of the force that knocks me down. It's a woman. I know because she smells of perfume and her sounds of surprise and discomfort are higher in pitch rather than lower. "I'm sorry, so sorry," she says, as I struggle to free myself from her and her smooth woolen coat, a piece of which has somehow flapped over my head like a hood. I can't see anything. I push the fabric away and rise up on my elbows to see if Evander has left. Cars are pulling away, I can hear them, but I'm still on the ground with this woman on my back so I see nothing.

"All right, all right," she says. "Patience, Svetlana."

The voice is familiar, though I can't place it. Finally she removes herself, and I push back and up, scrambling to my feet. The navy-blue car that I think Evander unlocked is gone. I've missed my chance.

I turn to glare at the woman who sidelined me. It's Miranda. My next-door neighbor from Ashbury Falls. The Southern one who called the Jovians instead of calling an ambulance when I went into labor—only she seems to have lost her Southern accent.

"What are you doing here?" I say with the same level of disgust I'd have for something that smells like a garbage truck.

She's dressed in business clothes. No longer the happy housewife. Playing a new role, apparently.

Miranda's pretty blue eyes crinkle around the edges in the charming way they did when I thought we were friends. "It's so nice to see you. I might ask you the same question. Shouldn't you be in Russia, living in a small farm town?"

I give her the "I hate you" scowl and scan the lot once more in case I'm wrong about Evander having left.

"To answer your question, I'm not doing anything," she says. "I just work here, honey."

There are no words for how angry that *honey* makes me.

She fluffs her wavy hair a bit and straightens her coat, dusts off her purse. "Are you hurt?"

I can't answer that, so I don't even try.

"When did you get into town?" she asks in an all-too-pleasant tone of voice.

"I'm sure you know exactly when I got into town. When did you leave Ashbury Falls?"

"Leo was transferred. I guess it's been about ten years now."

"Ten years, of course," I say with a *pfft* of dismay. "Well, I'm here to see Edmund." I start to walk in the direction of the building's entrance.

She follows me. "I heard you shout Evander's name."

"Yes, I saw him."

"That wasn't Evander."

It's several minutes past 5 p.m. now, and a steady stream of employees exit the building. A pretty Black woman waves to Miranda. "Have a nice weekend," she says. Other people glance in our direction but don't look familiar to me. I stop walking when I reach the sidewalk in front, and Miranda catches up.

"I think I would know my own son when I see him," I say.

"I have no doubt that's true," she says as if paying me a compliment. "But you couldn't have seen Evander because he's on assignment."

"On assignment?"

The last time I was told someone was "on assignment," it was Uncle Jimmy. And soon after that, the Jovians sent him back to Mintaka. His home in the sky. "Evander was right here," I say. "I just saw him."

Miranda stares into the distance, then focuses back on me. "Listen, I'm going to tell you where he is because you're a good friend, and I know you think I wronged you in Ashbury Falls. I want to make it up to you, Sveta."

I snigger in a way I hope bothers her but probably doesn't. "That's impossible."

"He went to the mother planet," she says, in a dire tone I've never heard her take.

A bomb goes off in my mind. I stagger forward a step, feeling like a balloon that has suffered a fatal puncture and now spins in circles as it deflates. *She's lying.*

"That . . . can't be," the syllables lurch out of my mouth.

"It's okay. *He's* okay. There's no reason to wor—"

"Where's Edmund? I need to see Edmund."

She shakes her head. "He went, too."

"I saw him in Russia."

"Yes, I know."

"He and Evander weren't together."

"But they are now."

"Okay, if that wasn't Evander who just got into his car," I gesture with a trembling pointer finger toward the lot behind us, "then who was it?"

"Another young man who works here. I think it was Christopher. He resembles Evander to a certain degree, but—"

"He looked *exactly* like my son."

"Are you certain? You saw him from a pretty far distance, across the entire length of this parking lot. Sometimes when we really want something, our mind makes it seem—"

"Don't say *we* as if you and I are the same," I say.

She wants me to think Evander left Kirksberg. She wants to throw me off the trail. But I've found him. He's right here, at Starbright.

"I can see that you're trying to figure all of this out like it's a puzzle, but it's not." She lays a hand on my shoulder and directs me toward her so that we're face-to-face. "Evander went willingly. He *wanted* to go."

The word *wanted* lands like a boulder upon my shoulders.

I stand there, dumbfounded. She can't be right. He wouldn't *want* to go. He wouldn't go willingly. Not without at least saying goodbye, not without letting me know he was all right. I know my son.

I step back and her hand slides from my shoulder. A strand of hair blows into my face and I swipe it away with a shaky hand. "Okay," I say, and before I know what I'm doing, I've turned and I'm striding toward my car. It's far too late to get in and chase after the person I assumed was Evander but may have been another young man according to the liar that is Miranda.

When I start the engine, Miranda is still standing near the entrance to the building. Hands in the pockets of her woolen coat, a fiercely blank look on her face, she gazes at me across the lot. For all I know she's dreaming of the mother planet.

8

A block from my house, I almost crash into a car that stops in front of me at a stop sign. The grasshopper's tires screech and I scream "Jupiter!" for no reason at all except that it's the only thing I can think of right now. The driver's distraught eyes check the rearview. I raise my hand and mouth the word *sorry*. I'm jittery and my insides feel sick hot—and I want to punch someone. An image of Miranda comes to mind. I should have done it when I had the chance.

The car in front of me crosses the intersection, and I creep up, then look both ways with deliberation. No one's coming. I drive the rest of the way home without hurting anyone. I pull into the driveway, then click the button and wait for the garage door to go up. I roll in and close the door behind me, then turn off the car and sit there.

They've taken my son to Jupiter.

If it's true, there's nothing I can do. I may never see him again. This is so much worse than I could have imagined. Or maybe they just want me to think he's gone to Jupiter. Maybe I actually saw Evander in the parking lot, and

Miranda has knitted this story together to keep me from coming back and stalking the Starbright employees. The young man had Evander's hair, his build, his way of walking and smiling when he talks to friends. . . . Then again I could be mistaken because I *was* far away. Miranda was right: my mind may have showed me what I wanted to see.

And then I remember the boy at the airport. The one I saw only from the back, walking with a bunch of girls. I swore he was Evander, too. I ran after him but didn't catch up, didn't get close enough for a good look.

I have the sensation of someone or some*thing* creeping up on me now—a shadow or some force of evil. My heart races and the pulse bangs in my ears. I close my eyes and picture the small notebook of Andrew's that I'd found just after Evander was born. The one where he'd written, "The SON" and "The CLONE."

Ten years ago, Uncle Jimmy told me the family wanted to clone Evander. He also said, "Don't let them do it, Svetlana."

Where's my cell phone? I thrust my hands into my coat pockets and pull it out, press the buttons to get to the contacts, then find Edmund's listing. It rings and rings. Edmund doesn't pick up. Voicemail doesn't pick up. I grab the steering wheel and squeeze it as if doing so might help me get the call through. But of course, it doesn't.

Edmund's on assignment with my son, who supposedly went willingly.

I enter my parents' house through the back door, remove my coat, and hang it on a vacant hook. I try to calm myself because I need to appear normal. I don't want Dana and John to know how upset I am.

"Oh good, you're home," Dana calls to me. "Can you help me make a salad?"

"Sure," I say and join her at the counter, my mind churning with thoughts of Jovians.

"We're having a casserole. It's in the oven."

"Okay," I say, adding, "smells good," as an afterthought.

John comes in and sits at the table with a section of the newspaper, probably the crossword, while Dana pulls the lettuce, onion, carrots, container of feta, and jar of olives from the refrigerator and puts them all on the counter in front of me. "Did something happen?" she says, in a gentle tone. "You seem a little out of sorts."

I shrug and shake my head. "I'm fine. I'm just . . . " I stop myself. Now that my mother has asked what's wrong, I feel like crying. "I thought I saw Evander a little while ago, but it didn't turn out to be him."

"Oh, sweetheart, I'm sorry to hear that. I'm sure you're going to think you see him just about everywhere you go."

"Yes," I say, and maybe that's true.

Or maybe it's true because Aunt Constant found a way to clone him after they forced us to leave our American life. I know for a fact the Jovians took a sample of Evander's cells days before we left, and I also know that the technology for cloning humans wasn't where they needed it to be. But they were trying. They were working on it.

"I went to Starbright just to, I don't know, spy, I guess you could say. And I ran into an old friend. Or, I should say a *former* friend. She's not my friend anymore. Her name is Miranda."

Dana hands me a vegetable peeler and pulls some leaves from a head of Romaine. "Someone you knew when you lived here?" She rinses the lettuce under the faucet.

"When I lived in Ashbury Falls. But she and her husband have since been transferred to the Starbright office here. They're Jovians—even though that's not their last name."

Dana's perplexity shows in her hesitant, "Oh, I see," as if she's failing to grasp how that makes sense. "And what happened with Miranda?"

I pick up a carrot and glide the peeler over it.

Dana slices the onion.

The moment strains under a pause that emerges while I sort out what to say and how to say it.

"She told me something about Evander," I say.

Dana stops chopping. "She knows something?"

"I haven't told you enough about the Jovians for you to understand. And I'm afraid to tell you because you'll think it's bizarre. You might even think I'm, I don't know, losing my mind."

"That's ridiculous. We've met so many people from so many different walks of life. I doubt there's anything you could say that would make us so much as raise an eyebrow. Isn't that right, John?"

He looks up from his crossword. "Yup, that's true." Then he folds the paper and places it on the table with the pencil on top. "If the Jovians are strange, it has little to do with you. You certainly didn't make them that way."

"Mm, thank you," I say, but I'm still afraid to tell them. "Um, I'm not sure where to start." I gaze at my hands, taking a moment to draw the courage. "Well, the truth is that the Jovians are not like other human beings, not like you and me, and I mean that literally."

Dana's neck retracts and her eyes widen. "I don't get it. They're not people?"

"They are, but they're not like . . . " I pause for a breath. "When Andrew was alive, he saw a file at work that basically said their DNA closely matches the DNA of the alien that crash-landed in Kirksberg in the sixties."

"There was an alien aboard that ship?" John says. "The common understanding is that it was basically a drone, an airship guided by remote control."

"There was at least one passenger on board," I say. "Maybe more. NASA has had it all this time. It's a secret, of course. No one is supposed to know outside of the senior employees of Starbright and some of the people who work for NASA, I assume."

"Isn't that interesting?" Dana says. A moment passes where my mother appears to have frozen. Then suddenly she's in motion again, throwing chopped lettuce and onion into the big white salad bowl. She puts the bowl down beside the chopping block I've been using and slides in the pieces of carrot I made into shreds. Then she pauses again, furrowing her brow in my direction. I can see that she's stuck in a moment of disbelief. "What does that mean exactly? Are you saying the Jovian family has some ancestral connection to—"

"They do. Yes. The Jovians' DNA and the DNA of the extraterrestrial are basically the same. I know it sounds crazy, believe me. Even Andrew had a hard time accepting what he read in that file."

Saying this out loud brings a blush to my face.

"I like to think I have an open mind," Dana says, glancing back at John, "but this is kind of scary."

"I agree," I say, with a nervous laugh. "And what's worse is that I think they're from Jupiter."

"From . . . " Dana stops what she's doing and looks me directly in the eye, probably to check whether or not I'm joking. "Can this be possible?" she says.

My head bobs my answer. "Yes, that's where they're from."

"You mean *Jupiter* Jupiter?" John says. "Fifth planet from the sun, Jupiter?"

"Yes, and that's where they've taken Evander. According to Miranda."

Dana's jaw drops. She clutches her cotton sweater in front of her heart. "How's that even . . . I'm not sure I can wrap my head around all of this."

"I know, I know," I say, trying to both acknowledge how unreal this is and that it's absolutely true, all while feeling like I've thrown a steaming hot pot of frightening facts at her.

I give them a moment to decide whether I've gone off the deep end while my nerves shift into slower gear.

When I look at John, he averts his eyes. He must be embarrassed for me. Or maybe he just needs more convincing.

"Is it even possible for humans to travel to Jupiter," he says. "I mean, physically?"

"Who knows what humans can do with the help of the Jovians," I say.

In the silence that follows, I feel John eyeing me. I have to say more. "Trust me when I tell you that I've seen things that make me believe it's entirely possible. They're *not* regular people. And neither is Evander."

John picks up the pencil and taps it on the tabletop. "Okay," he says like a father who's trying to be supportive in spite of his skepticism. Then he brings a hand to his mouth and bites a hangnail he's been picking at since the conversation started.

"The point is, the situation is far worse than I thought," I say. "Evander's not just sightseeing or spending quality time with my in-laws on his way to Kirksberg."

John presses his lips together, radiating seriousness and resistance—I sense him thinking his daughter might not be quite as balanced as he'd once assumed.

"I know it seems crazy," I tell him.

"No, not crazy," Dana says. "Just hard to accept. Not because we don't believe you. I want to take your word for it, so I will." She can't seem to hold my gaze. "And you will, too, right, John?"

"Thank you for keeping an open mind," I say.

"Something unusual is going on, that's for sure," he says.

They're trying, and that's all I can ask for right now.

A moment of awkward silence descends. The conversation has reached a standstill. John stares into the table. Dana takes in a tired-sounding breath. Neither of them seem to know what to say or do. Even I don't know where the conversation can go from here. The sudden buzz of the oven timer makes all three of us jump.

"That's the casserole," Dana says, and she goes about getting dinner to the table.

We linger after we've finished eating. The plates have been cleared, and only drinks remain. Suddenly I'm exhausted.

Dana tells me that whatever is going on, and wherever the Jovians have taken Evander, she's sure they will bring him back. "Edmund promised you. Why would he lie?"

He might lie for many reasons, but I won't argue with her. I dumped a very hard-to-believe reality on both of my parents today, and I sense it's not time to reveal more. So I'll go with the flow, to use one of Dana's favorite phrases.

"You're right," I say. "I'm sure they will come back, though it may be a while before that happens."

"And even if he went willingly," Dana continues, "like your friend Miranda said, that's perfectly normal for a boy of his age. Young men need to spread their wings."

"You're right," I say, determined not to worry them any more than I already have.

Dana passes me a bittersweet simper, as if mentally sending the message that children grow up and leave the nest, and this is just an ordinary fact of life. I won't remind her that there's nothing normal about one's son being whisked away to Jupiter.

"Fran came by earlier," John says, as if he just remembered. "Sorry I didn't tell you sooner. Sort of got lost when you shared your news."

"He came to the door?"

"Not at first. I pretended not to notice him when I went for a walk after lunch. He was in his car, parked down the street, so I guess he's keeping an eye on the house."

"I was hoping he wouldn't do that," I say with a sigh.

"He came to the door a couple hours later, and I told him you haven't called or come by, and that I would phone him if you did. He thanked me and left." John takes a sip of his drink. "Outside of his scruffy looks, he seems like a real upstanding guy."

"He is. He always was," I say. "He used to look exactly the way an FBI agent should. Big and smart. Buzzed hair, muscles out to here, clean-shaved face. He was the kind of guy you'd want for protection, if you needed it."

"I wonder what happened."

Whatever it is, I hope it didn't have anything to do with me or the Jovians.

"I should call him," I say. "He deserves that much and more, but I can't risk it. He might send me back, and I can't go, especially now."

"Do you really think he would send you back?" Dana says. "He seems so nice."

"And concerned," John adds.

The temptation to call Fran swells within me. "I don't know. Maybe. All I know is that if the FBI sends me back to Russia, I'll never find Evander."

9

The following morning, I take the grasshopper to Starbright again. I want to see if the Evander look-alike shows up, or Caroline or David, or any of the Jovians for that matter. I want to know if it's true that Evander has been taken to the mother planet—and if so when he'll return. On the way over, I dial Edmund's number. I'm feeling bold, ready to demand answers, but of course he doesn't pick up.

I'm there by 8:30 a.m., one of the first cars in a short line heading toward the security guard. My palms sweat as I consider the lies that could get me through. It's not the same guard as yesterday. This one resembles a marine. A wide-shouldered buzz cut of a man, with a frown like a drill sergeant. I drive up to the booth and roll down the window, about to explain how I'm here to see one of my in-laws when he says, "Good morning, Mrs. Jovian. Please pass through."

"Yes, okay, thank you," I stammer in a jittery, relieved way as he salutes me.

So the first time wasn't a fluke.

Similar to the prior day, I back into an empty space, this

time in the middle of the lot, much closer to the front entrance. I shift into park, then let the motor hum while I watch a sporadic line of cars enter in an orderly manner: one going this way, one that. Soon the line becomes consistent, flowing into the lot and filling most of the free parking spaces. Suited people emerge and come together in their fancy shoes and woolen overcoats, converging near the entrance and streaming through the front door.

No one looks remotely familiar. No Evanders, Edmunds, or Mirandas.

As the minutes slowly tick past, I wish I'd stopped for a cup of to-go coffee.

I sit for an hour, feeling drowsy and like I could easily fall asleep. The last car arrived at twenty after nine. Since everyone's already at work, there's nothing for me to watch. I wonder if I should go inside. They must know I'm here. Obviously they don't care. Maybe they're watching me as closely as I'm watching this building. I might be able to see Caroline and ask a few questions. Demand that she tell me where the hell my son is. But if I go inside, they may decide to keep me here, or make me live with them, or . . .

I can't do it.

By 9:40, I'm losing the battle to keep my eyelids from falling closed, and for this reason, I consider paying my old house a visit, the one Andrew and I renovated before running away to Ashbury Falls in order to put some space between us and his suffocating family. It's the house Edmund wants me to live in now.

My body warms with anger as I fall backward into the past, remembering how Andrew's family tried to manipulate us even when Andrew was still alive. What I wouldn't do to see him come through the front door of that house after a long day of work, briefcase in one hand, mail in the other. The way he always came home so hungry, sniffing the air and saying, "What's that cooking?" even when it was something ordinary, like store-bought lasagna. His eyes would widen with anticipation. "Dinner, now please!" he'd shout in his adorable way. And then he'd grab me and spin me through the living room until we bumped into the breakfast bar, stumbling over each other in the most ungraceful ballroom dance as he told me how much he appreciated that I'd made dinner. "I'll do cleanup," he'd say, as if looking forward to it.

It still feels like he should be easy to reach, like he's just beyond a corner I need to round in order to get back to him.

I pass the security gate and head back up the road through stretches of forest until I arrive in one of the neighborhoods on the outskirts. I turn onto Main Street and come upon all of the old landmarks, including the ice cream shop where Helena and I worked, and Andrew and I exchanged our first longing glances. It's strange driving past the shop. I can see that it's a lot smaller than I remember, that my memory of it has distorted over time. Being here whisks me back to my youth, when Helena and I went about the world single and free, our lives bristling with opportunity. It's a state of mind that's so distant to me now. The life I had before marrying Andrew, having a baby, running from the Jovians.

I drive through town and then turn into our neighborhood with the sprawling front yards and charming old ranches, creeping up the street at about 20 mph. It's Sunrise Court. I'd forgotten the name. Even before I get close to the house I sense that it's abandoned. What I can see of the front lawn is the color of wheat, which is normal for winter, but the grass is overgrown as if someone forgot to mow it one last time before winter arrived. My attention hovers over the room above the garage. Andrew's exercise room. The one he never used because I made him move to Ashbury Falls before it was finished. Closer now, I see that the bushes against the house are overgrown as well, and there's a pile of soaking-wet newspapers lying in bags on the front path to the door. Even more surprising, one of those gray realtor's lockboxes hangs on the doorknob.

It's for sale?

Maybe the Jovians just want people to think it's for sale.

I turn into the driveway, wondering which family members have lived in this house over the past ten years, if any, and what they did with my things after I left with Evander. I hope if anyone is here they aren't planning to ambush me, but it *is* a possibility, so I've got that "on guard" feeling. In my mind, I go through the self-protection moves I learned in a class I took soon after we returned to Russia. It's been a while since I've practiced them, but I still feel better knowing how to kick and punch and twist out of someone's hold, if the need arises.

The last time I was here, David was my keeper—and Evander and I stayed in the master bedroom with a video camera watching us in the corner. Back then, David pretended to be just another Jovian, Andrew's cousin, the son of Uncle Jimmy and Aunt Constant. I would still think so today if he hadn't transformed into the supreme being right in front of me. I remember how I trembled when I saw the supreme one the first time. He was on the stage at Chateau L'Origine, a solid and yet transparent *thing*, wavering like mottled light—up and then down—in an unearthly, indescribable way.

As I get out of the car, I button my coat to my chin. A gust of wind attempts to blow me back. The place feels vacant, dismal. A manifestation of the sad story that Andrew and I became. I walk up the path to the front door. If the house is for sale, why is there no sign? I knock. Should someone I don't know answer, I suppose I can say I'm interested in a tour of the house. I can act like an eager buyer who thinks it's for sale.

Edmund wants me to live here, so it can't be for sale. Or, was that a lie? I can't imagine why the Jovians would sell any of their homes. There's no need. They have so much money.

No one answers, and the door is locked. I walk to the back, and my heart clenches when I reach the deck where Andrew and I spent so much time talking and observing the night sky. A circle of wood planks embedded within the boards indicates the place where he set up the telescope—we called it the "sacred circle." Whenever we went out there, he would find something to show me, his passion for outer space practically tangible. "Look, it's Jupiter's largest moon, Ganymede," he'd say, beckoning me to the telescope as if he'd just discovered a mine filled with gold.

I cup my hands around my eyes and peer through the sliding glass door. The interior looks just as I remember, except that it's empty. Not a piece of mail on the counter, not a pot or pan on the stove. I tug on the door, but of course it's locked, so I go back down the stairs and take a slow walk to the garage. The side door here is locked as well. I look through one of the square windows of the wide garage door. A variety of lawn equipment clusters together: a couple of rakes, a shovel, a partially folded tarp, two ladders, and a broom. Beside the broom, a For Sale sign leans up against the wall. Kirksberg's New Moon Realtors—the same one my parents used when they tried to move to New York.

The lockbox is on the front door, so why would the For Sale sign be in the garage instead of planted in the lawn? And why would the house be for sale if Edmund wants me to move into it?

In the car again, I head to the Jovian mansion, Caroline and Edmund's home. This will be a more dangerous mission. Theirs is one of the largest homes in Kirksberg, your typical suburban manor house situated behind a fence of tall trees that obscure a clear view. For this reason, it will be more difficult to determine whether anyone lives there. Unless, of course, there's a For Sale sign out front, but I'll be surprised if there is. The Jovians have to live somewhere, and Edmund said they never left Kirksberg.

I suppose they could have kept their houses and simply purchased new ones in other parts of town.

I park four homes away so that I can walk by and observe as if I were a random pedestrian. I cross my arms over my chest and step at a fast pace, not turning my head toward the property until I'm right in front of it. When I look up, I see curtains in the upstairs windows, a holiday wreath on the door, a garland of pine twisted around the short length of bannister. That's normal considering it's December—or it would be normal if the Jovians celebrated Christmas, which they don't. When I'm one house away, I stop and fiddle with my boot, pretending there's something wrong with it—a rock in my shoe, something stuck in the heel. I lean against the brick wall to sturdy myself and gaze back. I can't tell if anyone is home. But so what if they are? Caroline might be there, and if she is, I could slap her face the way I've imagined slapping it for years now. After that, I could try to scare some answers out of her.

Then again, she was never afraid of me.

If someone is in the house, there's a good chance they're alone considering no cars occupy the drive and none are parked on the road out front. So, yes, I'm going to the front door. I hope Caroline is there. I really do.

Before I knock, a zingy nest of nerves constricts my stomach. Of all the Jovians, Caroline is the most intimidating and hardest to interpret. In some ways, she's even scarier than David.

I ring the bell.

No sound of footsteps or general movement occurs. I continue to listen.

No one answers.

I knock loudly, the way Uncle Jimmy used to.

Still no sign of movement.

I twist the doorknob just to see if I can—and, oddly, I can.

The door opens, and I continue to stand there because I'm worried it could be a trap. Or maybe they simply forgot to lock it?

I lean in and say, "Hello?"

No one answers.

What I see of the inside appears to be furnished the way I remember. Grandfather clock in the foyer, Oriental rug in the entry, a huge painting of flowers in a vase at the top of the opulent open staircase. So someone may live here, which means that someone could be here now.

I step inside. "Caroline?" My voice sounds small, but I refuse to bow to my fear.

I cross the foyer and enter the kitchen and breakfast area. "Hello?" I call out, imagining a huge dog with fangs and frothing drool waking from a deep sleep to bite me. But the Jovians never had any pets that I can recall.

I continue into the living room, where a trail of footsteps imprints the carpet. A man's large tread. I continue to the den, where an enormous flat-screen TV, muted, broadcasts the news for no one. I head into Edmund's office. When I was here last, there were shelves to the ceiling filled with books of all kinds. It was like a miniature library, with globes of the earth, maps of the stars, ancient calendars decorating the walls. Now it's basically a shell of a room with a wooden floor, a lone office chair, a set of abandoned bookends, a paper shredder on its side in the corner. No papers or books or filing cabinets to be seen.

I leave the office and pass through the living area once again. Then I head up the curved staircase, which is carpeted. It occurs to me that the house has no smell. Nothing distinctive to bring back memories. Not that Andrew and I spent a lot of time here. A handful of holidays, a couple of lunches and dinners, the "drinks on the lawn party" where the two of us fell in love.

I reach for Andrew's ring attached to my necklace.

Drinks on the lawn was also the party where I met Fran Vasquez.

I move quickly into the master bedroom, which seems staged. If I had to guess, no one has slept in the four-poster king-size bed in months, or maybe years. A decade, to be precise. But who knows? Being upstairs puts my nerves on edge, and I'm imagining where I'll hide should I hear the sounds of someone walking through the front door or coming out of the bathroom down the hall. I could leap into the closet to my left, and there's plenty of space under the bed.

It's not like the Jovians will appear out of thin air. They climb stairs and walk across floors just like humans do. Still, I drop to my knees and check under the bed. It's probably a strange thing to do, except that I find something there: a necklace below the headboard.

I have to reach all the way to the middle in order to get my hand on it. It's a gold chain with a sizable diamond for a pendant. Caroline's. I remember this necklace. It has significant weight and is no doubt genuine. And yet she's left it behind. Why am I not surprised? Even if it's a stellar diamond worth thousands, to her it's just another prop to round out her pretend humanness.

I put it in my pocket because unlike her, I need the money

I can get for it. Then I check the rest of the upstairs: the two guest bedrooms, which are mostly empty. The one Andrew and I once slept in has no furniture at all. There's also a room with a treadmill, and three full and sparkling baths. Nothing unusual.

I walk back to the stairs. I've taken the first two steps when the sound of a dropped water bottle clatters across the wood floor. Someone must be in the office. I freeze in place as a plan of escape flashes together like a puzzle picture in my mind: run down the stairs, bolt out front door, don't look back.

Before I move an inch, a baritone voice says, "They live at Starbright, as far as I can tell."

Fireworks ignite within my chest. I peer over the side of the staircase, and Fran steps out of Edmund's office wearing the same black trench coat from the other day, the same aura of a damaged man.

"When did you get here?" My voice vibrates with fear.

"A few minutes before you did."

I clear my throat. "Did you pick the lock?"

"No need. It's been open for years. I've been here a hundred times, and it's always the same. The house still belongs to them, but no one's home."

"But the television . . . "

"Sometimes it's off, sometimes it's on."

His voice is the same, but the scruff of beard doesn't suit him, and his eyebrows have sprawled like untended vines because he's now a man in his early forties, no longer young and vain, apparently. His hair, too, grows unruly and thick around his face. I wonder why he doesn't just buzz it the way he used to. He was so good-looking. So well groomed. I guess he's not interested in being handsome anymore, just like I'm not interested in being pretty.

As he approaches me, there's a catch in his gait, a limp. I

pretend not to notice as I reach the bottom of the staircase. He remains near the center of the living room. I could still run out the door and get away from him, I'm pretty sure.

He's big. The size of his body, still impressive. There's no doubt about that. But he's changed; he's a different man from the one Andrew and I knew.

"There are vacuum marks in the carpet." I point to the far corner of the living room.

He turns to glance at them. "Yeah. Someone definitely sneaks in here every now and again and cleans."

"But the family is actually living in Starbright? All of them or . . . "

He stops beside a lone armchair and lets out a sigh. "No idea. I came across Caroline at Town Hall five years ago. I had a personal matter to resolve and wasn't prepared to encounter her. I lingered around while she sat in the waiting area—I guess she had an appointment to see someone—and when she left, I followed her. It wasn't long before her driver lost me. I ended up here, but she didn't come back. I camped out for most of a week."

The hard edges of his face make him look mean, and I almost feel like I'm the one who's upset him, but I know it's the Jovians who have done that.

I meet his gaze, but I don't know what to say.

"Living at Starbright is the only thing that makes sense," he says. "I've seen them enter the building a few times. Miranda, Edmund, David, Constance. Not all at once. Never together. With others. They're a slippery bunch."

I'm staring at his missing arm. His prosthetic, which peers out the sleeve of his coat. It's the kind that's a dull beige color with a metal prong at the end. A few seconds pass before I realize he notices, and I glance away.

He tugs the sleeve of his coat down so it covers everything but the tip of its metal end. "Yeah, they've managed to elude me," he says. "Sorta like you."

I look away, ashamed. It's too quiet in here. I feel like Fran can hear my thoughts. "I'm sorry I didn't call. I didn't know if you would make me go home. I couldn't risk it."

He frowns. "You know me better than that."

I grab for Andrew's wedding band and play with it self-consciously. "I once knew you, yes, but I haven't heard from you in more than three years. I didn't know what happened. And from what I see, it was something serious."

He drops his head, then puts his hand into the pocket of his coat and jiggles some loose change. "Yeah, that's fair."

"So what happened?" I say.

He's staring at the floor. "You mean to my arm?" He speaks in a dull, mechanical way, very low volume. "I lost it."

"I'm so sorry." My words fall flat. I want to do more. Run over and hug him. Ten years ago, I would have. I would have found some comforting words to say. But I'm not the same person I was ten years ago—and neither is he. There's too much time between us, too much that's unknown. I clear my throat and wait for him to continue the story of how he lost his arm, or maybe just mutter a few words of explanation, but he doesn't. I don't like the silence that persists, so I say, "What are you doing here, anyway?"

"Waiting for you. I wanted to ask you what *you're* doing here, other than posing as your sister."

I run my hand through my hair. "Yes, well, I had to. I'm looking for Evander. They came for him in Russia. The one time I let him go out with a girl, they took him."

"They've been in touch with you?"

"Edmund came to see me. He said they would bring him back here *soon*, to Kirksberg, and that the two of us can live in the house Andrew and I renovated when we first married. But then I ran into Miranda at Starbright yesterday, and she said Edmund took Evander to—" I stop to take a breath because, though Fran was with me that day in the park when David showed his true form, saying what I have to say is difficult—"the, uh," I look at the ceiling, "mother planet."

"Whoa." Fran grabs his forehead. "She actually said that?"

"Yes, that's what she said."

"Jesus." He sinks into the velvet armchair and lets out a crazed laugh, then rubs the scruff around his chin in a nervous way, uttering the word "holy" under his breath. This is all very unlike the Fran I knew, who appeared invincible and fearless.

I'm still standing near the bottom of the stair, a clear line to the front door in my peripheral vision. "I was surprised she told me," I say, "but maybe it's not true. I don't trust any of them."

"Is that what your gut tells you? That it's not true?"

I wish it told me that.

"I don't know what to think," I say. "I'm feeling pretty numb at this point."

"How can he be back soon if they're taking him all the way to Jupiter? I'm no scientist, but I'd think a trip like that would require more than a few weeks."

I take in a slow breath and bite the inside of my cheek. "I suppose it depends on how they travel. You saw what David could do, what he became. Who knows what they're capable of. I think they'll bring Evander back, but I don't know when. I could be dead by the time he returns," I say, my voice cracking.

"Believe me, I get what you're up against."

I say nothing.

"Man, I wish we could talk to Andrew," he adds.

"Yeah, me, too."

He gives me the eye, like he's asking a question without actually asking.

"What?" I say.

"Have you heard from him?"

"Andrew? Oh, uh, the night Evander was taken, he told me to 'Wake up.' Prior to that, he hadn't spoken to me since we arrived in Russia ten years ago. I'm not sure—it may have just been a dream."

"So he warned you," Fran says, overriding my insecurity.

Then I remember: Fran believes because it happened to him, too. Andrew came to him in a dream when I needed help getting away from the family. He told Fran to go to Kirksberg, the UFO Festival. Otherwise, I would have faced David by myself.

"I was asleep when they took Evander, so yes. I guess it was a warning. It's been so long since he's spoken to me."

"But you said your father-in-law showed up right after. So it had to be."

I do like to think Andrew and I have this connection. I'm just not as sure about it as I used to be.

"Even if it was, I never know when he'll chime in," I say. "He's unpredictable."

"Right . . . but he's still out there. He's still getting through."

I hate to tell Fran, but hearing from Andrew once in ten years isn't much better than being on my own. I wish it were.

"Do you have a picture of him?"

I'm confused. I have no pictures of Andrew.

"Of your son," he says.

"Oh! Yes. At home. I'll have to show you next time."

He startles a little, like he's been fishing and I have tugged at the line. "Will there be a next time?" His dark eyes beam his intention, saying, "You better say yes."

I nod, but that might be a lie. "Are you going to make me go back to Russia?"

"I don't work for the bureau anymore, so no."

This makes me feel better and worse at the same time. How could he *not* work for the FBI?

"Why don't you work for them?"

"Long story. You don't have any photos of him on your phone?" he says.

"I haven't owned a phone in years. Edmund gave me this one the other day." I take it from my pocket. "I own only one picture of my son—a paper photograph. It's in my backpack at my parents' house."

"Let me see the phone," he says, extending his bear paw of a hand. "I'll put my contacts in."

I'm nervous to get that close to him. In a way, I feel as if I've been talking to a stranger, a broken one who isn't too happy with me. I know I shouldn't feel this way, but I've grown leery of people in general over the years.

"I'll stay in the chair," he says. "You come to me."

I cross the space between us and hand him the phone, then stand there, watching him cradle it in his palm and tap the numbers with his thumb. Then he hands it back.

"If you don't work for the bureau, who do you work for?" I say.

"Myself."

"You're a private detective?"

"Something like that."

"Where do you live?" The sound of that question has a startling, too-personal cadence. I follow with, "I mean, do you and Lisa live in Kirksberg?"

"Yeah, I do. Don't hide from me, okay?"

He stands, and I back up a few steps to the staircase as he continues toward the door. His legs seem stiff, like he's consciously trying not to limp.

"I'll be in touch," he says, and he doesn't look back.

10

Someone chose an interesting ringtone for my phone: the old, blaring traditional landline. Probably seemed like the most "human" choice, the most old-fashioned choice. I'm sure that's how Jovians see our race, like relics from an uncivilized era.

It's Fran calling at 6:15 a.m. He might know something about the Jovians or even Evander, so I click the accept button as fast as my still-sleeping hands can manage.

"Let's do breakfast," he says before I get a word out. "I have something to tell you. Bring the photo."

Downstairs, I run into Dana in her robe. She's filling the teakettle. "You're up?" she says with startled eyes. "Is everything all right?"

"Yes, fine. I'm going out. Breakfast with a friend."

"Oh?" she says, her face stuck somewhere in between surprise and worry.

"It's Fran. I'll be back soon."

She stands in front of me, eyeing me closely. "Are you sure?"

"Yes," I say. "He's okay with me being here. And it's just breakfast."

Reluctantly she moves out of the way.

Outside, the grasshopper purrs to life and speeds me over to the Sheridan Café, which is as busy as it was a decade ago. I park in the back and walk around to the front entrance. The fat floaty snowflakes dropping on my coat and in my hair would have delighted me years ago, before I moved back to Russia and experienced snow showers every day for six months at a time. Painted on the windows of the café, sprawling red ribbons and the words "Merry Christmas" in pine-tree green remind me it's the holiday season. I vaguely recall Dana baking cookies last night and John hanging a few strands of lights; they don't believe in decorating trees, real or plastic—neither is good for the environment—so I know what little they're doing is for me and hopefully Evander, if he makes it back in time for the holiday.

I slip into a booth near the door and order coffee from a waitress in a mustard-colored uniform with a white apron. I don't normally want coffee before eating, but I haven't been sleeping well, and I'm laggy from anxiety. Before she turns away, Fran slides into the seat in front of me, his eyes burrowed in puffiness, as I'm sure my own are, and when he removes his wool beanie, he has a bad case of bed head that I'll never get used to. Makes me wish I'd brought an electric shaver.

"Coffee, please, Char," he tells the waitress, and she answers, "Of course" and rushes away.

"I saw Caroline and Miranda," he says, a bit winded. "They entered Starbright soon after midnight last night."

"You were there?" I look at my cell phone. It's 7:05 a.m. "You called me at six this morning. When do you sleep?"

"Sleep's not a priority right now."

Char the waitress is back with two cups that she fills from

the black plastic pitcher in her hand. Fran says, "You're a life-saver, you know that?"

"Yeah, that's what they tell me." She gives a little chuckle and takes off again, as Fran lifts his cup and makes half of it disappear.

"Where's the photo," he asks.

I pull my backpack toward me and unzip the outer pocket. Before I hand it over, I glance at Evander's blue-green eyes with the kind of longing that comes with worry wrapped in guilt for letting him go out that night. The photo trembles in my hand as I pass it to Fran.

He stares at it. "This is your ten-year-old?"

I plant my elbow on the table and prop my chin in my hand. "I know. He's big for his age."

Fran's get-real expression can't be ignored.

"Okay, okay," I admit, "he's *old* for his age. But he's still my baby."

"I guess he inherited the Jovian . . . " He shakes his head, at a loss for words. "Whatever. He's a good-looking kid. The question is, why'd they take him now?" He places the photo on the table, pulls his phone out of his coat pocket with his good hand, hovers it over the photograph, and snaps a picture.

Then he places the phone on the table, picks up the photo again, and hands it back to me. I zip it safely away.

Char returns to take our order, scribbling maybe two words on her pad before retreating. The café bustles with hungry customers, and she obviously can't afford to take her time.

Fran lifts his coffee cup again, finishing it off. "What else can you tell me?" he says.

He's back in FBI mode. The professional attitude and eager-for-answers boldness are intimidating, but nothing I can't handle. I'm happy to see this tougher version of Fran. Yesterday he reeked of despair.

"You remember what I told you ten years ago? How they want to spread their DNA around," I say. "They want Evander to have many children, to take a leadership position in the community, teach people to truly care for the planet and to notice and respect the stars. The universe needs Earth for some specific reason Uncle Jimmy didn't tell me."

"Okay," he says. "Anything else occur to you over the years?"

"What do you mean?"

"After that day in the park, you told me that when David struck you with that bolt of energy, or whatever it was, you felt some connection to the family. Did you learn anything about them that way?"

He remembers everything. I didn't expect him to.

"Until recently I suffered headaches pretty often. A strange buzzing that ranged from hardly there to very obviously there. Also, I often daydreamed about outer space, which wasn't normal for me until David did whatever he did to me."

He blinks a few times, as if trying to grasp what I've said. "What does that mean, 'daydreaming about outer space?'"

"It was like I'd be eating my breakfast or reading a book, or doing whatever, but in my mind I was floating through the cosmos, drifting past stars and planets. Black holes."

"That's interesting."

"I know," I say as I stir milk and then sugar into my coffee. "It's weird. That's why I never told you. I think it was all part of my connection to them. Like a mental kind of . . . I don't know, telepathy? Their thoughts combining with mine. And—" I stop there, considering how to put it into words.

"And?"

"It's not like I could tell what the family was doing. It was more like they knew what *I* was doing, what I was thinking. Like they were keeping tabs on me. I sensed their presence in my head. The day before they came for Evander, I thought I was losing my mind. Their attention beamed at me like a stage light, and the buzzing became so loud that I *knew* something was up, but I was also distracted because Evander had met this girl and—"

We pause while Char delivers our scrambled eggs and toast.

Fran points to his coffee and says, "Please."

She rushes back for the pot, and as she pours, she says, "All good?"

He gives her a thumbs-up before digging in, feeding himself like a starving person would. In the midst of chewing, he says, "You're speaking about it in the past tense. It's not happening anymore?"

"No. The night they took Evander, Edmund appeared in the yard, and it stopped. The constant hum, the buzzing, or vibration, whatever you want to call it stopped. And I've had no daydreams since I arrived in Kirksberg. I'm thinking that now that they have Evander, they have severed our connection."

"You're probably right." He spreads butter on his toast, which is already buttered. This takes more time than it would for a person who has two hands, but I can see that he's had a lot of practice.

I'm not as eager to eat as he is, but I take a few small bites. "All this time, I thought they would come for me and Evander both, but really they only want him. I'm worried they think they don't need me."

"I'm sure Evander doesn't feel that way," he says, reaching out with a soft swell of empathy in his eyes. "You two get along well, right?"

"We do. But he probably doesn't have much say in the

matter."

Saying this out loud opens the door to the hopelessness that's been pulling me down since I left Russia. It could be worse, I realize. I could be in this alone. But Dana and John have acted stiff and awkward since I told them about Evander's trip to Jupiter, as if I'm a mental-health bomb that could detonate if exposed to the wrong words or suggestions. I shouldn't have revealed so much so soon.

"From what I've observed at the Starbright office lately, I think something big is going on," Fran says, stirring his coffee though I didn't see him put any sugar in it. "In the past ten days, there's been a noticeable uptick in Jovian activity. Add to that the fact that you're back and Evander may or may not be on an intergalactic vacation—" He laughs in an ironic way. "It's obvious they're prepping for something."

I roll my eyes. "Plotting to take over the human race."

He scoops a pile of home-fried potatoes into his mouth.

Feeling somewhat dejected, I fall back into the plump pleather booth. "Uncle Jimmy told me I can't understand the Jovians because I'm human and therefore incapable of seeing the whole picture."

"He didn't mean it as an insult, did he?"

"No, you're right, he would never say something so unkind."

A child cries and I glance across the café. A family of five is squeezed into a booth meant for four; three young children have orange juice and cereal. The toddler, red-faced, makes a horrible squawking sound and the parents, with frazzled expressions, tempt him with a doll that has a bell on its head. They look uncomfortable, but I still wish I could be more like them right now, jumbled into a booth with my young, fidgety children and husband, worried about ordinary things like "Did I buy enough wrapping paper, or I hope young Evander likes his remote-control race car."

"I miss baby Evander," I say. "Days when I could take him everywhere with me and the simplest things kept him busy, like bouncing balls. Don't you miss those days when Max was young?"

Fran looks over his shoulder at the family in the booth, and his eyes glaze over. "Doesn't interest me, to be honest. Not anymore."

His despondency pulls me deeper into the bleak and unbearable place I often find myself. He used to be such a family man. This isn't the Fran I knew.

"You haven't mentioned Lisa and Max," I say.

"Yeah, that's intentional," he says, concentrating on his plate.

"I'm only wondering how they are. *Where* they are."

"Lisa has the same number, far as I know. Call her."

I level a look at him. "Did you two get a divorce?"

His dark eyes grow darker, and I know he's angry with me for asking.

"Can you at least tell me if they're okay?" I say.

He looks away, huffing a little. "They don't live with me anymore. That's all I'm gonna say."

Something terrible happened, and I assume he can't talk about it without getting emotional. Helena's Ivan does the same thing when he's upset, huffing and acting angry.

Fran picks up his fork and resumes eating. His overgrown hair falls in front of his eyes.

"I'm sorry for bringing it up," I say. "And for the fact that you and Lisa aren't together. I always thought you were a great couple."

"Uh-huh," he says, his eyes still on his plate. "You were telling me all you know about the Jovians." His blunt tone advises me to return to the subject at hand. He lost an arm, his family. He's tortured by whatever happened—and because we haven't kept in touch, his life is not my business.

"Svetlana?"

I shiver out of my thoughts. Moving on. "The family wants to influence the human race to be better, more connected with the rest of the universe, that's what Uncle Jimmy told me. Will their leadership be good for humans, or will it be bad? I have no idea. I hope it will help us save the planet like he said it would. But does it worry me that they want to change the human race by making it more like them? Yes, because they are strange and have a shallow depth of emotion." I pause to take a sip of my coffee. "Does the fact that their plan involves Evander worry me? Of course it does. I don't know what they'll expect him to do for them. They have never answered my questions, and when they speak, it's in riddles. They act as if I could blow up their entire plan if I actually knew what it was."

Fran jolts a little, as if I've just made an important declaration of some kind. "Maybe you can."

"What? Blow them up?"

"Screw up their plan, whatever it is."

I'm shaking my head. "I mean, I guess I could, equipped with the right army."

His blunt-faced expression remains intact. "I'm saying they're afraid of you."

I widen my eyes. That's funny.

"Trying to stop the Jovians and their plan, whatever it is, has never struck me as a possibility," I say. "I don't care for their plans. Of course I care about the human race, but all I ever wanted was a normal life for me and Evander—and my husband, if only he had lived."

"Right, but hear me out. You're a good mother, and your son loves you."

"Uh-huh."

"That's your power." He jabs his index finger in my direction.

It's nice of him to say. I sip my coffee. "Unfortunately, I don't feel very powerful."

"You're not hearing me."

"Yes, I've been a good mother. I know."

"No. Look." Now he's shaking both his hand and his prosthetic limb at me. "The Jovians have taken some pretty big steps to make sure you stay out of the picture, to keep you away from Evander. No doubt there's a reason."

"I do have a huge influence on him, so I guess you could be right. You know I gave birth to him on my birthday, right?"

"You did?"

"Even when he was an infant, he understood me better than anyone I've ever met. I swear he knew what I was thinking. We're built the same way. On the same plane, or whatever. I'm convinced he helped me escape that day at the UFO Festival. He ran into the crowd, Fran. *He* was the reason I was able to call you."

"I didn't know that. That's helpful to know."

I don't know if Fran means it's helpful for getting Evander back or helpful in some other way.

"Uncle Jimmy told me Evander and I would be very close, and he was right about that. We get along well when we're not arguing about the girls I won't let him go out with."

The temperature inside my body rises, reminding me that I'm embarrassed for what I've done, for keeping him from those girls, for keeping him from friendships he could have had. "You know what it's like to be a parent," I say.

Fran neglects to agree or disagree. Instead he says, "Jimmy made it a point to tell you that you and Evander would be very close. He must have known that closeness would come into the picture down the road."

My shoulders creep up. "He told me lots of things."

Andrew left me a warning about the cloning, but it was

Uncle Jimmy who said it was true. Maybe that's why Edmund has taken Evander to Jupiter. Maybe he's going to clone him there.

I look up and meet the intensity of Fran's stare.

His voice is deep and stern: "Years ago, you said they wanted Evander because of his special DNA."

"Yes, because he's a human and a Jovian," I say. "He's exactly what they'd hoped for in a grandchild. A mix of exceptional DNA that will pass from one human to the next. 'Evander the Mighty,' that's what Uncle Jimmy called him right before he left us. You haven't met Evander yet, but when you do, you'll see: he's the kind of person who can't go anywhere unnoticed. He has this attractive way about him, this even temperament, and he's very smart, capable. Girls twice his age ask him out. He's honest, too, and loyal. Fair. A dream person."

"Charismatic like Andrew? And charming, like you?"

"Yes, he's like Andrew. Very much."

"Svetlana, what you're describing is a natural-born leader."

"Oh, yes." I chuckle thinking of all the second glances he's accumulated over the years. "Evander's like a rock star."

"Perfect for the leadership position they want him to take," Fran says.

At first I'm flattered by this idea, but then my breath catches in my throat. "But he's so young. What are you saying? He can't exactly run the country."

"I know. Do you think they're getting him ready for a job as mayor, or, I don't know, something else? Even if he's in the body of a twenty-year-old?"

"I can't picture it," I say. "They may start teaching him, but he won't be ready for years. There's no way."

And then I think of the Constitution and Evander's American history class.

Fran wipes his mouth with his napkin. "So, they could be prepping him for a leadership position, but they can't do it if you talk him out of it. Do you think you could talk him out of it?"

I couldn't even talk him out of taking that course. But this would be different. This would be me telling him not to fall for the Jovians' tricks.

"Yes," I say. "I think I could."

Later that day, I have a late lunch at home with Dana and John, who inform me that I'll be going to the food kitchen with them to put together holiday meals for the homeless. This is something I would be more than happy to do if I wasn't busy solving the mystery of the Jovians and the whereabouts of my ten-year-old prodigy. Still, I reluctantly agree, and at around 6 p.m., just as we're walking out to the garage, Fran pulls up to the curb at the end of the drive. I tell Dana and John I'll be right back and jog up to see what he wants. The window goes down, and he leans over and says, "I'm headed to Starbright. Care to join?"

"Definitely." I pull my phone from my pocket and text Dana that I'm going out with Fran again. I get in the sedan with the sizeable dent in the front bumper and tell him to "Go, go, go," as my phone pings. *What about the food kitchen?* Dana writes back, adding a frowny emoji, to which I respond, *Sorry, important Evander business.*

Fran's car looks about as bad on the inside as it does on the outside. Only dirtier. More lived in. There's a duffle bag in the backseat that's packed tight. A laundry bag, I suppose. And some paper fast-food bags on the seat beside it. A pile of napkins, packets of sugar and ketchup. A paperback book, its pages curled. I try not to be obvious when I strain my neck to see what the thing on the floor is: looks like a wool blanket.

"You live in this car," I say as the realization hits me.

His eyes remain steadfast on the road. "Oh, cause of the blanket? It gets cold in here during a stakeout."

"If you live in this car, I'll be very worried about you."

He breathes out a loud sound of annoyance. "It's my job to worry about you, not the other way around."

"It's *not* your job. I'm perfectly capable of taking care of my—"

"Yeah, sorry, that came out wrong." He passes me a sideways glance with a face that tells me he's afraid he has offended me. "But I'm glad you've opted to accept my help with this thing we're doing."

On the drive up the hill that leads to Starbright, I reach for the grab handle when Fran takes a sudden turn off road. It's a dirt path that passes over flat ground that may have been farmland at one time. Along its perimeter, there's a pine forest that we follow for several minutes until the dirt road ends. He puts the car in park and twists the ignition. "Grab your stuff," he says.

I look around myself. "I only have a phone."

He gets out and opens the trunk, removes a set of binoculars and hands me a blanket. Then he leads the way through a thicket of trees grown so dense I can't avoid branches that poke and scratch at my sheepskin coat.

"It's not far," he says. "Get behind me so you don't get whipped." His wide girth blocks most of the skinny branches that would otherwise lash me.

After a five-minute walk, we come to the edge of the forest and a clear vision of the back of the Starbright office in all of its technical glory. The adjacent parking lot designated for the Jovians, guests, and other VIPs is empty at the moment.

Fran points to a tree near the edge of the forest we had just hiked through and whispers, "I usually sit up there."

A wooden platform extends between several thick branches about twenty feet up. It's only a square of wood planks, and I'm surprised it holds his weight.

"All the way up there?" I whisper. "If you fall asleep, you'll kill yourself."

"I don't sleep."

"It could happen against your will."

"Don't worry. I catch maybe two, three hours a night. At home. In my *apartment*."

No wonder he looks like hell. But at least he has an apartment.

"The platform's not big enough for both of us," he says, "so we'll have to take cover by those bushes. Come on."

We sneak across the grounds like kids playing paintball, leaning into one tree, then running to another before taking refuge beside a thicket of evergreen bushes at the perimeter of the landscaping. The two of us literally squat down and peer through the brush. It feels silly, but a few minutes later, headlights dart across the lot, and I hold my breath, praying whoever it is has brought Evander with them—and that they don't see us.

The car responsible pulls into an empty parking space, and three people get out.

"Here we go," Fran whispers. "They're early tonight."

From what I can see, one of them is built like David, thin and young-looking, but I can't see his hair because he's wearing a knitted hat. Fran hands me the binoculars, but they don't help much because everything looks green and alien-ish through them—and that makes sense in more ways than one. Still, the face isn't David's. And the way he walks isn't what I remember. He's with a woman and a man who don't look familiar, but they're all wearing bulky winter coats, so I can't see their bodies very well.

The click of a camera surprises me.

Fran is taking photos with a tiny camera with a little zoom lens sticking out. I wonder how photographs will be helpful.

The group has reached the back door of the building. The woman puts her hand up to what I suppose is a scanner, and the door opens.

"At first I thought the small one might have been David," I say, "but it wasn't really his face. And David wasn't so skinny the last time I saw him. He was more like Andrew."

"Probably wasn't him. There are plenty of them, believe me."

"Plenty of Jovians?"

"A lot of people visit this building in the middle of the night and wee hours of the morning. Whether they're Jovians or not, I don't know."

"And you've photographed them."

"Some of them. But I hardly ever catch their faces. They wear hats and turned-up collars. They may know I'm out here. Either way, they're tough to identify."

"Did you ever see anyone who looks like Evander," I ask.

"I don't think so."

The idea that Evander might have been cloned (or soon will be) won't leave me alone, but I don't want to bring it up to Fran. I don't know why. I guess I'm hoping it's not something to worry about.

"I thought I saw him here the other day," I say. "I forgot to tell you. It was the day I spoke to Miranda. I was parked out front when the employees were leaving the building."

"I've never seen him here. I would have told you if I had. You know you can trust me, right?"

"Oh. Yes. I know that," I say in a stiff tone that's unconvincing.

"It's important that we're honest with each other," he adds.

"I know," I say.

He's glaring at me the way a skeptical parent stares down a rebellious teen.

I press my lips together, then say, "I've been on my own for a long time, Fran. I'm sorry, but I've learned there's only one person you can trust, and that's yourself. Even *you* disappeared from my life, and I understand that you have your own problems, but . . . " my voice reaches for a deeper octave when I say, "I don't know you very well anymore. And I thought you'd make me go back to Russia."

"I would never." He reaches out and squeezes my hand, holding it for an elongated moment that draws my eyes to his. "I would never," he says again.

"What if you were still in the FBI?"

He readjusts his position and smirks a little. "Maybe eight or nine years ago, I would have thought about it," he says, pausing there. "Because back then I would have felt like—"

"You had to. That's what I thought."

So my instincts were right. I *am* alone when it comes down to it. Then again the Fran in front of me here and now is on my side—or at least he wants to be. I also believe that.

"Yeah, I would have felt like I had to back then, but more important I would have thought it the safest thing for you at the time."

He's probably right about that.

"I want to see Evander again," I say as firmly as possible. "I *have* to get him back, especially if you're right in thinking I'm the only one who can stop them from using him. I'm afraid they're going to keep him from me, and there will be nothing I can do about it."

He tips back his head and then rights it and sighs.

"Believe me, I know how you feel. I can relate to the agony of being cut out of your kid's life."

This gets my attention. "You don't see Max?"

His face goes long, and he shakes his head.

"Lisa won't let you?"

"Oh, it's more than Lisa not letting me. *He* doesn't want to see me."

I sit back on my heels as the weight of disappointment presses down. I can't help but be suspicious of what Fran may have done. Did he cheat on Lisa? Could he have hit Max?

"I fucked up. Royally. I don't blame him."

"The Fran I knew never fucked up royally," I say.

"Yeah, well, it happened. And as you can see," he raises his prosthetic arm, "I'm not the man I used to be. Not by a long shot."

"Please tell me what happened."

He stares into the distance, then scowls and shakes his head. "Maybe later."

"Fine, but I'm sure whatever horrible thing you did, you had good reason."

"Doesn't matter. What happened, happened. Can't change it. Can't go back in time and fix it." His eyes droop a little when he says, "Not a damn thing I can do."

I understand wanting to go back in time. I still wish I could backstroke my way to a time when Andrew lived.

"Let's go," he says.

"What about the Jovians?" I gesture toward the parking lot.

"I've been doing this for years and have never seen more than one group per night."

"Really?" I say. "That's strange."

"We're talking about Jovians," he says. "Strange is to be expected."

11

As soon as I step into the kitchen the following morning, Dana asks if I would like to get my hair done. My noticeable swatch of natural medium-brown roots creates an unsightly furrow through my highlighted blonde. Dana isn't one for criticizing my looks, so I am not offended but will take it as a subtle hint.

"I don't have time right now," I say, lingering behind the breakfast bar. "Fran is picking me up. Or meeting me somewhere."

"I beg to differ," she says. "I think you have plenty of free time these days. Maybe too much."

"What do you mean?"

"I mean that I can see you've been overthinking. You've been scowling so much that your elevens are showing."

Elevens?

"The lines here, between your eyes," she says in response to the confusion that I'm sure has surfaced on my face. I will check these so-called elevens in the mirror later. But I don't really care. My son is missing. Of course I'm scowling.

"And there's ample time for sleeping, too," she continues.

Obviously Dana woke up in mother mode.

"I know you're stressed, but staying up all hours of the night won't make Evander get here any faster. Have you seen the purple petals beneath your eyes?"

"I always have that. That's a Russian thing. It's hereditary."

"Okay, well, sometimes it also means that you need sleep. Maybe you'd be less grumpy."

Never one to start a fight, Dana winks at me, but I don't respond.

"You've become very serious in your more-mature age, Sveta."

"Yes, this is true. Where's Dad?" I step up to the pantry and grab a box of cereal, any will do. I want to get out of here before Dana insists I spend the day at a spa.

"He took the car for an oil change."

"The grasshopper?" I say, disappointed. "I mean, *your* car?"

"No, his. Don't worry, the grasshopper is still available to you—love the name, by the way."

I sit in a chair and start eating the cereal straight from the box. "Uncle Jimmy had the same car. Did I ever tell you?"

"He was the eccentric one, right?"

"Yes, but also kind. The kindest Jovian of all."

"I'm going for a walk. Would you like to join me?"

"I can't. Fran's going to be here soon."

This isn't true. He didn't text this morning, so I have no idea when he might show up—or get in touch. But I want to be available if he does.

"This is what I mean," she says with eyes that accuse me of . . . I'm not sure what. "You're nonstop on this mission, and you and I haven't so much as taken a walk together since you got home three weeks ago."

I'm surprised I've been here that long, but I'm not going

to stop doing what I'm doing. "I'm fine," I say. "I promise I'll color my hair tonight."

"You know this isn't about your hair."

She crosses the kitchen and heads toward the back door, to the rack of hooks offering an assortment of coats. She grabs her parka, then pulls on a wool hat and fusses with what little of her short hair peeks around the sides. On the way back, she stops in front of me. "How's the search going, anyway? Getting anywhere?"

"Not really," I say with a frown. "But I can't quit. He's my son."

"I understand. Please let me know if there's anything I can do."

Her business-polite tone lets me know she's disappointed in me. The least I can do is take a walk with her. "If you'll wait a second, I'll come with you." I press a fist full of cereal into my mouth and then put the box of cereal away before running down the hall to get my coat from my bedroom. If Fran wants to do something today, he'll just have to wait.

"Ready," I say as I join her by the front door.

She stares at my feet, and I look down . . . to find slippers there. We break into laughter so fierce it hurts my stomach. When I can breathe again, I say, "Hang on one more second."

"Six inches of snow fell last night," she says. "You better wear my extra pair of boots."

Dana sets the brisk pace of a person who has conquered this fitness challenge many times before. She informs me that we'll be going to the high school track. In some places where the snow plough has built up mounds, we have to lift our legs high as if we're marching. Dana's boots are too big for me, so my feet shift around inside of them. The school is about four blocks away, and by the time we get there, I'm sweating in my coat and close to panting. I'm not in as good shape as I would like to be. Maybe Dana is right. The not-sleeping and feeling sad and stressed all the time may be taking a toll.

The track has been cleared, probably shoveled away by some serious runners who came before us.

"It's nice, right?" she says. "No worries about crossing streets or cars pulling out of driveways. No icy patches to maneuver."

If you like walking in circles is what I'm thinking, but I tell her, "Yes, it's nice." The surrounding school grounds unfurl like a peaceful holiday dreamscape of brick buildings with a blanket of untarnished snow at their feet.

We're the only ones here, and I'm glad. Dana and her five-foot-zero svelte figure flaunts a lot more energy than I do—she has always kept in shape for the humanitarian efforts she's involved with—and I'm struggling to keep up, even though I've got six inches on her and thirty fewer years. Dana must be in her sixties by now, but everything about her seems well preserved. Come to think of it, she's pretty amazing for an older lady.

"What's your secret?" I ask her.

She looks at me with lips pressed together, and says, "Hm. What do you mean?"

"You're in really good shape. I'm huffing and puffing over here, and you're ready for ten more laps."

"Oh that," she says, with a chuckle. "I've been walking every day for I don't know how long. Since I was about your age."

"And you eat organic."

"Uh-huh, that could have something to do with it."

"Also, you do a lot of good deeds."

"Yes, but do you think that affects overall health?"

"If it doesn't, it should. You spread your goodwill all over the world. You and John are amazing people."

"I'm glad to hear you say that. I wasn't sure how you felt about our humanitarianism after we fell off the map at such a crucial time in your life."

"I'm proud of what you and John do. I always have been."

"See? This is why we need to spend more time together. So we can talk like this."

"I'm sorry I've been obsessed with finding Evander, but I'm sure you understand. It's horrible not knowing where he is and when I'll see him again."

"Of course I understand, but you also have to practice self-care. Sleep normally and exercise, get some air. Eat at home instead of at the café all the time. I just don't see you taking care of yourself very well."

It's nice to be mothered. Feels oddly foreign, but I like it. It reminds me, once again, that I'm not alone, that I still have my family.

"Thank you," I say.

"For what?"

"Being my mom."

"Oh, honey," she says, and she places her hand on my shoulder and gives it a squeeze. "I wouldn't trade being your mom for the world."

This paints a smile on my face, and I take a few sniffly happy-cry breaths.

Then I say, "Also, just so you know, I do try to stay in shape. In Russia I sometimes went for a jog, and twice a week, I used Ivan's free weights to tone my muscles." I do a few pretend bicep curls to make my point.

She nods her approval and says, "That's good."

I don't tell her about the buzzing headaches I've had to withstand, and how they left me too lethargic to exercise consistently. A lot of the time I couldn't get off my bed. Still, I managed to take a six-week self-protection class, so now I know how to break free of a hand hold and push an attacker's nose into his brain. I'm also good at kicking male dummies in the crotch, something that amused Helena quite a bit whenever she asked me to show her my new "superhero moves," as she called them. Ivan used to say no one in their right mind would mess with me, though I'm not sure he meant it as a compliment. I'm afraid he thought of me as one of those kooky in-laws you simply have to tolerate.

Anyway, I feel like I could free myself if someone tried to abduct me. Not that I think the Jovians will attack me in a violent way. They're nonviolent people.

"What are you thinking about?" Dana says, noticing the lapse in conversation, I suppose.

It's not a good time to tell her I've learned how to fight—she's already worried about my mental state, and picturing me kicking my way out of a problem isn't something I want her to do, so I go with, "It's almost Christmas."

"Yes, I know. That's something I keep meaning to discuss with you. Your father and I don't do much by way of observing the holidays anymore," she says. "I hope you don't mind."

Dana took to Buddhism long ago, and John describes himself as an atheist. Though they once went all out, decorating our home with a tree indoors and many lighted wreaths and reindeer outside, Helena and I both knew they wouldn't have bothered to celebrate at all if it wasn't for us.

"That's fine. Evander and I have been celebrating with Helena and her family because the children enjoyed the presents, but Evander's not here, so there's no reason at this point—"

"Good. I'm glad to hear it," she says with an abruptness I hadn't expected.

"Will we have dinner, or do anything?"

It seems weird not to do anything at all.

"Only if you want to. Do you want to?"

That would mean staying in for one night, which I might be able to handle but would rather not. "How about breakfast? I want to make French toast for you and John."

"Lovely. I'll buy the powdered sugar and some thick-sliced bread. I'm going to the store later today."

"Okay," I say, "there's no rush."

She looks at me with wide eyes. "It's tomorrow, Svetlana. Christmas is tomorrow."

I keep forgetting what day it is. To me, all of the days without Evander are the same. "Oh, wow. I guess I'm still out of it," I say.

We round the bend for the fourth time when someone appears on the sidewalk not far beyond the fence that separates the track from the rest of school grounds. The road passes close to the track, and this guy is on the adjacent sidewalk. He's tall, wearing a wool beanie. Looks pretty young. My alarmist brain tells me it may be Evander.

Before I know what I'm doing, I run straight off the track and onto a surrounding untouched swath of snow.

"Where are you going?" Dana shouts behind me.

I twist partway around and motion with the one-second finger, still running.

Coming upon the four-foot fence that stands between me and the world beyond, I experience a flash of panic because there's no easy way out. I'm going to have to hop over, which I do, by planting one boot through the diamond-shaped wire pattern, then the other, then swinging one leg over, then the other, and landing in an ungraceful heap on the other side. The bottom of my coat has snagged on the wire coils on top, and it pulls me back, stitches ripping. I stand up as much as I can in order to free myself, pulling and twisting until the coat lets go. I then ascend a short hill as fast as I can, slipping and sloshing my way up to the top in Dana's too-big boots. She's still shouting at me, but I can't tell what she's saying over the swoosh of melting snow that has turned brown under the wheels of the traffic driving by. I've reached the sidewalk, and the young man has continued on his way, but he's not out of earshot yet, not if I yell loud enough.

"Wait," I shout, still heading in his direction. "Hey, wait!"

He stops, turns around, removes an earbud from one ear. "Huh? Are you talking to me?"

I jog over to him. It's the strangest thing: Evander's face; his long, lean body; his cheeks pinkened from the cold. The expression, however, seems not quite right. I'm close enough to study his blue-green eyes, and I can tell from the numb unknowing that spreads thick across his face that he doesn't recognize me. Where there should be affectionate familiarity, a blank sort of confusion lingers. The hair peering around the edges of his woolen beanie matches my natural deep-brown color, and when he half-grins in an insecure way, his unsure features exude skepticism.

My heart races with joy, though my brain knows better—and yet I can't help myself, I open my arms wide and pull him in a hug. "Evander," I say.

"Um, I think you've, uh—" He doesn't hug me back. "I'm sorry, but I'm not whoever you think I am."

He nudges me away as he steps backward, and I let go. It's definitely Evander's face.

"I'm not Evander, ma'am. And I don't know you."

Dana has caught up by now. She's panting large clouds of warm air in my direction. "What's going on?" She turns to me and passes a stern look that seems to be unsure and hopeful at the same time.

"This is Evander," I say.

She looks at him, and he shakes his head.

"He's saying no," she tells me.

It *has* to be him. The Jovians told him to pretend otherwise. They're making him do this.

I grip his arm above the elbow. "Please don't pretend you don't know me."

He stares. "I *don't* know you. I've never even seen you before." He looks to Dana. "I'm not whoever she thinks I am."

"Edmund said it was all right," I say. "He said we could live together in the house on Sunrise Court, where your dad and I used to live."

Dana puts her hand on my shoulder. "It's okay, Sveta. Come on."

She doesn't understand. I can't leave.

I step away from her, sloughing her grasping hand from my shoulder. "Give me a second," I say before turning to Evander once more. "If you're not Evander, who are you?"

"Doug. Doug Hardacre."

He has Evander's eyes, his jawline. The hair. The body. "Oh my God," I whisper, "are you a—"

Dana puts her arm around me and jerks me back. Her face appears close to mine as she says, "You need to rest, that's all." Then she nods at me the way people nod into the faces of the infirm. "Let's go home, okay?"

I say nothing as she addresses Doug. "Sorry about this. Thanks for your time."

Doug resumes walking up the street. He's Evander, but he's not Evander. And I know this, but I can't accept it. *How many Dougs are out there?* I wonder.

"Come on, now," Dana says, her voice soft with disappointment and pity. "It's okay. *You're* okay."

She's still holding me close, and I'd like to shake her off, to use one of my self-protection moves to get free of her, but I can't be that callous. Instead, I twist around so I can see Doug one last time, as much as that's possible with Dana wrapped around my upper half. "Who are your parents?" I yell.

Dana groans. "Leave him be, for goodness sake."

"Who are your parents? What are their names?" I say again.

Doug walks backward now. "Bill and Samantha Hardacre," he shouts.

Dana takes a firmer hold of my arm and pushes me in the opposite direction. Unless I want to wrestle her, I have no choice but to continue.

"They've done it," I say, because I know she thinks I'm acting crazy, but she would understand if she knew the truth. "They did it a long time ago. I can't believe this."

"What? What did they do?" Dana says.

"They've cloned him. They've cloned Evander," I say.

Dana makes one of those exasperated sounds—like a breath of air crashing through her throat—and then, in an impatient tone, she says, "You don't actually believe that."

"Uncle Jimmy told me they would do it. I thought that by taking Evander to Russia, he'd be safe, but they helped themselves to a skin sample before we left. Right here, right under his arm. They must have figured out how to clone humans."

She stares at me with a look of wide-eyed outrage. "Stop this," she says using her stern voice. "Just stop!" Then she stamps her foot. "I do not want to hear another word."

I'm shocked into silence. Dana, so open, so supportive . . . Dana, my mother, is shutting me down.

I feel like a misunderstood teen as she continues to hold me with one hand and presses me forward with the other. We walk in this manner until arriving at the end of the block, the end of school grounds. We need to cross the road. As we wait for a few cars to pass, she's still holding onto me. I look at her, and she looks away. "You don't think he looked like Evander?" I say.

She shakes her head. "He was young, and there were some similarities maybe with the eye color, or the coloring in general, but he was fully grown. Your child is only ten."

I'd forgotten that she and John have never seen Evander in person. They don't know he's six feet tall. They've seen one photo of him from the chest up. "I told you, he's advanced for his age. He's big. Like an adult. Like Doug."

"I know that's what you told me. But you worry me, you really do." She squeezes my arm again as if I might make a run for it. "And I don't want to hear any more talk of aliens or clones, or any other outrageous things. We're going home, and you're going to rest."

I've pushed her too far. I shouldn't have told her. I don't know what to say. I know the truth; I know I'm as sane as she is. But the truth has upset her, so from now on I will have to lie.

There's not much more I can do at this point than play the dutiful daughter.

When we get home, Dana follows me to my bedroom and lectures about sleeping more and eating better and putting absurd thoughts powered by fear and worry out of my mind. According to her, I must take a few days off from agonizing about Evander. She insists that I stay home tonight, and that she's going to color and trim my hair herself this afternoon. "The three of us will have an early dinner," she says, "and after that you can go straight to bed."

"I don't want to go to bed," I say with the sassiness of a child as I whip off my coat. "I'm thirty-five years old. *You can't tell me when to go to bed.*"

Her face droops. "It's Christmas Eve. You should be with your family."

The laugh I stifle gets twisted in my throat, and I end up choking. "Are you serious? After the conversation we just had about not celebrating?"

I don't appreciate being reprimanded. And I'm miserable because I know for sure that my son has been cloned. It's not worth arguing, however, because if I want to go out, I can simply climb out the window. Problem solved.

"Otherwise," Dana's strident voice interrupts my thoughts, "I'm going to call a therapist I know and make an appointment for you."

She sounds exactly like Helena. I feel right at home.

It takes all the courage I can muster to struggle through the rest of the day at home with my parents. I don't bring up Evander. I don't speak much at all. I allow the inner workings of my mind to do the thinking while the outer workings go through the motions of acting normal. I comb through my tangled hair, watch Dana mix the brown dye and apply it, sit still while she trims the ends, accept John's compliments when he sees the new/old me, and later, when we're eating, I tell Dana how delicious her Chicken Diablo tastes.

After I wash all of the dishes by hand, Dana and John retreat to the TV room and switch on the evening news. I sneak a mostly empty bottle of vodka out of one of the uppermost kitchen cabinets and wedge it into the back waist of my pants so my sweater hangs over. I pass through the living room, peek my head around the corner of the den, and make the announcement that I'm going to bed.

Dana smiles as if there's no trouble between us: "Goodnight, Sveta. See you in the morning."

Once I'm in my room with the door closed, I check my phone, a screen void of messages. Fran didn't call or text all day. I don't know why. I think back to our last meeting. The way I asked about Lisa and Max. Maybe he's annoyed with me, too. Still, I want to call him and tell him what happened today and how Dana reacted when I told her the truth. If he's with Lisa and Max tonight because it's Christmas Eve (I doubt he is), he can ignore my call.

He answers with a gravelly "Yeah, hey" that's very unlike him. I'm not even sure it *is* him.

"Fran?"

"Sv'lana," he says through a heavily exhaled whoosh of air.

"Hi. What are you—"

"Um drunk."

"Oh, okay. You sound—"

"Yeah, thas why I sound weird. I wanna'd you to know right off the bat."

Music thumps in the background.

"*Where* are you?"

Please don't say a strip club.

"Holy shots. They're closing early tonight."

"Because it's Christmas Eve."

He grunts, followed by a moan. "Yeah, thas right. Chrissmaas Eve. Ho ho ho."

"I feel the same way. I was wondering if you might go see Max and—"

"Nah, no. Not doing . . . that."

"I'm sorry."

"Don't," he barks, and I'm jolted into silence. "Do not say that."

A moment of tension stretches between us before he says, "Look, I know you're s'prised about what a loser I turned out to be—"

"Fran, no, that's not what I think."

"Yes you do. I'm the def'nition of loser. And I'm missin' the arm to prove it."

"Please, don't talk like that. God, Fran, I would never think that."

"Yeah, well, you doan know what hapnend."

I hesitate one second before saying, “Then why don’t you tell me?”

“You really wanna know?” he says as if it’s nothing. “I’ll tell the whole dumb story right now. Stupid-ass story will haunt me till the day I die.”

“Okay,” I say.

“It was ’bout three en a half years ago. I was in charge of the newbies, the recruits, you know, the youngsters. They were my ’sponsibility. We were in training. A live fire exercise. You know what that means?”

“I think so.”

“Means guns, bullets. Real ones.”

He pauses. The music in the background fades and a man shouts, “Last call! Last call for alcohol, people.”

“You were shot in a training exercise,” I say.

“Yeah.”

“I’m so sorry—”

“Kid would have taken one in the head if I didn’t get in the way.”

“So, you *saved* someone?”

“Tried to.”

“I don’t understand. How can you call yourself a loser? You *lost a* limb trying to save—”

“He died anyway. Bullet went right through my arm. Wrecked it. *Splintered* it. And hit him.”

He takes a noisy breath in and out.

“You got in the way on purpose,” I say. “You’re only human, and you risked your life.”

“It was my job to keep them safe. *All of ’em,*” he says sounding more sober by the second. “After that, I was depressed, to use a word I thought would never apply to me. Couldn’t get out of bed, couldn’t do anything, just lingered around the house like a sad sack of—” He stops there. “Got so bad the FBI fired me. And Lisa, my lovely former . . . ” A groan escapes with his next breath. "Well, I was already on thin ice with her after that day in the park—"

"The day with David?"

"She didn't believe me, Svetlana. She said she did, but she didn't. Might a been cause I started, um, sorta collecting data after it happened. You know, I did the thing where you put a desk in the basement and hang photos on walls and just scribble whatever you can find about the Jovians on papers and sticky notes and notecards. Shit, I had notes everywhere, like I was wallpapering the place. Lisa thought I'd lost it. Thought I made the whole thing up. Like I had a beautiful mind or was doing drugs or, I don't know, just plain lying."

I could have helped him with this.

"You should have told me," I say. "I would have talked to her. I would have told her it was—"

"And then I lost my arm, my hand," he says, spitting out the words as if he hates himself for saying them. "And she didn't look at me the same. I had no job. I couldn't get out of bed. Lisa was angry all the time, as if I'd done something to make it happen so people would feel sorry for me. She said I brought it on myself. Can you believe that?"

"You would never."

"No, I wouldn't."

"I don't know what to say. Except I'm—"

"Don't!" He fires the word, sharp as a gunshot. "I don't want your sorrys."

"What about Max? He was just a young boy when this happened."

"Eight years old when Lisa took him away from me."

"But you can still be his father. He needs a father, Fran."

He exhales loudly with a bit of a growl at the end. The voice that follows sounds dead, hollow. Without inflection. "I let someone's son die. A mother and father lost a son on my watch. How can I ever enjoy my own son again?"

I close my eyes and shut my mouth as his pain washes over me, an ocean wave of emotion that mentally knocks me off my feet. The brute force of his statement leaves me without breath, waiting for the swell to pull back, for my throat to relax, for the pain in my chest to diminish. *No wonder he walks like a man who's crushed. No wonder he doesn't take care of himself.*

"I'm sorry that the only person who can help you get Evander back is such a loser," he says.

I jump up, grab the jeans draped over the end of my bed. "I'm coming over. We need to talk."

"Nope. I'm leaving. Just paid my bill and stumbled out the door."

"You shouldn't be alone. You're not in a good way."

"That's definitely true, but you don't have to worry. No one should waste their time worrying about me, so don't you do it."

"Listen," I say through gritted teeth, "do not get in your car and drive right now. I swear to God, Fran, I will—"

He chuckles. "I live in the one-bedroom upstairs. I'm halfway to my shitty home sweet home already."

"Above Holy Shots? But isn't it noisy? How do you sleep?"

"I told you, I don't. I'm usually stalking Jovians well past midnight."

"We need to talk about this tomorrow," I say.

"No, we don't."

"Fran."

"Night, Svetlana. Merry Christmas."

12

In the morning. I make the Christmas French toast, as planned. I stretch my arms to the ceiling and say that "I feel so much better now that I've slept," though all I can think about is Fran and what he's been through, and Evander and how I failed to stop the family from cloning him—and how awful it is for us to be apart during the holiday.

Dana and John have put some music on and hum along to Christmas tunes while they move about the house. Dana pretends nothing happened yesterday and that she has a perfectly sane daughter, and I pretend we are a happy family with no secrets. John acts his usual level-headed self, so I assume Dana didn't tell him about the fiasco that occurred during our walk. Or maybe she did tell him, and she also told him not to bring it up. I actually do feel much better thanks to the full night of sleep (helped along by two or three ounces of vodka, all that was left in the bottle).

To my relief, my parents made plans to visit some humanitarian friends in Philadelphia but haven't invited me to go. Probably because they're afraid of what stories I will tell.

As soon as they leave, I call Fran.

"Vasquez," he says as if he's still in the FBI.

"You're alive. Good. I need to talk to you. Something happened yesterday."

"You mean other than me getting drunk and making a fool of myself?"

I expected him to regret the prior night's conversation.

"Nothing to do with that, actually."

"What about Christmas?" he says. "Shouldn't you be with—"

"It's already done."

"Cool. I'll pick you up in fifteen."

I lace up my combat-style boots instead of Dana's oversize snow boots and grab my sheepskin coat, then wait in the foyer.

When I hop into his black sedan, Fran says, "Nice haircut." As it turns out, his beard has been shaved and he's sporting a trim as well. His hair's not buzzed like it used to be, but it's pretty short, and he looks a lot more like the handsome Fran I remember.

"You, too," I say, surprised that he has spiffed himself up considering the shape he was in last night.

"Took a visit to Earl's barber shop before finding a barstool at Holy Shots."

"Oh, I see. Well, I had no choice about my new look. Dana made me."

"She *made* you?"

"She's fed up with me and my problems, and she took it out on my hair. I guess she doesn't like me as a blonde because she brought chestnut brown number twelve home from the pharmacy. Where do you want to go?"

He hasn't eaten, so we drive to the café, where a handful of lost souls sit at the counter and stare at the television hovering over the milkshake mixer. I'm surprised the café is even open. Then again, this is America, where plenty of places refuse to close for the holidays.

I'm mixing sugar into my coffee while Fran scarfs down the farmer's breakfast, which from the look of it is a little bit of every kind of breakfast food scattered across his plate.

"I was under the impression you get along with your parents," he says.

"I do. But then a few days ago, I tried to tell them where the Jovians are from." I eye him knowingly, considering there are waitresses within earshot. "They went along with it, but I don't think they believed me, and then yesterday Dana and I went for a walk, and I accused a random stranger of being my son."

A veil of confusion overtakes his expression. "You thought you saw Evander?"

"He looked *exactly* like Evander," I say, with a flush of intensity warming my cheeks. "But apparently he was someone named Doug."

"Was this up close, or—"

"I hugged him. So, yes, very close."

He takes a swallow of coffee before saying, "This just keeps getting better and better."

I sigh and drop my head. "Yeah, I know. And he didn't just resemble Evander. He looked *exactly* like him—aside from the way he acted like I was a crazy lady he had never met before."

Fran eyes his plate. "Are you saying—"

"Yes. I think he's a," I pause and lower my voice, "you know what."

Fran puts down his fork and rubs what used to be the scruff on his chin but is now only stubble.

"This is the third time I've mistaken someone for my son," I continue. "First at the airport, once at Starbright, and now right in front of me. Who knows how many others are out there." My jaw clenches with the thought.

Keep it in check, Sveta.

"The question is," Fran says, "what do the Jovians want with all of them?"

I hunch low in my seat and look around to make sure no one's listening. "They want them to spread their DNA around. It'll be faster that way. The change they're hoping for. The kinder, more-aware human race and all of that."

I hate saying it out loud. I'd rather not think about it. It's too big.

"I think we need to know more before we jump to conclusions." Fran resumes eating. "Did you get to ask Doug anything other than his name?"

I put my coffee cup down. "Just who his parents are, and he said Bill and Samantha Hardacre."

"Have you heard of them?" he says as he chews.

"No, you?"

"No."

He eats the last bite of pancake, then wipes his mouth and takes a gulp of coffee. "I think we're going to have to find out where the Hardacres live and pay them a visit."

I'm glad he said so because I think the same thing, and I'd rather not go alone. Thank goodness Fran found me, considering my parents no longer think I'm sane.

Fran removes his cell phone from the black trench coat he always wears and places it on the tabletop. He presses the home button, holding it down, and says, "Bill and Samantha Hardacre, Kirksberg, Pennsylvania."

I stare sadly at his solitary hand.

"Got 'em," he says. "They're on Oak Leaf Terrace, four blocks away."

"So we'll go this morning?"

"No time like the present."

"Even though it's Christmas?"

"Yeah, we got this."

He's not worried, so neither am I.

The plan is to "feel them out." First we'll see if they actually exist. If they are a family. Second, if Doug is home, I want Fran to see him.

"If someone answers the door, what will we say?" I ask. "Maybe I should stay in the car since Doug has already met me?"

"No. We'll go to the door together and say that our dog ran away and that we live just a couple blocks over. I'll do the talking, and you can stand there and look worried, so even if Doug answers, he'll think it's just a coincidence."

"He may not recognize me. I was wearing a hat when we met. And my hair was still light, too."

"Even better."

We park down the street so they won't see our car. Outside, Fran tells me to walk fast so I get a little winded. I jump up and down a few times, then try to keep up with his longer strides. It occurs to me that he's not limping today. At all.

"Your leg," I say.

"What about it?"

"You're not limping."

"Oh, that. That's arthritis. Comes and goes with the weather. Snowstorms are the worst."

Sounds like an old-man thing to say, but I'd rather hear that than learn his limp came from another FBI injury.

The cold air numbs my cheeks and the tip of my nose. We reach the front door adorned with a silvery wreath.

Fran rings the bell.

Some movement beyond the door creates thumping sounds. Approaching footsteps. A man answers. His thin body and face bring to mind nicknames like "bean pole" and "slim." Other than that, he's generic looking, with ordinary short brown hair, brown eyes, a winter-pale complexion.

"Good morning," Fran says in a rushed way. "Sorry to bother you on Christmas Day. We live just a couple of blocks that way." He points in the direction of the parked car. "And our dog jumped the fence a few minutes ago. Someone down the street said he came this way, so I'm wondering if you'd let us check your backyard?"

I'm impressed by his acting skills.

"Sure, sure, of course. Can't say I've seen him back there. Then again, I've been chopping vegetables. Christmas dinner, you know."

Fran rubs the top of his head and passes me a knowing look. It happened to him: the Jovian jolt of electricity, the phenomenon of hair raising when a Jovian looks you in the eyes.

"Thank you," I tell the man, who turns in my direction and stares straight at me—and nothing happens. I'm not surprised. At some point after Andrew and I moved to Ashbury Falls, what Fran and I call "the Jovian jolt" stopped being a reliable tell for me.

He leads us through the house, which has few pieces of furniture and even fewer decorative items. No Christmas paraphernalia whatsoever, not even in the dining area that we pass on our way to the back of the house.

A woman calls down from upstairs. "Who is it, honey?"

"Some neighbors lost their dog," he says.

He opens the sliding glass door to the deck, saying, "I hope he's out here."

We step out. The deck's floor holds an untouched block of six-inches-thick snow. The yard next door is pockmarked with dog prints. "Could have been out there," the man says. "They have a dog, too, but some of those prints could be your dog's. What's his name?"

"Roger," Fran says without hesitation.

"If he comes back, I'll be sure to grab him. He big?"

"Midsize, a mutt." Fran holds his hand about a foot above the ground. "Mostly black with one white spot around his eye." He points to his own eye, making a circle with his finger.

I shout, "Ro-ger, here boy! Ro-ger!"

Then I look to Fran, who says, "We better move on before he's halfway to Philadelphia."

The three of us reenter the house, and Fran strides across the living room with me close behind.

The man follows. "Wait, let me ask my son." He stops at the bottom of the staircase and shouts, "Hey, Doug?"

"Yeah." The boy's voice appears at the top of the stairs. He must have been up there, listening to us.

I drop my head, and reach for the knob of the front door, ready to bolt.

Bill says, "Have you seen a dog, medium sized, mostly black, next door most likely."

"I heard one barking a few minutes ago."

Next to me, Fran faces the stairs, his head tipped back.

I squat down and pretend to tie my shoe.

"That was probably him," Fran says. "Thank you, thanks a lot. Merry Christmas."

I open the door and step out, eager to get away.

"What's your number," the man says. "We'll call if he comes around."

Fran's behind me. He turns and shouts some numbers that I'm sure are not the real thing.

My nerves spin as I rush down the shoveled path. I start to head in the direction of the car and Fran grabs my arm.

"This way, hon," he says.

I turn, follow him. We jog down the street. Once we're safely around the corner, he says, "Oh, yeah, they're the real deal. Every hair follicle on my scalp stood at attention. Did it happen to you?"

"Not even a little."

We jog around the block, until we arrive at the car. I'm warm, panting.

"I guess your Jovian radar is defunct," he says, talking over the top of the car as he unlocks the doors.

"I felt something when Edmund showed up, but only a little bit. It doesn't work for me anymore."

I open the door. As we sit, he says, "For me it was full volume." He feigns pulling his hair. "Spike city."

"So they're part of the family."

"Absolutely. And that kid looked exactly like your photo of Evander."

"Thank you. It's nice to know I'm not losing my mind."

Fran starts the car and adjusts the heat. Then pauses to look out the driver-side window. "So why didn't Dana think so?"

I open my mouth to answer and realize I have nothing to say. Seems like I should, but I don't.

He looks me in the eye and says, "He really looks like Evander."

The defrost reaches midway up the windshield, clearing a flame-shaped space on the fogged glass. "I guess because she was expecting a ten-year-old. And Doug looks more like he's twenty."

"That's true. Do your parents know the Jovians?"

What the hell is he suggesting?

I smirk. "Everyone in Kirksberg knows the Jovians."

"Right. But could Dana and John be—" He pauses and glances at the doubtful face I've made before he says, "Just hear me out. Do you think they could be working with them?"

"Working with them? I don't understand. How? Why? They're my parents, Fran."

"Yeah, I know. It's a ridiculous thought. I'm just checking around every corner. Dana saw the same photo you showed me."

Suddenly I'm uncomfortable. The heat blasting through the vent surrounds me, but I'm no warmer.

"Dana thinks I'm overreacting about this whole thing, that I'm being dramatic. She expects Evander to be big for his age. A big ten-year-old boy. Even though she saw the photo, she assumes he's still a kid. And I don't blame her. She thinks I exaggerate and make things up. About him. About the Jovians. Telling her that they've cloned him was the last straw."

He dips his head up and down a few times. "You're right. I'm sure that explains it."

I give Fran my imitation of the Jovian stare with dead eyes and a tilted head: "He's a *marvelous* child, you know," I say, deepening my voice in a humorous manner.

He laughs and raises his newly trimmed brows. "Is that what they call him?"

"When he was a baby, they did." I look away. The adrenaline of visiting Doug's house has worn off and reality has settled back in to haunt me. "He's so marvelous that they've made reproductions and kept the original for themselves."

At that, Fran's smile disappears, his moment of good cheer joining my own in falling off a cliff. "There was nothing you could do to stop them," he says. "Jimmy told you it would happen."

"He said they would have trouble doing it without his help."

Fran's hand grips the top of the steering wheel, and his

knuckles emerge like the peaks of small mountains. "I guess one of them figured it out."

"I know exactly who it was. Aunt Constant. I should have stopped her. I could have, had I stayed."

"Here? In the US? No. No way. Look, this isn't on you," he says so sternly that if I didn't know him better, I might mistake his insistence for anger. "You were booted from the country. And even if you weren't, the Jovians literally disappeared. How could you have stopped them if you couldn't even find them?"

"But they're here. Right *here* in Kirksberg. They haven't gone anywhere. And we don't have any idea how many Evanders are out there, spreading their DNA around."

"I'm not going to let you feel guilty about this. Do you actually think you could have made a difference? Do you think you could have changed their minds?"

I look down at my lap when I say, "I don't know. We'll never know."

Fran leans toward me and reaches awkwardly across his chest to hold my hand. "Andrew would be *proud* of you." He squeezes my fingers. "You beat the odds and got Evander out of the country. You raised him your way. Seriously, most people would have given up."

Then he lets go, sits back again.

With a tired groan, I press my head backward into the headrest. "I keep waiting for Andrew to speak to me, to tell me Evander's okay or even just that I'll see him soon."

"I'm sure he'll be there when you need him most."

I don't tell Fran that the truth is, he's not close, not like he used to be.

"I can't sit around until he does," I say. "And I can't just 'let it happen' like Uncle Jimmy told me to. Evander is out there somewhere. They'll probably bring a clone to my house and try to pass him off as the real thing, but they won't be able to fool me again."

Fran adjusts himself in the seat and presses the brake. He crosses his left hand over his body and shifts into drive, then places it back on top of the steering wheel. Before today, I tried not to notice all of the adjustments he has to make because of his missing hand, but now that we've spoken about it, it's out in the open and there's no reason to look the other way.

"Should we go back to Starbright?" he says. "See if we can devise a plan to finally get in there?"

I was worried he would call it a day and take me home.

"You've read my mind," I say.

13

Fran and I drive to Starbright the usual way, not the back way that leads to the rear of the building. It's Christmas Day, and the gate is raised. No guard on duty, either.

"Should that be up?" I say.

"Never has been before."

We pass through and glide into the empty parking lot, stopping directly in front of the entrance, which makes me uncomfortable. It's not something I would do, but I'm not driving.

"Maybe it's open because it's Christmas?" I say.

"Do you think they're expecting guests for dinner?"

"They might be expecting *us*. Or maybe they're not in there at all."

"They're in there," Fran says. "I bet they're all in there. And this is a high-security facility, so the blatant lack of coverage is extremely suspicious."

"Is it, though? A high-security facility, I mean?"

"They work with NASA, so yeah, it's supposed to be."

Fran reaches into the back seat and passes me a bag of black licorice. "Would you mind opening it?"

I do, then hand him a stick.

"Thanks. I need sugar."

"The pancakes weren't enough?"

He cocks a brow in my direction. "Are you mocking me, Mrs. Jovian?"

I chuckle. "So why are we here again? Do we *want* them to see us?"

"Yeah. I'm hoping one of them comes out, talks to us." Fran leans forward so he can see through the top of the windshield into the sky. "By now, I'm sure they know you saw Doug."

"You're right. And they probably don't care. That's how they are."

"Or they might think we're preparing an attack. Maybe building an army." He pushes the rest of the licorice stick into his mouth and puts his hand out for another.

"Again, I doubt they care," I say, passing him three more.

"Why not? You think they have technology that could thwart anything a human army comes up with?"

"Yes, and his name is David," I say in what I call my "doomsday voice."

Fran rubs his chin. "I wonder if everyone in the family can do what David did that day in the park."

"You mean transform into a ball of energy and cause an earthquake? Who knows? But, no, Uncle Jimmy said David is special. David is the supreme being. He can read minds, he's obviously powerful. I never got to see what magical things the others could do. They're nonviolent, that's all I know."

He makes a grunt of a sound that tells me he's not so sure.

"I've thought about showing up in the lobby and demanding they let me see Caroline and Edmund, or even Constant, *anyone* I know," I say, "but even if they allow me in, they'll make sure I don't see anything important. Nothing will come of it."

"I guess we'll have to get in on our own so we can search the place."

"Can you imagine how many secrets are in there?" I say.

"Plenty," Fran says. "The FBI tried to enter the building two days after David attempted to take Evander, but we couldn't get clearance. The higher-ups dragged their feet and finally gave us the go-ahead to investigate Jovian homes, but not their offices. Starbright was off-limits. I'm sure that's why the family moved in there."

"The FBI wouldn't even *try* after that?"

"We wanted to, believe me. I led a team, and we were set up in the parking lot, ready to go, when my boss called it off. The command was 'Stand down,' and there was nothing I could do. The next day, I was given a new case—in Colorado."

"I have to get in there," I say.

"You know I've scoped it out thoroughly. The weird thing is, like you said, sometimes it seems like there isn't much security around."

"The few times I came to visit Andrew, there was one guard at the entry and one standing at the far side of the lobby, beyond the spiral staircase. I'm sure there could have been more, but that's all I remember."

"A team of six or more guards man the building most of the time, from what I've discerned. How well do you know the layout?"

"If I go through the front door, I know how to get to the wing where Edmund and other family members have their offices. Miranda and Leo brought me through the back when I came to see Andrew's body. But that was in Ashbury Falls, and I don't think the two buildings are exactly the same, so . . ."

Fran's eyes soften. It's like I did something to let the air out of him for a second. Then I realize that I've reminded him of the day he lost his best friend.

"Did you see a security guard in the back?" he asks.

"Leo used a card to get us in, I'm pretty sure. And I didn't see any guards right away. That doesn't mean there weren't any. I was overwhelmed that day and may not have noticed."

"They use touchscreens and eye recognition now."

"Of course. So I guess we can't enter through a door?"

"Oh, I didn't say that."

I grin and say, "Good."

"I may be able to get past the security system with some help from you. Since you have both your hands." He's sheepish as he lifts his prosthetic arm in my direction. It's the first time I've had this close a look, the first time I can study its beige-colored base and silver prong at the end. "This thing isn't the most graceful when it comes to picking locks."

"But it helps you do some things?" I say.

"Yeah, some things."

He's staring at the arm like it's someone else's.

Then I remember: "I read an article about robotic limbs that can pick up items as small and delicate as a flower stem. Scientists make bionic arms. Maybe you could get one."

His face becomes rigid, and he turns away when he says, "I don't think so."

"I'm sure the FBI will pay considering the accident occurred—"

He's shaking his head. Then he lets out a breath of air laced with an underlying grumble.

I can take a hint, so I say, "Okay," and look out the passenger-side window.

When he speaks again, it's in the tone of our prior conversation, before the subject of the arm came up. "The truth is, I'm not sure what kind of risk we'll be taking if we do this, if we enter the building. The security guards are pretty well armed."

"With guns?"

"As far as I can see. And batons. Pepper spray. One of them had a stun gun."

"But the Jovians are nonviolent people," I say with exasperation. "To tell you the truth, I'm not worried about getting shot."

"If security catches us breaking in, you don't think they'll fire?"

"Not if they're Jovian. And even if they aren't, they work for the Jovians, who wouldn't stand for it. The guns have to be for show. It's the Jovians pretending to be human. That's all."

Fran scratches his head. "Okay, so let's say they don't shoot at us. You still think they'll take us and lock us up somewhere."

"If they catch us, they'll probably escort *you* off the property, but they'll have me where they want me. And if they think it's best to lock me up, that's what they'll do."

"Because you can bust their plans wide open," he says. "Because you have the power."

I roll my eyes. "If you say so."

His face flickers with a thoughtful expression, as if some flash of wonder just lit up his brain. "Maybe it wouldn't be the worst if they were to take you into custody."

If I didn't suspect him of joking, I would slap him. But then I realize there's zero hint of humor in his face. "You can't be serious," I say, glaring at him.

"I mean, if it ends up we can't get in or if we do get in but we don't find anything, then maybe Plan C should be for you go live in your house under their watch like Edmund wants you to."

I'm not hearing this. How can he say this to me?

"At least you'd be in their circle—and you'd be safe. You might even have access to . . . "

He continues to double down on this plan as a swell of panic rises up my neck and lights a crackling fire in my brain. By the time he stops talking, my head has filled with angry flames of bewilderment and betrayal.

"I *can't* live with them," I say far louder than necessary. "You don't understand. I can't be a prisoner in one of their homes. It's not an option."

"It wouldn't be like last time because I'd know where you are," he says, using an even deeper, more insistent tone than before. "I'll keep an eye on you every second, and your parents would know, too. The chance that the Jovians would be able to pull off an abduction is—"

"Highly likely," I say, once again too loudly.

"*Slim,* actually."

I don't know how he can remain so calm and unwavering. *Doesn't he realize how angry this makes me?*

"After I had Evander," I say, "David wanted me to produce more children for them. Did I ever tell you?"

Now I have his attention.

His nostrils flare and mouth twitches. "David said that?"

"Yes, David said that."

His jaw clenches and he sits back. "I didn't know."

"Why are we here right now, by the way? Were you hoping to drop me off?"

"Of course not." He rubs his forehead and then pinches the bridge of his nose. "I want to help you get your kid back, and so far avoiding your in-laws isn't helping. Action is the cure for fear. We have to do something."

"I thought the plan was to get into the building," I say, slicing the air with sharp enunciation.

"It is."

"But you thought about dropping me off, didn't you?"

"You think I would do that?"

I slump in the seat, aware that I may be pouting.

"Just help me get in," I say. "I'll find out what's going on with Evander and where he is. The answers are in there, and I'm not the innocent girl I was ten years ago. No one is going to lock me in a tower."

"Okay," he says.

"Whatever happens, they won't take me willingly."

"That's fine, but you're not actually KGB, you know? I'm not sure you have the skills to take on—"

"I have the skills," I say. "And I know more about them than anyone else on this planet."

We hold a look. His brown eyes sharpen and his upper lip quivers. I wonder what he's holding back.

"What?" I say.

"Are you sure about that?" His voice is gravelly low.

"Who would know more about the family than I do?"

"NASA. Employees and former employees, some of which I interviewed when I was still with the FBI."

I'm sure that could be true, though he's never told me the specifics of his FBI work, nothing about interviews or what the interviewees had said.

"Have you been in touch with someone recently?" I say.

"Maybe."

"Fran, you either have or you—"

"Okay," he says, shoulders drooping with abandon. "Not very recently, but in the last year or two. I haven't said anything about her because I'm not sure we can rely on her intel. A lot of it is pretty far out there. She's retired. Nearing ninety."

"Ninety!"

"Yeah, she's old. She met the Jovians in the 1970s according to her employee file, when she was forty-five and had already worked at NASA for about twenty years. She was one of the employees who helped build NASA's partnership with Starbright."

"You never told me about her. Why didn't you ever mention her?"

"She was the only former NASA employee who didn't shut down completely when I brought up the subject of the Jovians. But she didn't tell me much, believe me."

"What's her name?"

"Ida Moore. Ever heard of her?"

I shake my head. The name doesn't sound at all familiar.

"Okay, so you know that in the beginning, Starbright played a small role in supplying parts for NASA telescopes and that was it."

"I didn't know anything about their partnership. Andrew hardly ever spoke about work."

"Like many business relationships, theirs changed over time. What little I could see of the files that were available to me indicated that with Ida's help, Starbright eventually became crucial to several of NASA's ventures. Again, I don't have the specifics. My pay grade was never high enough to see anything that had been redacted—and a lot of it was. I couldn't find anyone, frankly, who had the clearance necessary to see more than I could, not even my boss. All I know from what I saw was that a controversy occurred that involved Ida and Starbright, and it happened in the nineties. She was working on something that had to do with space travel when NASA put an abrupt end to the project. Her connection to Starbright was severed, and soon after, she left her job."

"She was fired?"

"According to her—and her file backed this up—NASA did not fire her and never even asked her to retire. She claims she worked as a consultant for them for about fifteen years after she 'joined the Jovians,'" Fran uses air quotes.

"She *joined* the Jovians?"

"That's what she told me, though there's no record of her employment at Starbright. And then a year ago, when we last spoke, she said NASA still reached out to her on a regular basis."

I'm not sure any of that matters, considering I only want to ask her if she knows what the Jovians plan to do with Evander. "Can we call her?"

"If I thought we should call her, I would have done it already," he says, frowning. "I'm afraid Ida may be mentally unstable, and I won't be able to verify anything she says, so what would be the point?"

"What do you mean, 'mentally unstable'?"

"Exactly what I said. She's unstable, and that makes all of her information *unreliable*."

"Does she live in a mental institute or something?"

"No."

"Then what makes you so sure—"

"Okay. Well, the first time I called her, she acted like she knew me, like we were good friends who hadn't spoken in a long time. She said she knew I was going to call and that she'd been waiting by the phone."

"That's weird, but—"

"And when I asked what she meant by that, she said we were friends—good friends—in another dimension."

"In another dimension," I echo.

"Another world, another time, who the hell knows? But I think we can agree she's not all there."

"She could still know things," I say, hearing the weakness in my argument.

He leans toward me, rests his hand on my shoulder. "Look, getting in and out of the building undetected is the first plan. Plan B is getting caught and fighting our way out.

And Plan C is you moving back into your old home and waiting for Evander."

I bring my fist down on the armrest of the door with such force that I recoil due to the pain. "There is no Plan C," I say, my voice shaking.

Fran turns away, exhibiting an impressive amount of composure. "We probably won't need it."

I want to slap the back of his head, but I can't. He's trying to help even if Plan C is the dumbest thing I've ever heard come out of his mouth. "I'll never agree to it," I say.

"Noted." He shifts the car into reverse. "Let's get out of here."

"You're going to have to call Ida Moore."

He raises his brows. "Am I?"

"To ask about Evander. Please, Fran."

He draws in a deep breath that expands his already broad chest, and says, "Yeah, okay. But don't get your hopes up."

In the morning, I take a shower and blow-dry my hair, which I must say is much shinier and healthier than it's been in a long time. A fresh sweater and pair of black leggings that Dana bought me last week does a lot to present a more put-together look than the one I've presented lately.

At the breakfast table with Mom and Dad, I start a conversation about life in Russia. The farm. Ivan and his brothers. What a great mother Helena is. I figure these are safe topics. But Dana and John don't seem all that interested, listening but not asking any questions, which is strange.

Something is up, so I stop talking.

John clears his throat. "We wanted to let you know that we have our next trip planned. We're going to Peru."

I sit back. *Having them out of the house could be a very good thing for me.*

"That's a new part of the world for you," I say with purposeful calm. I don't want to appear too happy about this. "What will you do there?"

John clears his throat again; either he's nervous or has a tickle. "We'll work with charities to help empower the people, exercise their rights, diminish poverty. You know, the usual." He smiles and I smile back.

Then Dana says, "We want you to come with us." When she looks at me, it's with a powerful attitude that tells me she means business. I'm not prepared for this. They have never asked me to come along on one of their humanitarian efforts, never so much as mentioned the possibility of my joining a trip.

In the void of my nonanswer, Dana sits straighter and pulls the neck of her sweater into line.

I brace myself for the take-charge mother I knew as a teenager, the "I know what's best for you" Dana.

"You need a fresh environment," she says. "A place where you can concentrate on other things. It's not one of our long trips, only a month at the most. And when you get back, maybe Evander will have arrived in Kirksberg like Edmund promised. Most likely, you won't miss a thing, and it will be good for your mental health to get away."

"My mental health is fine," I say with a grumble. "I told you I feel very good now that I've been sleeping."

"We know," John says. "We just think you could use a break from the worry." John used his gentle voice, which makes me realize Dana has told him what happened at the track, how I thought I saw Evander and what I said afterward about cloning. Of course John wouldn't believe it. Why would he? He thinks I'm on the verge of a breakdown.

"Besides," he adds, "it would be nice for you to come with

us, see what we do, how we do it. Maybe you'll join us on trips in the fu—"

"I can't go with you," I say, because these are the only words that will unstick from the sides of my mouth.

"Is it because you think they've cloned Evander?" John asks in a cautious tone. "Because Mom says the young man you ran into didn't look much like the photo you showed us. Maybe you were mistaken?"

I tilt my head in Dana's direction. I'm afraid I may be scowling at her. "That's because Mom thinks Evander is an average ten-year-old, but I told you he's actually very big for his age, and the guy we met on the street *did* look like him."

"Anyway," John says, steering my focus back to him, "Evander may not get to Kirksberg for weeks from what you've told us, and Dana and I think it would be nice to travel as a family."

I push my butt to the very back of my chair, the backrest bumping the apex of my hip bones. "I see what's happening. You don't want to leave me alone in this house. You think you need to keep your eyes on me."

"You're under an enormous amount of pressure," Dana says, in a tone that's not as patient as John's. "We know you can take care of yourself. We just want to help you get through this difficult time."

"And if I don't want to go to Peru?"

"Promise you'll think about it. We leave in ten days."

Seems to me she's trying to sound like a person who doesn't care one way or the other, but I know she expects me to make the "right" decision.

"Of course I'll think about it," I say with promise in my voice.

I can promise her whatever she wants right now, but I'm pretty sure she won't like my answer when the time comes.

14

The next few nights, Fran and I drive to Starbright under the cover of darkness. We're more serious about staking it out now. We need to watch how they enter the building, whether they touch or look into the screen and in what order. Crouched in the bushes near the tree with the platform, we whisper our conversations. On the left side of the building, the telescope is an enormous bubble of metal parts and gears that adjust from time to time, making buzzing sounds and clicking movements as it allows the viewer to focus upon all the stars in the galaxy.

After the first teeth-chattering night, I learned to wear long underwear beneath my jeans (some of Dana's that I found stored in my closet) as well as a woolen scarf and my bulky coat. We've muted our phones and complain about our feet going numb in our boots. No one arrives or departs. Nothing happens for six hours.

Serious stakeouts, I learn, are quite boring.

The third night, though, I've just peeled a banana to stop my stomach from growling when two men approach the staircase that leads to the entry. One of them resembles Leo,

Miranda's husband, and his bulkier build, but when I look through the binoculars, I can see that it's a much younger man, and I'm doubtful that the hair under his knit hat is Leo's silvery-gray mix. I'm still looking through the binoculars when he turns in our direction, and his eyes glisten neon green.

"Crap!" I say, startling, and my banana falls to the ground. "He sees me."

"What?" Fran whispers. "Stop fidgeting around."

I freeze, afraid to so much as breathe.

The Leo lookalike starts to move toward us.

"He's walking this way," I say.

"I can see that."

The man continues toward us, and I notice his lips are moving. He's saying something, *reaching* for something.

"There's something on the ground. A cat. He's petting a cat."

"Stop talking," Fran whispers.

After a moment, this younger Leo retreats, heading up the stairs to the entry where the other Jovian waits. He hovers in front of the small screen beside the door, and they enter the building. That's the last we see of them.

The next night, a man and a woman run up the stairs to the door, touch the small screen, and slip inside as if late for an appointment. By the fifth night, I'm so bored and tired that as soon as we settle in behind the bushes, I close my eyes and drop straight into a dream. I'm in the park in Kirksberg, hurrying down the paved path like I did the day David found me and Evander there, only this time I'm alone, and I'm the one who's late.

I'm meeting someone.

Not David, but . . . *Uncle Jimmy.*

It's the summer: the lawn smells freshly cut and flowers quiver in the breeze, yet the park is void of people. I'm nearing the bench where Andrew and I ate cheesesteaks on our first date. I haven't seen nor heard from Uncle Jimmy in years, not since the Jovians sent him back to his home of Mintaka, and I can't get there fast enough. I'm pretty sure he wants to help me. Why else would he want to see me?

I round the bend past the small grove of pines. The bench comes into sight, and . . . someone is there. Someone thin and young. Not Uncle Jimmy. I slow to a walk, then come to a full stop. It's David looking like he did when I met him at the "drinks on the lawn party" at Caroline and Edmund's house. I want to turn and run the other way before he transforms into the supreme being—powerful, cunning, a mind reader—but he sees me now, and I know if I try to get away, he'll come after me just like he did a decade ago.

"Come," he says, putting his arm out and gesturing me toward him.

My legs don't want to obey, but somehow I'm moving toward him. He pats the space on the bench next to him, and I sit.

He looks not at me but at the grounds in front of us. "Remember the UFO that crashed in 1965?" he says. "It was a hoax."

"Yes, you told me," I say.

"But you didn't believe me." He turns, and his sharp eyes see into my mind; I feel him flipping through memories of me and Andrew. Our first date on this very bench, the drive to our new home in Ashbury Falls, the embrace we shared when I learned I was pregnant.

I break the connection by gazing at the ground by my feet. Suddenly my head fills with a buzzing headache like the kind I experienced in Russia.

"We're going to have to keep you away from that spaceship," he says with a blank demeanor that leaves me cold. "Promise me you won't go near it."

I could care less about the spaceship.

"I don't even know where it is," I say.

"It's buried at Starbright." The words come not from David but from Uncle Jimmy, who has taken David's place seated beside me. He's wearing a cardigan, and his balding hair is in the usual absentminded whirl.

I reach out and put my hand on his shoulder to make sure he's really there. His flesh feels warm, solid. It's not a trick as far as I can tell.

I say, "Andrew told me the Pentagon has it."

"Oh, sure, sure." Uncle Jimmy's head bobs up and down. "There's a lot Andrew didn't know."

This sends an angry flare through my brain, though it fizzles a moment later.

"There's something on the spaceship for you," he says, "something you'll need."

"Something for me?"

"Yes, yes, for you," he says.

"But I wasn't even born when that spaceship landed."

"You can't understand. Not yet, I'm afraid."

"How will I get into the building?"

"The Baltic Sea will work," he says, grinning the way he always did at this little joke about the color of my eyes. "I programmed the software."

"The eye recognition software? Do you mean my eyes will open the door?"

"It's in the eye of the beholder," he says, looking straight through me like a blind man would.

I don't know what to say to that. This conversation feels like a bad connection. I'm not sure of anything he's saying.

He stares into the distance. "Nothing is lost. Nothing is created. Everything is transformed."

"That's what you said the night you went back to Mintaka. I remember everything you told me. 'The only constant is change. Find the freedom within your confinement.'"

"Yes. Good, good," he says with a seriousness that wasn't present the moment before. "And here's another: The light you see in the present is light that comes from the past."

I consider what the significance of that might be but can't come up with anything.

He nods, sure of himself. "No worries, my dear."

The wind picks up and blows back my hair. Little dirt devils rise from the ground and flash past us like spinning tops that go on to pull the yellow flowers from their comfortable bed. Uncle Jimmy is biting his lower lip and gazing forlornly into the sky.

Our eyes meet and he says, "Don't panic."

I wake with a loud suck of air, looking this way and that as if I'm under attack, trying to figure out where I am and why it's so cold and whether I'm in danger.

Something heavy falls upon my shoulder. It's a second before I realize it's Fran's hand.

"You okay?" The binoculars hang like a necklace upon his chest, bouncing a little as he laughs at me. "You dozed off. Happens to me on occasion, too."

"How long was I—"

"Three maybe four minutes, at the most. Were you falling?"

"What?"

"Is that why you yelped? I hate those falling dreams."

"Uncle Jimmy," I say, rubbing my eyes. "He said the spaceship is in there."

The next morning, I enter the kitchen in the same clothes I wore the day before and didn't bother to get out of after a night of staring at the Starbright building and trying to make sense of my dream.

John sits at the table with a cup of coffee and a cereal bowl with leftover milk. He's reading his phone. It's 8 a.m. I'm wide awake and compelled to get my day started, though Fran brought me home at four-thirty in the morning after we drove down the Hardacres' block to see if their house might be worth staking out as well (it wasn't).

There's no need to be up this early, but I can't stop thinking about Starbright and the fact that *the* legendary Kirksberg spaceship dwells in its basement—and that the Uncle Jimmy of my dreams told me there's something for me on the ship. Something important.

Also, the lack of sleep makes me hungry.

I put two pieces of rye in the toaster and grab a glass for orange juice. Then I retrieve the butter from the fridge and find a butter knife on the cutting board, already used and surrounded by crumbs.

Dana comes in. "There's strawberry jam, if you want."

"Oh. Yes. Thanks." I don't want it, but I've been trying to be agreeable to Dana since she and John asked me to travel to Peru with them. I stare into the fridge but can't find the jam on a shelf or in the door.

"In the pantry," Dana says.

I don't like the way she's watching me so closely. I feel the intensity of her interest getting stuck in my unbrushed hair. When I'm this tired, acting normal and agreeable requires special attention. I should have brushed my teeth and changed into pajamas, or at least slipped into my robe before I left my room. I could have showered. Or, I could have just stayed in bed until I knew Dana and John had left the house, off to the organic grocery store or the high school track.

The toaster pops, and I spin around. With the cabinet open, I grab a plate and it slips from my hand onto the floor with a heart-stopping clatter. It's not broken, but now both of my parents stare at me with grim frowns that reveal their even grimmer worries.

"Sorry, sorry," I say, hunched over in a forced giggle. "Just call me butter fingers."

Everything I say has a pathetic ring to it.

I put the dropped plate in the sink and more mindfully reach for another one. The toast is stiff by now, and I have trouble applying the cold butter because it's not softened at all. I feel my parents' concern surround me like a blanket thrown over my shoulders and decide to go without the jam. God forbid it ends up on the floor as well.

Finally, I take my place at the table, where Dana and John seem to have been waiting for me to settle.

"What is that scent?" Dana says in a positive tone, though I can tell she's directing the question to me in a negative way.

My jeans have pine sap on them from the previous night. Before Fran and I drove to the Hardacres' this morning, I climbed the tree to his lookout platform. I wanted to see the view from up high.

"I don't smell anything," I say, and I crunch on my toast.

"Okay, well," she says, "we've made a decision about Peru."

I swallow and put the bread down.

"We're going to need you to come with us."

"You can't make me," I blurt out, realizing I've just uttered the phrase of a toddler.

"We're leaving in five days, and I'm sorry, Svetlana, but you're wound tighter than ever. John heard you come in last night—or, I should say, this morning. You're dirty, you haven't slept, you're losing weight. And I found an empty bottle of vodka under your bed. Why won't you let us take care of you?"

I can see why she's worried when you add a bottle of vodka to coming home at four in the morning and arriving disheveled for breakfast. But I haven't been drinking. Just that one night, to help me sleep.

"You know I can't leave the States yet," I say. "They may not let me back in. I have to use Helena's passport because I'm on the 'do not enter' list. It may not work next time. I was lucky it worked last time."

Dana leans in and taps the tabletop with a pointer finger as she speaks. "I'm sure it will be fine."

This is not the response I expected. If she's willing to take that risk, I'll have to come up with another, equally good reason not to go.

"Evander should be here any day now," I say as if this were a fact I'm sure of.

"And we hope that he is," she says with enthusiasm. "But it won't hurt if he comes back and you're away for a little while. At least you will have taken some time off from the worry, gotten out of your own head, away from all of the reminders of your predicament. Away from the Jovians."

"My problems won't go away just because I'm in Peru," I say.

She slumps with impatience. "Yes, I realize that, but I'm afraid whatever is going on with you is going to hit rock bottom very soon, and I'm not comfortable leaving you alone right now. I'm sorry."

She's too good of a mother. This is what a good mother, worried for the sanity of her child, would do. And I love her for it. At the same time, I'm rolling my internal eyeballs. Outwardly I act like I get it because Dana's chin trembles as if she's near the verge of a cry—and she *never* cries—she's as tough as they come. She has to be in order to deal with the poverty and hardship she encounters around the world.

"Fine," I say. "I'll sign up for therapy so you don't have to worry while you're away. I'll place myself under a doctor's supervision."

Dana's face has gone blank. The suggestion, I can see, has surprised her.

"If you let me stay here, I mean," I add because her silence persists. "I'll even take a yoga class. Deep breathing, meditation, relaxation. I'll do it all. Whatever you want me to do."

Dana eyes John, who wears the same "at a loss for words" expression.

Pressing forward, I say, "We can even have the therapist phone you with updates of my progress."

I pass John the hopeful gaze of a teenager.

He says, "What do you think, Dana?"

She clears her throat and stares into the tabletop as if she'll find the appropriate answer there. "I'm not sure a therapist will agree to it. Seems like a tremendous responsibility for a doctor who hasn't even met you yet."

"I don't see why not," I say, as if I know a thing or two about therapists. "This is something people do these days."

I have no idea what normal people do these days, but I can't go to Peru right now. Not when there's something for me on that spaceship.

Once my parents leave for Peru, I can reschedule my appointment ten times and never get there—or I could just go to it. Discuss my feelings with the doctor. I'm sure I can think of something to talk about. How bad could it be?

I've been looking out the window, staring at the garage, and when I turn back to Dana and John, I realize they're sitting in complete silence, watching me like two cats watching a beetle cross the carpet. Now that I've noticed the lack of discussion, the silence strains between us like an overstretched rubber band.

Dana's lips curve slightly, though she doesn't look happy. "We'd rather you come to Peru," she says.

My shoulders droop, and I toss my head backward in frustration. "I'm thirty-five years old. Sometimes people have to work things out on their own. Without their parents."

I thought I needed them to protect me. I wanted to stay with them because I wanted to feel safe and surrounded by people I know and trust. And I'm so grateful to them both for everything—especially adopting me when I was a teenager—but the twine that keeps my anger wrangled has begun to fray. I love them, but I want and need to get my way, even if they can't understand why.

"Svetlana," Dana says with determination equal to my own. "You're still our daughter no matter how old you are." Her stubborn eyes bore into my face like little hands pinching my cheeks.

It breaks my heart that she cares so much. Usually we get along so well.

I drop my head into my hands and let out a grumble. "I'm sorry. I know I've brought all of this on you, but he's my son. I can't switch it off."

"We understand," Dana says as if it's not that big a deal after all. "Just, please, watch the video about Peru. There's something very gratifying and *healing* about helping others. I think it's probably just what you need right now. And it's warm there. We'll be surrounded by beautiful blue water, pristine beaches."

I can't tell them no. They're worried about me. They care. I would have ended up on the streets of Moscow without them.

"Okay," I say, knowing I'm only delaying the fight that's sure to come. "I'll watch the video."

John retrieves his laptop from the den and sets it up for me where I'm seated at the table. Standing beside me, he clicks a button, and a video begins with many dirt-stained, bony children, some of them crying, some lying down, others sitting propped against a building. Their sharp knees and elbows pierce my attention as they sit unsmiling with their small bowl of rice or . . . whatever kind of food that is. Most of these children, the narrator says, are parentless.

For a second, I'm tempted to drop everything and run to Peru. Before my husband died and the Jovians tried to steal my baby, I wanted very much to help children in need. Now that the opportunity has come to me, I can't deny my natural reaction to what I'm seeing. The video continues, delving into the city ghettos and dirty water of poverty-stricken neighborhoods. It pans across beaches, fishing villages, and resorts. The sun blares upon the jungle with sharp-as-a-razor brightness, and I can't help but worry about all of those thirsty, hungry children going without clean water or bread or fresh fruit—or adults who care for them.

Then again, I have a spaceship to find, a message that waits for me on board; that is, if the Uncle Jimmy in my dream really was Uncle Jimmy and not something my imagination willed to life.

The narrator explains the hardships of the Peruvian people and how they can be helped, how their standard of living can be raised. When the video comes to an end, John explains his goals for the trip, and once again I think how lucky I am to have him and Dana for parents. Of all the couples who could have adopted me . . . I feel bad for involving them in my problems.

He reaches in front of me and closes the laptop. "So, that's it," he says. "What do you think?"

"It's very persuasive."

He crosses his arms. "So you want to come with us?" His words are bright with optimism.

"I do. I really do. But even if I wasn't waiting for Evander to arrive, I don't have a passport. What if I get to Peru and when I try to come home, they realize the passport is fake. That's a federal offense. They'll send me straight back to Russia, and I'll miss my chance to get Evander back."

"Yeah," John says, pressing his glasses up the bridge of his nose. "I understand that you might worry about something like that, but you know what? When you travel like we do, with the humanitarian groups, they don't look at you as closely as they do ordinary citizens. That's not a fact that's well-known, of course, but I can all but promise you won't be taking a big risk. You'll get back in."

That does not sound good for the security of the nation.

"Are you sure? I'm surprised to hear that. It seems like—"

"It's just stuff you learn when you're in our line of work," he says. "And you know how long we've been doing this. I'm on a first-name basis with several of the officers in customs."

"I don't doubt that. I'm sure you know all of the ins and outs of international travel. I'm sorry to be so difficult," I say. "If all of this wasn't going on with Evander, it wouldn't even be a question. I'd love to go. It's just the timing."

The sight of him drooping with disappointment is almost enough to make me say yes.

"Let me sleep on it," I say.

"Sure." He lifts the computer from the table. "Give us an answer in the morning."

No doubt he was hoping to put the discussion to bed, but I can't lie to him, can't agree to this plan. The truth is, if they want me to go, they'll have to knock me out and carry me there unconscious because there's just no way in hell I can say yes right now.

15

Fran and I text back and forth several times that day in preparation for the following night when we'll attempt to get into Starbright. He mentions details like possibly carrying pepper spray and wearing leather gloves in case we have to deal with broken glass.

I tell him how my parents want to take me to Peru.

Dana is practically insisting, I text.

But they know you're waiting for Evander.

They're worried for my mental health and don't want to leave me alone.

Tell them I'll babysit. Smiley emoji with tongue sticking out.

We have to get into Starbright as soon as possible, I write.

Tomorrow night. Just have to firm up a couple of things.

Did you call the old lady who worked for NASA?

Ida Moore? I tried. Couldn't reach her. Either she's ghosting the world or something happened. She's been wiped from the internet.

I'm calling you. I tap his contact, and he picks up right away.

"She vanished?"

"Her telephone number has been disconnected, and I found nothing about her online, not even what I used to find. It's like she's gone off-grid." He pauses there. "And there was nothing about a funeral, either."

"Okay," I say, with reluctance. "I was really hoping she could tell me about the spaceship and where it is."

"Don't take it as a loss. I told you I'm not even sure anything she said was valid."

"Right, I know."

"I mean, the more I think about her, the more I realize how unreliable she really was. She claimed to be in touch with the Jovians on a regular basis after she left NASA, which definitely could be true, but she also said that it was because they had a part they wanted her to play."

My ears perk. That's a Jovian phrase. David, Caroline, Miranda, all of them have mentioned the parts they play.

"That's actually—" I start to say, but Fran interrupts in a loud, blunt manner: "She also said what they wanted her to do involved a solar system over twenty lightyears away."

"As in they wanted her to go there?"

"I think that's what she was saying."

"Evander is traveling to the mother planet."

"Right, but Ida is eighty-nine years old, an ordinary human being—not a human-Jovian— and you know how far a lightyear is?"

"I was married to an astronomer, so I do know: it's something like 6 trillion miles."

"Exactly. I don't think Ida could survive the trip."

That makes sense.

"When did she say she was supposed to go," I ask.

"She never said. Why?"

"Because she's missing now. Maybe it was the Jovians who erased her from the internet."

Fran makes a *hmm* sound. "I'm thinking it's more likely that her old brain has been making up stories."

"I guess it doesn't matter either way. Do you have any other contacts?"

"Wish I did."

"Okay," I say with a sigh.

"You'll be fine," Fran says. "We'll go in, have a look around. You'll find the spaceship and whatever waits for you, then we'll head up to Edmund's office and see what we can dig up on Evander."

"I'm not afraid," I say, though he didn't say that I was.

"Good. Me either."

We hang up.

Late that afternoon, my phone beeps again.

Fran texts: *All systems go for tomorrow.*

I'll be ready, I type.

Get some sleep.

So I'll have one night of rest, and then we'll do it.

I spend the next couple of hours lying on the bed staring at the ceiling, recalling the handful of times I've visited Starbright in the past, trying to remember the layout of the building. Then I go over my self-protection moves, the best places to kick, the best ways to incapacitate. I'm picturing the walk to Andrew's former second-floor office when a strange noise outside my window draws my attention. It's a deep and hollow thump, like a small meteorite has landed in the backyard. I extinguish the lamp on my night table, roll off the side of the bed, crawl to the window, and carefully press my face to the glass. Something must have dropped to the ground. *Uncle Jimmy.* Not that that makes sense, except I did just see him in a dream, and he came to my window the night they sent him back to Mintaka.

The backyard lighting creates a shadowy picture of the lawn and foliage, trees here and there. Nothing appears out of—a strange yowling sound occurs, and I brace myself. An animal? Or ... a person? The yowl transforms into something like a stifled moan, possibly stifled crying? One of the neighbors maybe. Whatever it is, it's pretty close. Maybe in the bushes that line the back fence, but it's dark along the far edges of the property, and I see nothing but mottled light around the apple tree. Helena and I used to climb that tree when we were teenagers. And once, also when we were teenagers, a wayward bear traveled through Kirksberg. Could it be a bear? Bears climb trees. Maybe a bear fell out of a tree?

Whatever it is has hurt itself.

I leave my room. The hall is dark, as is the kitchen. I snap on the ceiling light and find one of the kitchen chairs on its side on the floor—the world blurs into fast-forward danger mode.

"Mom?" I shout. "Dad? Where are you?" I enter the living room, which is also dark except for the light that streams through the partly open door of the master bedroom. "Dana, John? Are you still up?" *Why would one of them knock over a chair and leave it like that?*

I cross the living area and approach the guest bathroom. The door is ajar. I hold my breath and proceed with caution, careful not to make a sound. *Where are they?* I creep up to the guest bath with my heart pounding in my throat, and peek inside.

My head buzzes with nerves or some kind of energy or static electricity the instant I lay eyes on it. What I see is black . . . and *shiny.* Some kind of glossy vinyl or glassy . . . I don't know what it is. A creature, not much fleshier than a stick figure. It has the drawn out body of the supreme being, but in much smaller proportion. Its back faces me. I'm trying hard to see clearly, but it's like a halo of electricity dances around my head, and I have to squint. Everything's fuzzy. The thing reaches with its elongated arms to one of its legs, which appears to be twisted in a strange manner. Broken, maybe?

I breathe shallow sips of air as I observe, hoping it can't hear, or sense, my pounding-the-door-down heart. In a stumbling panic, my thoughts slip and slide through my brain, and I'm wondering if what I see can be real. Maybe I'm dreaming again.

The thing turns its blurred, featureless skull in my direction—and in one fell swoop the bathroom door slams shut in front of me. I'm knocked backward onto my ass as the electric buzz that swarms my head breaks into pieces like a glass bottle smashed against a wall. As quickly as I can, I get my feet back under me and stand, wobbly like a drunk. I run the rest of the way down the hall into my parents' bedroom, my nerves so high-octane that I'm wheezing.

I stop a few feet in, breathing like a madwoman and shaking with epileptic severity, unsure whether I possess the ability to form words.

John lies prone on the bed, his tablet on his lap, a news station babbling. He's waiting for me to say something. "Honey?" he says, calm as ever.

I raise my arm and point down the hall. "I think there's . . . " I stop myself. He's never going to believe me. He didn't believe my story about the Jovians being aliens or Evander going to Jupiter or the cloning, so why would he believe this? "Something's in the bathroom." My eyes bulge with unrestrained fear, though I'm trying my best not to come across like a lunatic.

"Is it your mother?"

"Some*thing*, thing, thing," I echo. "Definitely *not* my mother."

He closes his eyes and exhales. "Svetlana."

"Go look. It's not Mom."

He puts the tablet down beside him and pushes his glasses up the bridge of his nose. He's got that "How do I deal with this kid?" look pinching up his face. "You're really worrying me, you know that?"

"Yes, I know, but I heard something outside, and then a chair in the kitchen was overturned, and just *please go look in the bathroom*," I say in a furious whisper that makes me cough.

"Look in the bathroom," he mutters. "Okay." He throws his legs over the side of the bed and stands, then sighs as he adjusts the waist of his pants.

As we march down the hall, he gazes back at me with an air of disbelief. "Are you okay?"

"Just . . . " I press his back with my hand, nudging him forward. "You'll see."

I'm a half step behind him like an eight-year-old who swears there's a monster in her closet.

In front of the bathroom door, he knocks. "Dana?"

We both stand there, silent. There's no answer, no sound at all.

I cut in front of him so I can try the doorknob, but it doesn't move.

He raps his knuckles against the door. "Dana. You in there, hon?"

"It might have gone out the window," I say.

He knocks harder, attempts to twist the knob. "Honey? Please open the door."

A slow shifting sound occurs. Then more-significant sounds of a faster, somewhat violent nature materialize. Something fumbles around. I picture an injured porpoise who finds itself out of water. A bottle falls and clatters against the tile floor. Something collides with the door, then swishes back and forth. There's a groan similar to the one I heard from the safety of my bedroom. The thing in there may be dying.

I meet John's gaze with a rumpled brow and horrified frown.

He puts both hands up, as if to say, "Don't panic."

"If Mom's in there with that thing," I say, "we have to get her out."

He leans into the door with greater force, leading with his shoulder and upper body. The knob jiggles but holds. "Dana? Svetlana is very concerned."

The sounds of movement stop.

"Dana?" he says.

When he doesn't get an answer, he takes a step back and plants his hands on his hips. "Maybe you should wait in the living room. If she's hurt, she probably doesn't want you to see."

I can't leave him here by himself. He has no idea what he's dealing with.

"I'm pretty sure it's not Dana in there, so you might need my help," I say. "I should stay."

He stares at the door. "Well, I don't know how to get this thing open without kicking it in."

"I think I can do it. Let me have a credit card."

He reaches around to his pants pocket in back and pulls out a wallet that looks like it's fifty years old. He takes out a near-to-cracked credit card and puts it in my hand.

I squat in front of the lock as I wedge the flimsy plastic in between wall and door, and jimmy it around. I'm starting to think it's not going to work when all of a sudden the knob twists and Dana barges past, in stumbling steps, in the direction of the bedroom.

Flung backward, my head hits the wall behind me, but

that doesn't stop me from noticing my mother's mess of short hair, scattered from back to front, completely out of shape and hanging in front of her face. She smells odd, too, like rich, wet soil. Like a muddy, scummy pond. Her complexion, what I could see of it as she passed, is gray, clammy looking—and her clothing appears to be damp. I also noticed the label of her shirt under her chin, so that means it's on inside out *and* backward.

Her right leg appears to be locked in an unnatural position.

As she struggles to move away from us, she stammers, "Sorry, sorry, I didn't mean to ... I'm sorry if I hurt you," sounding somewhat out of breath and using the wall to sturdy herself. She's limping and hunched over in pain. "I didn't mean to—" she says, stopping to squeeze her eyes closed and whimper. "My leg cramped up in the shower. I slipped and fell on the mat and then hit my head on the floor and couldn't hear anything over the ringing in my ears. I'm sorry if I frightened you."

"That's not what happened," I say, rising to my feet. "I saw something in there. It wasn't you!"

Dana startles, and her complexion grows yet a deeper shade of pale. John gets in the way so I no longer have a clear view of her. His brows create an angry cleft in between his eyes as his words hurl in my direction: "Don't yell at her like that."

"I'm sorry, but I don't think you under—"

"You thought you saw an intruder in the bathroom," he says at an uncharacteristically loud volume, "but now you see that it was just your mother, that there's nothing to worry about. It was Dana all along. You must be more tired than you thought. You should go lie down. I'll help your mother." He urges me with his eyes, as if desperate for me to accept what he's said.

But I know what I saw.

It was a shiny black creature. Unearthly. Alien.

He didn't see it, so he doesn't know.

"She's not who you think she is," I say. "You have to believe me."

"You're being ridiculous," he says, with unwavering assuredness.

"That's not Mom," I insist, my voice shaking.

His jaw tenses, nostrils flare, and his next words come booming out of his mouth: "Go to your room. I'll speak to you when I'm finished here."

I cower a little. In all the years I've known John, I've never heard him yell—and certainly not at me.

Whoever this Dana is, it's not the Dana my father and I know. But I have no way of explaining it to him because he won't listen.

"Ask her!" I cry.

By now the muddy-smelling version of Dana has reached the bedroom and looks over her shoulder at me, peering guiltily as she tries but fails to put on a smile, or even a normal countenance. "I'm sorry I worried you. I'll be fine in a minute."

John takes Dana's arm and drapes it over his back. "It's okay," he tells her. He leverages her weight, allowing her to take the pressure off her injured leg.

I hate to leave him alone with her. But he wants me to go, to stop looking, to get out of here.

Which seems wrong. All wrong.

And then he closes the door.

16

I enter the guest bathroom. Items have scattered across the floor: a hand towel, a wooden bowl and several pastel-colored soaps, a bud vase. What the hell happened in here? Did that thing have some kind of fit as it transformed into Dana's human form? I open the door to the toilet area, which is empty, then peek into the shower stall to make sure no one's hiding in there. Uncle Jimmy's words come back to me: "We're not at our best in human form."

So they can change. They can all change the same way David changed into the supreme being. But Dana's not Jovian, so this doesn't make sense!

John told me to leave, and then he closed the door. He told me I must be tired, that I didn't see what I know I saw. Could he know about Dana? But they're my parents. They're not Jovian!

The Jovians must have taken the real Dana. They took her and replaced her with this thing so that it could keep an eye on me. Force me to leave the country.

I'm shaking all over. Could they have cloned my mother?

If so, what have they done with the "real" Dana? Or—I suck in my breath—could the thing that I saw be the *real* Dana? Could it be that Dana has always been Jovian, and I didn't know?

No. She never raised my hair. There's no way. I'm in a panic. I'm not thinking straight.

I have to get out of here.

I run down the hall, through the living area and kitchen, past the small gym neither of my parents ever use, and into my room. I lock the door, strain my shoulder as I push the dresser in front of it, grab my backpack from the closet, and throw it on the bed. I struggle to unzip it with shaking hands, then toss a couple of shirts at it, and leggings, underwear, socks. I smash it all down to make it fit. Then I check for my Helena passport and my photo of Evander. I swipe the phone Edmund gave me from the top of the dresser and place it on top. Whatever is left of the money he gave me is in an envelope on the side of the bag. I also have Caroline's diamond necklace. I fish around the underwear drawer until I find it and zip that in, too.

Thank goodness I wore my coat into my room last night when I returned. I pull it on and unlock the window, raising it all the way. I throw one leg over, bump the side of my head on the window frame as I move through, and follow with the other leg. Outside, the air is cold but not frigid. It feels good on my skin, which is hot.

The light from the kitchen acts like a nightlight for the yard. Crouched in a skulking stance, I sprint past the patio to the far end of the lawn, stopping by the apple tree where I hop over a fallen branch that's about eight feet long, cracked at its connection. Was Dana, or whoever that was in my parents' bedroom, in the tree? Probably trying to get a better view of the sky. But right now the sky and its stars are hidden under a blanket of cloud, so . . . I don't have time to hypothesize. All I know is that the Dana in the house isn't human, and I hope John will be okay.

I plan to call Fran as soon as I make it safely down the street, but then his Plan C comes to mind, the one in which he suggested I move into the house I renovated with Andrew and wait for Evander to return while under the watchful eye of my in-laws. Plan C makes me wonder if calling Fran could be a mistake. Considering what just happened, he might be one of them, too. He could have been one of them all along, even when Andrew was alive. The Jovians could have removed his arm so I would feel sorry for him, so I wouldn't see him as a threat, so I'd trust him. Then they could have made up the story about losing Lisa and Max to explain why he's here, why he has no job and can spend all of his time with me. The Jovians no longer raise my hair, so there's no way to test my theory.

I'm so stuck in my thoughts that I step off the curb in front of a slow-moving car. Thankfully, it swerves away from me. Funny that this is not the scariest thing that has happened to me tonight.

But, wait, Fran always said the Jovians raised his hair, and he helped me fend off David's attempt to take Evander. He has to be my friend. He's my *only* friend right now. Then again I assumed Dana and John were my American, *human* parents, and now I don't even know that for sure. I don't want to believe Fran could be anything but an ally, but the safest bet is to assume anything is possible.

I'm on foot, passing through town without a destination, seeking the dark spaces as I move. Tonight's cold is the kind that numbs the forehead, cheeks, and nose, and I have nowhere to go, no car to drive. My mind flashes on the grasshopper—and my brain gets snagged once again. Could Dana's car be the one Uncle Jimmy drove ten years ago? If she's Jovian, that would make sense.

"That kid looked exactly like your photo of Evander," Fran had said earlier, *"so why didn't Dana think so?"*

Maybe this is why Miranda didn't come looking for me. Why Edmund gave me the phone but doesn't get in touch or answer calls. The Dana I've been living with has been watching me, finding out what I know, trying to influence my decisions of what to do while implying that what I surmise about the Jovians and Evander and the cloning is unrealistic thinking. Telling me that I must be stressed and tired! When I saw the shiny black creature, John told me to go lie down, that he would handle it.

He wanted me to go away.

He must be in on it.

But that's hard to accept. Dana and John never acted strangely, never angered me the way Caroline and the others do. They're caring people. *Humanitarians!*

Then again, ten years ago, when Andrew died and I gave birth to Evander, they were nowhere to be found. They stayed away much longer than their other missions kept them away.

Tonight I saw a shiny black alien in my mother's bathroom, and then my mother came out of that room smelling strangely and looking as if she were turned inside out.

And maybe she was.

The hairs on my neck rise to a stand: Dana and John tried to take me to Peru! They urged me to go. Something must be happening in Kirksberg soon. Evander must be coming home, and the Jovians want me out of the way.

The wind picks up, and the air smells like imminent storm.

Out of nowhere, I'm pelted in the back of the head with what feels like a pebble launched from a slingshot. I scan the area for anyone nearby. Then it happens again, and a colorless crystal drops onto the sidewalk at my feet. Hail. The wind begins howling like spirits in mourning, and I pull my coat around me, buttoning it to the top. A spray of frozen raindrops is thrust upon me. They bounce off my head, my coat, my face. They tap, tap, tap upon the rooves of the buildings I pass, the branches of trees that hover over me. I press forward, hoping this shower will end before ice balls the size of acorns come down and leave me unconscious with black eyes and lumps on my head.

I'm half a block from the Kirksberg cemetery when it occurs to me that a graveyard could be a safe place to plan my next move.

By the time I reach the wrought iron gate, the ground lies under a layer of hail that crunches like gravel below my feet and makes me leery of slipping. I pass through and start down the path. In the distance looms a stone structure with a roof that I can stand under, if not take shelter inside. My breath trails in long, steamy exhales. My chapped lips sting and nose runs. I stop under the roof of the mausoleum, a place for the urns of the cremated, and remember Andrew's ashes. Thinking of the small vial Aunt Constant gave me after the funeral draws my hand to Andrew's ring threaded around my neck. As far as I know, the ashes remain in my bedroom in Russia, where Helena will keep them safe for me.

I scan the neat sprawl of headstones and statues, some of them accompanied by solar-powered lanterns of the sort loved ones leave behind. I'm not afraid of the dead or the possibility of seeing ghosts. I don't care that it's a dark night and that I may spend hours here alone. If I'm able to get inside the mausoleum, it will be nice to have some light.

Beside one of the many graves in front of me, a solar candle flickers blue-white. I venture back into the wind that whips my hair in front of my eyes as tiny ice balls bounce off the chest of my buttoned coat. I'm not surprised when I trip at the foot of a plot and lunge sideways into the ungiving wings of a stone angel before dropping to the base of her pedestal. Instead of getting back up right away, I surrender, rolling onto my back while I wait for the sharp pain in my side to let up. As I lie there, my pants cling to me; much of my lower half is now damp from the icy, muddy ground I'm resting on, and I wonder why everything must go from bad to worse.

The view of the clouds above reminds me of the first winter after Andrew and I had married. It snowed three feet, and Andrew couldn't wait to get outdoors. Like a little kid, he grabbed my coat and jacket from the closet and threw them at me, shouting, "Put these on!"

I jumped up from the couch. "What? Why?" and threaded my arms through the sleeves because I didn't want to miss out.

"If you have to ask, you can't be from Russia." He reached the front door and sped through, throwing back his head and releasing a savage cry. I followed behind only to have a snowball explode on my puffer jacket. He was standing a few steps away, a wide smile under his knit hat pulled down so low I could hardly see his eyes.

"Oh, I see. You're looking for a fight. Well, I accept the challenge!" I bent over and pulled some snow together, then dodged his next throw. Though I aimed for his body, my snowball ended up connecting with the side of the head.

He tugged the neckline of his jacket, and whined, "Man! It went down my shirt."

"Sorry!" I shouted while I pulled together another round of ammunition. When I looked up again, he was heading for me, his playful aggression evident in his wild eyes and a mound of snow the size of a globe between his hands. I thought about turning and running, but he was practically on me already, so I simply fell back as if trust-falling into a swimming pool or onto a king-size mattress.

He leapt at me, arms and legs splayed like a tree frog in midair.

"What are you doing, you kook!" I screamed, thinking the impending collision would surely result in bumped heads or broken ribs, but he landed in a much more graceful way than I had imagined possible. No broken bones or headaches, just Andrew on top of me, his moist lips and cloudy laughter making my face damp.

"You fell back, so I assumed this was what you wanted."

"Why would I want this?" I teased. Then I pressed one of his arms until it slipped out of line, leaving him unbalanced and easy to roll over.

"Hey, whoa!" he shouted as he hit the snowy ground.

I danced in his lap, singing, "I've got you now."

"You'll always have me," he said, "but do you really think you can beat me in a wrestling match?"

Suddenly I was tossed into the snow, and this time we were kissing and I didn't even mind that there was ice melting in the waist of my jeans and my hat had fallen off and hair was getting wet.

And then an acorn fell from the tree above us and pelted my forehead.

I open my eyes and realize I'm alone. My Andrew hallucination and all of its warmth and good humor becomes powder carried off with the winter wind. The acorn that hit me was actually a piece of hail the size of one of those dinner peppermints, and I'm so cold my lips quiver.

I rub the bruise on my forehead and sit up. Beyond the angel and her extended wings, a headstone draws my attention. Engraved with large, almost Gothic-style lettering, it spells out the name *Andrew Jovian*—no middle name because the Jovians don't know how to properly fake a human name. *Andrew has a gravestone?* I scramble to my knees as the past presses up from my mind like a splinter pushed from my skin. This time I've fallen back to the day the Jovians and I made funeral plans while we breakfasted at the Sheridan Café: Andrew would be cremated (a family tradition, Caroline had claimed), I'd be given a vial of ashes, and a tombstone would be purchased and placed in the cemetery, where I could go to "be with Andrew." Aunt Constant promised to make it happen, and now I see that she has kept her word.

Finding his memorial on one of the loneliest nights of my life feels intentional. Like Andrew's still out there watching over me. My longing for him fills my insides like an empty bottle filling with water. The pain of his loss has never dulled, and I've yet to move past it the way others who have loved and lost claim to. I don't think I grieved him properly, never mourned him or put him to rest. He lives on in my mind and my hallucinations. He lives as a star in the sky. He communicates with me through my dreams. I want to swim backward in time and break whatever barrier separates us. The barrier between life and death.

I get up, stand before his headstone, and swipe my fingers across the letters of his name from beginning to end. "I miss you," I say.

To the right of the grave, a solar-powered lamp glows. I pull it up as if it were a flower pulled up from its roots. There's another in the shape of a lily a couple of graves over, so I carefully make my way and grab that one, too. The whipping wind no longer bothers me as I carry the lights to the mausoleum, mindful not to collide with the angel wings on the way back.

I need a plan.

Feeling the warm ache of sore ribs from the fall, I enter a short corridor that veers right and then right again, like a maze that circles around until it finds its way to the burial vault at its center. The wind can't touch me here. It's quiet, just the soft scuffs of my footsteps rise from the floor. The air comes and goes in whispers. I prop the lantern and flower against the wall and claim a concrete bench in front of the many panels and plaques that remind me no one lasts forever. One day my time will end just as it has ended for these people. My fight with the Jovians will end. I'll enter whatever afterlife awaits and hopefully join my husband . . . somewhere. In the ether, maybe, where our souls intermix.

It would have been nice to spend a lifetime with him.

Andrew and Evander are the only ones who ever deserved my trust.

Apparently Dana and John do not—a thought I don't want to explore right now—but it could be true. I think it's true.

I pull out my phone. It's already ten forty-five. I consider calling Fran. Part of me wants to even though I know I can't trust him. Part of me needs him to be who he says he is. But I can't chance it. The realistic side of me knows I can't. I click off the sound so notifications won't come through. Then I close my eyes and think. I have to get into Starbright. I have to find the spaceship. I need to know where Evander is. *I need to see my son!*

Waking up in a mausoleum isn't as pleasant as I thought it would be, I joke with myself. As a matter of fact, I've never had such stiffness in my back. I lift my phone from my coat pocket. Eleven-thirty in the morning. Can this be correct? I know I was tired, but how did I sleep for so long? I have received several text messages a few minutes apart. All from Fran.

. . .

Coffee?

Hello?

You up?

Where are you?

Text me. Starting to worry.

Svetlana!

You can't be sleeping. You never sleep this late.

I'm tempted to reply. I know I shouldn't, but I want to give him the benefit of the doubt. He was Andrew's best friend. Andrew trusted him. But what if Fran isn't Fran? Or what if he is Fran, and Fran has been a Jovian all this time? I don't know what to do. We're supposed to break into Starbright tonight, and I need that to happen one way or another, especially considering what occurred with Dana and John last night. I can tell him that something has come up, and we'll have to postpone, but he knows me too well. He won't believe me. I can tell him that Dana and John are taking me to see relatives, but then he may try to get me out of it. I could also act like nothing has changed and then simply fail to meet him tonight. That might work.

I write: *I'm fine. Sorry. Just slept in.*

I don't hit the Send button. Instead I stare at the words. If I start here, what will my next move be?

Meanwhile, he texts again: *If I don't hear from you in 5, I'm coming over.*

He'll talk to Dana and John, and they'll tell him I went out. Unless he's Jovian. Then he already knows what happened last night, and his concern is fake. I hit Send because I don't know what else to do.

Thank God, he texts back. *Thought I'd lost you. You ready for tonight?*

No. I can't do it.

Are you joking right now?

I'm scared.

You weren't scared yesterday. Did something happen?

I just can't risk it.

I'm calling.

Shit. I close my eyes as the phone's jarring ring collides with the surrounding stone. My hands shake. I should not have texted back.

I press the green button.

"What's going on?" he says in a taut, angry manner.

"Plan C. I can't agree to it. I told you I couldn't, but you insist it's an option."

"Are you—oh, man, I knew I shouldn't have—" He groans. "Look, I told you before, we're nowhere near Plan C. Plan C is a distant, last-ditch—trust me, it's not gonna happen."

"But you suggested it."

"And?"

"Now I don't know if I can trust you."

He would understand if he knew what happened with Dana and John.

"Are you serious?"

"You could be one of them," I say softly because I'm pretty sure he'll explode when he hears it.

"*Be one of them?* You have to be kidding right now!" His high-pitched fury presses through the phone like wind that presses its way through a crack in the roof. "I may be the only one in this world you *can* trust. You know that."

I say nothing because it's true.

"Something definitely happened. Tell me what it was."

I'm alone again. That's what happened. I'm alone with only myself to trust. My eyes water and cheeks heat up. Damn it! I don't want to feel like this. I need to be tough. I need to be sure of what I'm doing.

"You can tell me," he says, his voice dropping into a

gentler tone. "I'm not one of them. I will *never* be one of those blank-faced idiots. I helped you when David tried to take Evander. I was right there defending you."

"I know," I say, "but things are different now."

"How?"

"Dana and—" I stop to wipe my nose with my coat sleeve. "Dana and John cannot be trusted."

"What do you mean?"

I don't know if I should reveal this much.

"Svetlana," he says.

The words race out of my mouth: "I saw Dana in her true form."

I hear a short pull of air, then silence so complete I'm afraid we've been disconnected.

"Fran?"

"*Alien* form?"

"Whatever you want to call it," I say. "You failed to tell me Dana raised your hair."

"Because she didn't," he shouts. "She *never* did."

"How do I know you're telling the truth? Doug's father raised your hair. Caroline raised your hair. Why wouldn't Dana?"

"I would have told you if she had. I mean, how should I know why?" he says, exasperated. And then, "You know who else didn't raise my hair?"

I wait for his answer.

"Andrew."

It's a slap in the face. As much as I don't like to admit it, Andrew was 100 percent Jovian. And, no, he never raised my hair. Neither did Dana for that matter. I have no argument; none of this is logical.

Fran doesn't say anything for a moment. I suppose his thoughts are taking him for a spin the same way mine did when I peered into the bathroom at Dana and John's house.

Finally he says, "Dana didn't do anything to you, did she? She didn't become like David or anything?"

"No. Not at all."

"Where are you, by the way?" he says. "When did this happen?"

"I can't tell you where I am. It happened last night."

"There was a hailstorm last night. It was about ten degrees outside. Did you sleep in your car? Do you even have a car—shit, Svetlana, you should've called me. Where are you?"

The angst in his voice breaks my heart. I want to tell him where I am. I'd much rather be with him than alone in this cemetery. But I can't trust him. He could be the biggest fake of all.

My voice shakes when I say, "I won't be at Starbright tonight. I just want you to know. I can't do it. Not now. Not yet."

"Where will you go? You have to be somewhere."

"I don't know."

"Stay in my apartment. I'll make sure I'm gone before you get here."

"I can't."

"Please, don't say that. You can. Andrew would want you to."

"Don't worry about me." My voice breaks as I struggle to fend off the tears. "I'm fine."

"Oh, I'm going to worry, that's a given. And you have to eat, that's a given, too. Do you even have any money?"

I want Fran with me. I hate that I'm alone. But this is how it has to be. I can't take chances.

"Everyone I know either lies or leaves," I say. As the words hit air, I grab my forehead and gasp on a spate of emotion that feels like a knife in my heart. It takes a moment of intense determination to keep it together.

"I know you believe that, but that's not how it is," he says. "Look, there's no Plan C, all right? I wish I'd never said it. I'll *never* make you live with them. I'll do whatever you want me to do. Just don't go off on your own. Don't stop taking my calls."

"You've been a good friend from the first moment I met you." I'm having trouble speaking.

"I never raised your hair," he shouts as if that's enough to change my mind.

"It doesn't happen to me anymore. For all I know, I'm the only human on this planet, and this is all a big joke on me."

"It's not. *You're* not. Meet me at the cafe. We can talk."

I want to. I really do. It's killing me to feel this way. But I'm a strong person, and sometimes that makes life harder rather than easier.

"I'll call you soon," I say, and then I punch the End key.

17

After last night's storm, the noonday sun shines unhindered through clear air that feels a lot softer than it did the night before. On the five-mile (or longer) walk to Starbright, I find a package of chocolate chip cookies in my backpack. I remember taking them from Dana's pantry a few days ago, but then Fran brought me to the cafe, so I didn't eat them. I've prepared myself mentally for the possibility that Fran could at any minute drive up in his car. I'm pretty sure he believed me when I said I wouldn't be going through with my plan tonight, but then again, Fran's FBI instincts won't take no for an answer. I'm sure he's considering all the places I might be. It will occur to him that I may have gone to Starbright. He knows my eyes might be all I need to open the door.

When I reach the woods behind the office building, I need to rest. I can't just lie down anywhere, so I ascend the tree Fran built the platform on. Scaly chunks of bark fall as I reach for the highest branch I can grasp and my combat boots kick the trunk like the reckless feet of an oversize squirrel. The climb proves difficult after such a long walk, and I grunt as I pull myself onto the planks of the small platform.

After catching my breath, I remove my backpack and lean into the trunk, allowing my calves to overhang. It's quiet here, peaceful. The afternoon sunlight caresses my face. I sink into my tired muscles while the breeze sifts through long-leafed needles that brush the air. My eyes close as I listen to the chirp of birds and think of Evander.

Where are you? I need to know you're all right.

"It's probably going to be a boy," I hear Andrew say.

I remember the night he said it, soon after the doctor confirmed my pregnancy. We were at home in Ashbury Falls, sitting on the bench I bought him for his birthday, overlooking the lagoon.

"I'm pretty sure it's a fifty-fifty chance," I told him. "Mathematically speaking."

"Outside of that," he said, raising his brows, "let's just say I have a strong feeling."

Something in his blue-green eyes hinted that he had more he wanted to say. "You *want* a boy," I asked. "Is that what you—"

"Oh, no, that's not it. I'd love a girl. Or a boy." His shoulders rose toward his ears. "It honestly doesn't matter to me."

"But you think it's a boy, because . . . " I tried to puzzle together how he had come to this conclusion.

He gazed over the lagoon, not looking at anything in particular, and I sensed his drop into a more serious mode. The sun had reached the horizon, leaving behind pretty pink and blue ribbons. "There's sort of a Jovian prophecy," he said.

I flung back my head and laughed in an obnoxious way. "Of course there is. Sounds foreboding. Please go on."

"It's not a joke," he told me. "My mother and my father, for that matter, are convinced our child will be a boy."

"That's weird."

"I know. They *are* weird. I shouldn't have brought it up. You know how my mother is about family lineage."

"Relentless," I muttered under my breath.

He straightened his legs and dropped his head back in observation of the sky, which was deepening in color, becoming a mix of red and dark gray, more violent than tender. "She seems to think our child is going to change the world."

"All grandmothers think that," I said, knowing how his mother, a wealthy and arrogant woman, often made grandiose statements that ventured over the top.

Andrew breathed in and exhaled a sound of frustration. "Yeah. Maybe they're getting our kid mixed up with David's. I could see David fathering someone important."

"I agree," I said, as if putting the potential problem to bed. "Let's just let David create the Jovian who changes the world."

If only that were the case.

I stay up in the tree for a while. Maybe an hour. Maybe longer. When I feel rested, I climb back down (leaving the backpack behind) in search of something solid to help me enter the building should I need to smash the doorknob: a thick branch, like a fireplace log, or a sizeable stone that fits in my hand. During our stakeouts, Fran and I decided it would be impossible to enter the building through a window without drawing attention because none of them open. No matter how I attempt to get in, one of their security squad may be nearby. When they see it's me, I have no doubt I'll be welcomed inside. Getting out is the part I'm unsure about.

So I'm going it alone. That's probably the way it should be. I could end up disappearing from the face of the earth with or without Fran, and I don't want him to get caught in the middle. I'm ready to deal with whatever comes.

That said, as the sky darkens and the minutes swiftly pass,

I can't seem to rub the cold sweat from my palms, and I'm tempted to remove my coat because my temperature's rising along with my anxiety. I know there's no need for this wave of fear to drown me. It's possible I can enter the building, and no one will be around. Stranger things have happened in my dealings with the Jovians. If they've locked the offices inside the building, I won't find any of the information I long to find anyway, so they won't care if I wander the corridors. They'll stay wherever they are, in their mad-scientist laboratories or luxury conference rooms or bedroom suites (if this is really where they've been living), while I wander aimlessly. I won't even have to speak to them, which would be nice.

I check the time on my phone—5:30 p.m. and already it's as dark as night. Since Fran said we would head in at seven, that's what I'm going to do. He knows the security schedule, and he said seven would be best. Once I'm in, with or without alarms blaring, I'll exit whatever room the door leads to and find my way to the front of the building. Then I'll duck into the stairwell that I think leads to the basement.

I've never even seen Starbright's basement, so I don't know how difficult it will be to find the room with the spaceship—I'm sure that wherever it is, it will be locked tight. So, even if I find it, I'll have to figure out how to get inside before I can hunt for whatever message Uncle Jimmy says I need to see. If all goes well, after that, I hope to enter Edmund's office and search for information about his trip with Evander.

If I make my way out alive, I'll retrieve my backpack from Fran's platform in the tree, then head to the main road and call a car to drive me. I can probably stay in the Jovian mansion tonight if I want to, though I'm not sure I'm that bold. I wish I'd thought of it yesterday, but when I left Dana and John, heading into another Jovian property didn't cross my mind as a possibility.

Which reminds me . . . neither Dana nor John has tried to call or text.

And that dredges up some sadness that might break my heart, but I can't let that happen right now. I need to focus.

It's a moonless night. I'm crouched behind some bushes opposite where Fran and I usually take cover. No one has come or gone, and if I didn't know better, I'd assume the building was empty. But the telescope moves on occasion, vibrating with minor adjustments, a fraction left or right, up or down. Someone is in there, scoping the universe—that much I know.

By a quarter after six, I can't wait anymore. It's cold enough to turn my toes blue. I'm tired and hungrier than I've been in a long time. I'm afraid I won't have the energy I need to physically do what I need to do. I want to get this over with.

Fran didn't show, and I'm both happy about that and disappointed, but it's for the best that he doesn't come with me. Who knows what they would do to him if they caught us. I don't want to involve Fran any more than I already have.

In my search for a door opener, should my eyes not do the trick, I found a club-shaped stick, which I place within the large inside pocket of my sheepskin coat, then follow the fence line of the far reaches of the parking lot. The lampposts hum as they glow, and a shadowed area between the parking lot and the building lies ahead. I race across, reaching the cement staircase that ascends the side of the building. I spin around, scanning the surrounding area—no cars, no Jovians—then take the steps two at a time and propel myself onto the landing. That's when someone reaches out and grabs me around my waist. They must have been up against the shadowy wall of the building, watching me.

Every self-protection move I learned in class flashes like an accelerated filmstrip through my brain. I spin around and kick my leg at waist-height as hard as I can.

In a blast of breath, the victim expels a strained growl. "Oh, you weren't kidding." He grumbles. "Good one. You got me good."

It's Fran.

He's doubled over with his arm across his middle, his hand grasping his chest.

"What are you doing?" I whisper-shout. "Did I hit you in the—"

He wheezes the word *stomach*.

He's lucky. That's not where I was aiming.

"Give me a second," he says. "Knocked the wind out of me."

I stand there, equally pissed as I am relieved.

He unbends. Takes a chest-expanding breath.

"I told you not to come," I say, forgetting to whisper.

"You didn't tell me anything. And you're not going in without me."

Yes, I am.

I push past him and rush at the door.

He's behind me like an oversize shadow. I spin around and stare into his deep brown eyes, large like the rest of him. I shout, "Back off!"

"You know I won't."

His face has the soft, honest curves of someone reliable. I want him to be the Fran I know and love and trust, but how can I be sure?

I pull out the stick I've been carrying inside my coat.

He grabs my shoulder. I could probably hit him in the

head hard enough to knock him out, but who am I kidding? I'd hate myself if I did that.

"If you use that to try to open the door, you might as well just ring the doorbell," he says.

I turn away from him and stare into the eye-recognition device. It's a blank TV screen, about four inches wide and three inches tall. Nothing happens. The screen remains a dull black color. It may not even be hooked up. I bend over and study the doorknob, which is plain and round.

I grab it in my hand—and it twists.

"You have got to be kidding," I mutter.

Fran's breath reaches the back of my neck as he says, "We should have known."

I push open the door, and a room with dim lighting glows red in front of us.

It's the size of a classroom, without desks, tables, chairs, windows. No security guards. No art on the walls, no plants in the corner. Just an empty room filled with pale red light the color of blood in water. I drop the stick and step in.

An exit sign hovers above the door opposite.

Fran remains a step behind me. I'm lightheaded with the relief of getting into the building and finding no one, and yet my body pulses with adrenaline because we've only taken the first step. When we reach the exit door across the room, I crack it open.

"Scope it out," Fran whispers.

Beyond the door lies an immense space with a two-story-high ceiling and emergency-style lights along its perimeter. The spiral stairway to the right takes a corkscrew turn up to the balcony. It occurs to me that the stairs and their railings topped with bannisters on both sides resemble a strand of DNA. I have no desire to climb it at this time because I know it leads to the family's offices.

"What do you think?" Fran whispers, gazing over the top of my head.

"I think you should leave now that I've made it into the building."

"Fat chance," he says.

I turn to look him in the eye. "Please go, Fran."

His face hardens. "If you don't move—"

Sensing he's about to push me aside, I step out with him practically draped over my shoulders.

I see no one as I continue forward with my hulking shadow. We have just passed the staircase on the right when a thud reverberates overhead and bright lights blare down from the ceiling above. Hunched over as if they've doused us in cold water, I twist to see the balcony behind us. It's too bright, so I use my hand as a visor.

"Hello, Svetlana."

Caroline's voice sends liquid trepidation through my veins. Three silhouettes are lined up, three Jovians in a row: Caroline, Miranda, and Leo, as far as I can tell.

Instead of talking, I turn and run. I didn't plan for this. My head wanted to say something like, "You don't mind if we have a look around?" in the casual yet hateful tone I've hurled at Caroline in the past, but my body decided it was not going to wait. My hair spikes from the scalp the way it used to. I'm not sure whether it's in response to the family's close proximity or simply because my fear is playing a number on me, but it happens.

Once I've passed the receptionist's desk, I take a right turn and come to the heavy doors I was hoping to find. They lead to the stairwell that only goes down. I yank one open, then leap with abandon, taking six or seven steps at once, ready to fall on my ass and slide the rest of the way if that's how it has to be. But my feet land firmly, and I take the rest of the staircase the same way, dropping to the bottom. That's when I sense that Fran is no longer shadowing me.

I strain a look over my shoulder. He's not there. Not on the stairs, not at the top of the stairs. And I can't wait for him. I told him not to come. I wish he had listened. The Jovians don't want him; they want me. I rush down the narrow corridor that unfurls before me. Lit by floor lighting as white-blue as moonbeams, it buzzes the way my head did when I lived in Russia.

A door at the end of the corridor inspires me to run even faster. Uncle Jimmy said they buried the spaceship under Starbright, and it feels like I'm traveling into the belly of a dragon. I realize I may not get out of here. Any of the Jovians could easily trap me in this windowless, underground place, never to be seen by humans again.

When I reach the door, I wonder if it will be unlocked as well.

An eye-recognition scanner hangs to the left. Maybe this is the one Uncle Jimmy was talking about when he said my eyes would do the trick. I step up and gaze into the small screen. Nothing happens. I tap a red button on the bottom, and it buzzes, then the screen flashes, and I take a closer look. It must have seen what it needed to see because a loud clicking sound makes me jump, and the door pops open.

None of the Jovians have caught up to me, though they certainly could have. Which means they want me to enter this room—and that makes me hesitate.

I use the toe of my shoe to nudge open the door another inch or two and look inside. It's an office about the size of a walk-in closet of the sort you'd find in a Jovian mansion. Unattractive dark brown wood paneling encases the room, and as I step in, I feel as if I've entered a wooden crate. It has a rectangular fluorescent light on the ceiling that produces the harsh glow of what I imagine an office worker might have sustained in the 1960s. I close the door behind me. It's heavy, solid. If one of the Jovians has followed me down here, I won't know until they step in.

I wonder which one it will be. Probably Miranda or Leo. I can't see Caroline making the effort just for me.

A desk—medium size, gray metal, 100 percent practical—butts against the wall straight ahead of me. Beside it, a filing cabinet stands stoic and ordinary, four drawers tall. That's all that side of the room has space for. A bulletin board, nothing pinned to it, hangs to the left, and just in front of it stands an easel displaying a whiteboard; the sill across its bottom offers a black pen, but there's no writing on the board itself.

That's it. The whole room.

This is not where they keep the spaceship.

But maybe there's something to see in the files?

I step behind the desk, which is so close to the wall, I have to suck in my breath. No one could sit here, behind this desk. Which probably means they've staged the room.

When I pull the top drawer of the filing cabinet, it rattles like an empty garbage pail. Inside, sits a lone hanging file with a manila folder. I grab the folder, which has a label stuck to the tab. It reads, "Svetlana Jovian," made with a typewriter's black old-school ink.

Next I slide out the desk chair as much as that's possible and nudge the desk forward a few inches so I can squeeze in behind it. The seat of the chair creaks with my weight. The wheels resist rolling, as if rusted—frozen in time like the rest of this room.

Why would they have a file about me?

Because I am Andrew's wife, and Evander's mother, I suppose. It probably has the results to the DNA test Uncle Jimmy carried out when I first met Andrew. But that can't be all. There are many pages here, and Uncle Jimmy said the spaceship has a message for me. He did not, however, say I'd find it in a filing cabinet in a tiny, pretend office.

"Okay," I say, reluctant to open it.

The first thing I see is a picture of Andrew and me from my wedding day. Someone has stapled it to the inside of the folder. Seeing it hurts because we look so young and happy, and also because I haven't seen a photo of us in years. My eyes linger on Andrew. Then I glimpse the page on top of the stack opposite. It's a report of some kind. Looks like a doctor's report. As expected, the DNA information. I don't understand most of what I see, but one item is circled: "No predisposition for hereditary disease, genetic disorders." The next page details my home in Tula, Russia, with Helena and Ivan. A fuzzy aerial photo shows the house and surrounding land.

I haven't called Helena in weeks. A wave of fear washes over me because the Jovians know where she is, but then I remember they don't want her. They want me to *live* with her. As far as I know, she and Ivan are in no danger from the family.

The next several pages concern my pregnancy. Dr. Falugia's records and notes. Evander's growing weight. A photocopy of the sonogram. My complaints of back pain. Nothing interesting. As a matter of fact, I don't care much about this file. I flip through the next several pages, thinking I'll continue to flip to the end, but something stops me: a page written in Russian.

Adoption papers? I've never seen these before. I recognize Dana and John's signatures. Jovians who masquerade as Petermans. The next page is a letter from my caregiver at the orphanage, Miss Sonja, written in Russian with the translation in English stapled to it. Addressed to Dana and John, she says, "The orphanage does not normally allow the couple to request a certain child, but since you are willing to take Helena as well, an exception will be made."

A flash of heat rises into my face. *They asked for me?* I'm holding my breath. *This can't be. Of all the children in the orphanage, Dana and John requested me.* I grab my forehead and rake back my hair. *How could they even have known me? How would they have known I existed?* I hadn't met them before Sonja informed Helena and me about the "nice American couple" that wanted to adopt two teenagers.

I'd never met anyone from America before. Why would Sonja not find this suspicious? Strange enough that they were adopting two teenagers, but then asking for a specific child by name? Asking for me! This isn't how Russian adoption works. There are strict laws about this sort of thing.

Is this what Uncle Jimmy wanted me to know? That Dana and John are Jovian? He couldn't have known I'd see Dana in her true from, so maybe it is. "Uncle Jimmy," I whisper. "What does this mean?"

The words on the letter spin, and I realize I'm taking too-fast breaths. I place both hands on the desk to prevent falling forward. I haven't eaten, and now I'm upset, and I don't know if I have the strength to fight my way out of here, if necessary.

Dana and John chose me. They traveled to Russia and requested me.

There are more pages in the file, but I can't look now. I'm afraid of what I might find. I open the drawer of the desk and some office supplies shift around: paperclips, pencils, thumbtacks, rubber bands. I roll the file into a tube and secure it as best I can with a rubber band at the top and the bottom, then I place this paper cylinder into the pocket inside my coat. I stand, wavering slightly, my stomach sick and my head dizzy. I stumble backward, and my shoulder grazes the wall. When I throw my arm out to the side to catch myself, a piece of the paneling shifts, then drops a few inches to the floor. It remains upright, revealing a pane of glass behind it. A window. A window hidden behind six feet of paneling.

I turn around and pull, breaking whatever attachment remains, then slide the piece a few steps to the side and lean it against the adjacent wall.

Through the window a purple-blue light vaguely illuminates a room that spreads like a warehouse or underground garage, though it's not filled with shelves of merchandise or cars. The strange light numbs my eyes, and it's hard to decipher the object at the room's center. It's about the size of a backyard shed. I blink a few times, and my vision clears: I recognize the smooth, elliptical shape of an acorn, the band of decoration around the bottom.

It's the spaceship that crash-landed in Kirksberg fifty years ago.

I found it.

18

Behind me the lock of the office door clicks, and every nerve I have hits the ceiling of my brain. I reluctantly turn. I wish I had that piece of wood now, or any weapon really. The Jovians may not be violent, but *I* can be if I have to.

Caroline walks in on high heels and shimmering stockings, a black pencil skirt and gold-colored blouse. "You found your file," she says. Her chin-length bob frames her classic face: the thick lashes, tasteful eyeshadow, elegant blush.

"It wasn't hard to find," I say. "Did you build this room for me?"

She blinks. Once, twice. I notice the diamond necklace she wears, exactly like the one I took from her master suite. She must have bought a replacement for the one she lost. Or maybe she has a collection.

"What do you think of the file?" she says.

It's like we've never parted. The familiar angst between us comes crashing in, alive and well. Non-emotion on her end, terse derision on mine. "It's nothing I didn't already know," I say.

"You knew that your parents didn't intend to have you?"

"What?" I feel the strain of my eyes attempting to leap out of my head. "Why would you say that? Why do you always try to hurt me?"

Her expression remains unchanged. "I see you haven't read it in its entirety."

"I may have skipped a few pages. If there's something you want to tell me, feel free. I've grown impatient in my older age."

"It's in your best interest to read the file."

"Well, it's in my pocket, and I will take it home."

"All right."

"Are you going to let me go home?"

"Not quite yet."

I purse my lips. "What do you want, Caroline?"

"There's something we would like you to see. Please follow me."

She reaches for the knob of the door and opens it, then crosses her arms over her chest, expecting me to move.

But I don't want to. I've found the spaceship, and I need to see what's inside.

I say, "Uncle Jimmy told me there was something on the spaceship for me. He said it was important."

"James is not on Earth at this time."

"I know, but he still, uh, communicates with me."

Her eyes pierce my soul and send a shiver to the crown of my head. "Please follow me," she says again.

I don't move. Instead, I observe the way her precisely tailored skirt fits, how her body hasn't grown larger or rounder since the last time I saw her. How it doesn't sag or bulge. It's as if she hasn't aged at all.

"Maybe you could let me go out there, just for a second?" I point at the exposed window.

"You're not going to see the spaceship tonight."

She enters the corridor.

I catch the door before it closes on me. "So, another time?"

She's already several steps ahead of me when she says, "Perhaps."

I realize it's likely she doesn't want me to see whatever it is Uncle Jimmy told me to look for.

Then she says, "I thought you were here for Evander."

Her mention of Evander has the same effect that grabbing me by the shoulders and shaking me would. I rush to catch up to her. "Has he been living here the whole time?"

"Miranda told you where he went," she says, continuing up the incline.

I stop. "If you want me to be sure of something, you need to tell me yourself. I can't trust Miranda."

She stops as well, turns around. Clasps her hands together. "And you trust me?"

I don't answer.

She turns once again and continues toward the stairs. I'm staring at the back of her silky blonde hair, willing it to burst into flames.

"Exactly twenty-three days ago Miranda delivered the news that Evander traveled to Jupiter," she says. "You have known for over three weeks. That is what I understood. I cannot do anything about your unwillingness to accept information."

"All of the Jovians have lied to me," I say in my defense. "All of you have hurt me. Do you understand? I never know what to believe."

I wait for a response but the moment passes without one.

Her non-answer strikes a match in my chest, and heat rises to the top of my head.

"Caroline?"

"We don't mean to hurt you," she says, not bothering to peer back at me as she begins to ascend the steep set of stairs. "No one means to hurt you."

"If you didn't want to hurt me, you never should have locked me up. You never should have taken my child. I had to run halfway around the world to get away from you."

"Yes, and you and Evander have had your time together. Were you happy in Russia?"

She makes it sound as if we spent an extended holiday at a beach resort.

"You never understand," I say, my voice whiny with exasperation. "You don't get it because you were never a real mother to Andrew."

"We *all* loved Andrew. And I know you love Evander, but he's grown now. He doesn't need you anymore."

It's a punch to the windpipe, and for a few seconds I forget to breathe.

When I recover, I say, "He's ten years old."

We've reached the top of the stair. Caroline turns around. "Your child is far more mature than an ordinary human juvenile, quite capable of making his own decisions. I think you realize that."

I wish I had something smart to say, but I don't. He *is* capable. He *is* mature. He's great at making decisions.

With high-heeled strides, Caroline begins to cross the lobby.

I follow after, angrier than before, though this is all par for the course, as Dana sometimes says, and remembering that—remembering *Dana* and who she really is—makes me want to argue. "Where's Fran? Where did you take my friend?"

Caroline doesn't do me the service of slowing her pace.

"They're examining him," she says.

My stomach drops. "*Examining* him. What the hell for?"

She has reached the spiral stair that leads to the balcony, and takes hold of the banister before turning her cold brown eyes on me. "He went willingly," she says, void of empathy.

"Just like Evander did? I demand you release Fran immediately."

He never should have come. I wanted him to stay away. As soon as I learned about Dana and John, I knew I had to do this alone. Caroline wants me to follow her upstairs, to the Jovian wing. David's probably there, waiting for me in one of the family offices.

Her unaffected gaze settles on my face. "No one wants to hurt you."

Is she implying they'll hurt me if I step out of line?

"Please follow me."

I'm thinking about escaping through the front lobby when she says, "It's about Evander."

Of course I follow.

At the top of the spiral steps, she leads me down the Jovian hallway. All of the doors are closed. We pass two of them, and she stops in front of the third. I think it was Uncle Jimmy's when I visited in the past, but I'm not sure. I've never been inside.

She turns, her back to the door, so that she once again faces me. "We want you to join us, Svetlana."

My ears perk. *Why she thinks I'd join them for anything is beyond me.*

"It's what we've wanted all along. It's what we still want."

Her eyes soften and brows lift with hope. She appears somehow humble. She wants something from me—or maybe she *needs* something from me.

"All I want is to get my son back," I say.

"And you will."

She pushes the door open and invites me inside with an open palm.

I take just one step into the room, so bright white it's practically purple, thinking, *Is Evander here?* I have to remain close to the exit, especially now that I see this isn't an office but a laboratory with silver tables and stools. White aprons hung from hooks. Microscope stations, vials, test tubes, boxes of blue latex gloves and plastic goggles. The vinegary scent of chemicals sours the air. I turn my head and realize we're not alone. Four men line up in front of the wall. Four silent Evanders, each dressed in a white shirt and gray pants. Brown hair parted on the same side, eyes forward in a guard-like gaze, blank and unthinking. Silent.

"No," I whisper through a loud breath. I worry that my legs will fail me if I don't concentrate on remaining upright. If I hadn't already glimpsed two or three Evanders in the real world, I'd be passed out on the floor right now. Instead, the surge of desperation and disgust I experience, the kind I know I shouldn't display, bangs its way up my neck and lands on my face. I stand there and stare, fighting an urge to let loose a stampede of anger and accusation.

"Why are you showing me this?" I say through gritted teeth.

"Because you are a part of this family."

I turn away from the lineup and face her. "Whether I like it or not? Is that what you mean?"

"No one wants to hurt you, Svetlana."

"You keep saying that."

She takes a step backward and tilts her head. "Yes, because—"

"I don't want any part of this!" My mind speeds ahead so fast that it jumps the grid of normal thinking. I'm yelling and can't stop. "This is wrong! And you're not my family. *Evander* is my family. *Helena* is my family. Except for Andrew, I never wanted any part of the Jovian family. Please just give me Evander, and let me go."

I'm finished here, but I can't shut up. I have to make my opinion known. I'm human—I think Caroline sometimes forgets—and by showing me these clones of my son, she has set off a bright, burning flare comparable to those that break away from the sun. I have to let it out or I'll go up in a blaze. "Do you know what you're doing to Evander, your beloved grandchild? You're *ruining* his life. This person you supposedly care so much about. The one you love?"

I gesture to the row of Evanders. "What will you even do with them . . . " I'm having trouble drawing air, and therefore there's not enough for speech. I cough and expect smoke to rise from my mouth like dragon's breath.

Caroline says, "They do whatever we need them to do."

The sound of someone entering the opposite side of the room draws my attention. I raise my head as Aunt Constant approaches. "Hello, Svetlana." She wears a white lab coat and the same old-lady glasses that deceived me ten years ago.

"Stay away," I say.

She crosses the room and stands beside Caroline. "They have Jovian DNA, " she says. "They'll make a better human race. Humans like Evander, who are kind, intelligent, caring."

"Uh-huh, and what about the old race? What will happen to it?"

Aunt Constant blinks before answering: "It's called evolution. A natural process of change, over time."

"I know what evolution is," I say, sniping at her. "Is it natural even when the Jovians make it happen?"

"Yes, it is," she says without hesitation.

I turn back to Caroline: "When will I see Evander—the real one? Now that you have *them*," I tip my head in the direction of the boys, "you don't need him anymore. If you don't want to hurt me, you'll tell me and let me go."

No one moves or responds in any way. Not Caroline, not Constant, not the clones.

"Please, Caroline," I say, my patience waning.

Her face is void of expression. "He'll be back soon."

"Can you be more specific?"

"A week. Or two."

Unlike Caroline, I can't maintain an unemotional countenance. I huff and say, "That's not good enough."

"I'm sorry if I upset you. No one wants to hurt you, Svetlana."

She's sorry *if* she upset me. "Okay."

She stares. There's nothing there: no bewildered impatience, no scowl or clenched jaw.

"So you'll call me when Evander arrives. Or maybe you'll send some buzzing brainwaves my way?"

"We will call."

I return my attention to the Evanders—the boys with nothing in their eyes—and wonder, *Do they even know why they're here? That they're playing a role in the Jovians' plan to change the planet one human at a time? Do they have any idea?*

I step toward Caroline, I'm not sure why. I suppose I want to hit her or smoosh the makeup from her beautiful face or maybe just push her into the wall, but before I find out what my body has planned, the four Evanders surround me like a human cage. I'm boxed in—trapped.

I should have just left. *What the hell am I doing?*

The Evander in front of me stares coldly into my eyes, his jaw set with unflinching confidence.

"Is there anything else you want to say, Svetlana?" Caroline says.

The boys surrounding me are tall and muscular, young and ready to fight. They wear heartless expressions not at all familiar to me, not at all like Evander. More like guards. Soldiers.

"Can I leave?" I say, the words vibrating in my throat.

Her "yes" signals the clone in front of me to step aside.

"You're nothing like my son," I say through a sneer as I hurry toward the door.

A few steps into the hall, I realize I'm holding my breath. I take the stairs, letting gravity pull me like water downhill. Then I remember that they've taken Fran.

"Fran!" I shout as loud as I can. "Fran!"

I know it's for nothing. I know they have him, but I also know it's possible they've already let him go. He could be outside, wondering where I am, waiting for me to come out. Or, he could be one of them.

Either way, he doesn't answer. The lobby is empty, and I can't get away fast enough.

19

I leave through the room with the murky red lighting, hoping to find Fran waiting in back of the building. As I ascend the incline of the lawn, I remember that I have no car. I'll run to the road, maybe a half mile away, and call for a ride. I have to get back to Dana and John's. I'll break in and steal the keys to the grasshopper. I've eaten only two cookies all day, and I'm emotionally drained. I have no home, and I don't want to stay in the Jovian mansion. Maybe Fran's apartment? He could be there. I *hope* he's there. If not, I can sleep in the car in Dana and John's garage. My thoughts blast through my mind like shooting stars.

The cold air gives me some strength, but I'm numb. I'm moving on reserves, nothing more.

As I head over to the tree with the platform Fran built, I turn in a circle, checking all around for someone following me. No one is there. Once again the Jovians have let me go. It's a challenge to climb the tree—my arms and legs resist as I grasp and pull myself from limb to limb, groaning all the way—but my one photo of Evander occupies the side pocket of my backpack, and there's no way I'm leaving it behind. I manage to reach the platform and grab my bag, then climb down without hurting myself.

I'm back on the ground, doubled over, struggling to catch my breath when a motor bubbles to life in the distance. It seems to be coming from the opposite side of the building. The muffled roar of a motorcycle.

So they might be coming for me after all.

I put my arms through the straps of the backpack, and scan the area for a place to take cover. No sooner have I ducked behind some bushes, a single bright light appears from around the side of the building. The engine grows in volume as it nears, its headlight preventing me from seeing any details of the helmeted person on board. It jumps the curb and drives up the lawn, aimed straight for the bushes I'm crouched behind. I consider running, but it's too late. I'll never be fast enough.

Whoever it is stops the motorcycle and hops off. They're dressed like the security squad that once watched over me at Chateau L'Origine: all black with a collared leather jacket upheld by the squared shoulders of a man (as far as I can tell). Probably one of the Evanders.

He parks the bike and pulls a helmet from a compartment behind the seat, walks over, and extends the hand that holds it. "Put it on," he says.

I don't respond. I have no intention of getting on the bike.

"I'm going to give you a ride. You don't want a ride?"

"Not from you," I say.

He puts the helmet on the ground and grabs both sides of his own. Just like that, he pulls it off, his hair standing straight up as if stretching for a moment before it falls in front of his eyes. With one hand, he shoves the flop of hair to the side, then looks me in the eye.

It's . . . I can't be seeing what I'm seeing. I stand, take a step toward him.

This isn't possible.

With a rumpled brow and offended eyes, I'm staring into the face of Andrew.

His dimpled cheek and light-brown wave of hair.

A blast of hopefulness pounds through my heart but fades in the seconds that follow. That's how long it takes to remind myself he's not my Andrew in spite of how much I want him to be.

They have cloned my husband.

Those imbeciles have cloned my husband!

He lifts the helmet from the ground and reaches out once more, offering it to me. The angry thoughts in my head rear up and crash down like the hooves of wild horses, and I knock it clear out of his hand. It hits the ground and rolls a few feet down the modest incline.

For several seconds, we're locked in a stare down.

My head reels with the knowledge that they've made duplicates of Andrew and unleashed them upon the world. *I hate them. I hate every one of them.*

But this man is not my Andrew. This Andrew is bold. Ready to fight me. Ready to push me or track me down. This guy has "do whatever you have to do" written on his face.

"Do you know who I am?" I say, pretending I'm not afraid.

"Of course I do."

"How dare you masquerade as my husband. What is your name?"

"Andrew."

I clench my jaw and shake my head, strands of hair falling in front of my face like a madwoman's would. "You don't even have your own name! That is sad. Do you know how sad that is?"

"My name is Andrew, whether you think it's sad or not."

"Do you think you can trick me? You think that because

you look like my husband and have taken his name that I'll get on board and go wherever you want to take me?"

"I think you need a ride, and I'm going to give you one."

His calm response strikes me as demeaning. He doesn't speak like Andrew. He lacks a timber of kindness. Decency.

"Put the helmet on," he says with a blank alien stare that has the power to turn my skin blue.

I walk over to where the helmet lies and swipe it from the ground. I'm so angry I want to spit. And cry. And scream. "You're not real, you know that?" I say, stifling my emotion to such a degree that my voice emerges in a deep, grating whisper. "You're a copy. A cheap imitation. There are plenty of cheap imitations to go around."

My insults inspire no change in his expression, no response whatsoever. He's impenetrable. Like all Jovians.

"You need a ride, and you need food, and I'm going to make sure you get both."

I laugh to keep from crying. He's right: I'm tired and famished. I do need a ride. And I'm in no shape for argument, or even normal conversation.

"I won't thank you," I say.

The helmet pulls my hair as I put it on and settle it in place. It's heavy, not the easiest thing to balance on a tired neck.

The clone gets on the bike, and I follow. There are platforms for my feet, but I want something for my hands to hold. I would rather fall off the bike and slide into the gutter than wrap my arms around him. Maybe I can manage if I grasp the undersides of the seat.

The engine strikes a deep and rumbling chord, thunder that fills every empty place in my brain and all of the sad vacancies in my body. I can't think even if I want to.

And that is something to be grateful for.

As we pass through town, I succumb to the December wind, which finds whatever warmth I've generated and eviscerates it. The clone brings me to a twenty-four-hour diner on the highway, one I've never been to. It's already 1 a.m., though that seems impossible. I'd swear I was at Starbright for minutes rather than hours. He stops the bike out front and says, "Go eat."

I'm relieved he won't be joining me.

"Do you have your phone," he asks as I walk away.

I check my pocket. It's there. I pull it out so he can see. He motors away, gliding into a parking space as I climb the steps to the restaurant.

An older man hunches over a plate of fried eggs. The scent of bacon and butter makes my eyes water with longing. I glance across the room in search of a server. A moment later, a middle-aged woman with a bleach-blonde bouffant appears through swinging kitchen doors.

"Anywhere you like," she says in a cheerful tone.

I drop into the first booth I come to so I can look out the window at the clone while I think about how much I hate the Jovians.

The waitress slides a paper placemat and a rolled-up napkin of silverware in front of me. The coffee aroma makes my head swim.

She smiles with pink lipstick as she says, "Coffee?"

"Yes."

She pours.

"You know what you want?"

"Chiz omelet, rye toast. Thank you," I hand her the menu.

"Sure." She sticks the pencil in her hair and leaves.

I wonder if after I eat I should slip out the back door and break away from my . . . I don't know what to call him.

Captor? That would imply his intent to take me captive. But is that what he's doing? He said I needed a ride and he was going to give me one. So he's my driver. I suppose he could be both a driver and a captor, however.

My phone beeps a text.

It's Dana. *We need to talk.*

I close my eyes and grumble.

"Do we?" I say out loud. Dana and John chose me. Why would they? How would they have even known I existed? I suppose they could have seen me, met me when they visited the orphanage, maybe on one of their humanitarian missions. . . . But what difference would that make? I would like to know why they were allowed to choose, why they even wanted to. Maybe I should ask Dana. Another texts arrives:

I want to apologize. John and I both do.

Leave it to her to coerce me with kindness. My pretend mother. The one who is so good at make-believe that I actually loved her. The thought breaks my resolve to pieces and leaves me with a trembling chin. I'm too tired for this. I have no energy to fight the sadness. The truth. The fact that my whole life has been a lie! I beat back the urge to cry and then type my answer:

I know what you are.

I send it. I want to hurt her. I want her to feel as bad as I do.

That's why we need to talk. Please, Sveta. I'm worried about you.

She's Jovian. My life is littered with them. I feel for the file rolled up in the pocket of my coat. It's there, and it's real. Not just a part of some nightmare I had.

The waitress brings my plate of food. I thank her and put down the phone.

Then I pick it up again and type *Maybe*. I have more

important things to do than text with Dana right now. I have to think. I need a plan. I don't know where to go from here. In the meantime, I can't chew this food fast enough. It tastes so delicious that I'm piling it in, practically choking on it. No one is here to watch me but the man at the counter, and he seems to have fallen asleep.

When I glance out the window, however, I realize I'm wrong. The clone leaning against his motorcycle stares up at me.

So I guess someone is watching after all.

When I step out of the diner, what I see gives me pause. Fake Andrew's head tips up toward the sky with an all-too-familiar look of satisfaction as if he'd rather stargaze than do just about anything else. Maybe he's more like Andrew than I assumed. The sight of him spills a lethal dose of longing into my bloodstream. I want him to be Andrew, not just to look like him, and because this can't be, I'm angry with him. Screw him for being a clone.

"What are you looking at?" I say with a tone that implies I couldn't care less.

"Venus. And Antares." He tries to hand me the helmet, but I don't comply.

"Where are you taking me?"

"You need a ride, and I'm going to give you one."

"Yes, I know, but you haven't said where you're taking me."

He throws his leg over the motorcycle and pulls his helmet on. "Dana wants to talk to you. If you want to go to the cemetery afterward, we can."

"Why would I want to go to the cemetery?"

"Isn't that where you're staying these days?"

"I slept there *once*."

He nudges the helmet into my chest. "Yeah, smells like it."

When I don't take it, he stares without expression through the visor and says, "I wouldn't care if you cracked your skull open, but Evander might."

The urge to slap his face snaps like a whip through my body. Andrew would never speak to me like this. How dare he take my husband's body!

He smacks his visor closed and continues to hold out the helmet.

"You're not even a real person, are you?" I say. "You don't have parents."

He deserves this and more for impersonating my husband.

The helmet remains extended.

I grab it from him.

He rises up on the bike and stomps the pedal, jarring it to life. I pull the helmet over my head and climb on.

When we arrive at Dana and John's, I'm surprised to find the house lit up. The Dana and John I know are early to bed and early to rise, as John always used to say when Helena and I were in high school. The clone drives us all the way to the garage. "They're waiting for you." He sturdies the bike so I can dismount.

I guess he's staying outside.

"I'll be here when you're ready to go," he says.

Stubborn and dutiful. The Jovians must love him.

I climb the three steps to the back door, tap on the window, and enter before they can invite me in. It's warm inside, the light above the oven glowing like the wholesome American home I remember from my youth. That oven light has been a beacon for me, guiding the way to a late-night cup of chamomile or piece of apple pie. The scents of polished wood flooring and home-cooked meals envelop me as Dana limps into the kitchen, her lower leg in a cast. All at once I picture the glossy black stick figure in the bathroom and my nerves flare.

She has the stiff posture of someone in pain, but I won't say anything to comfort her. Too bad for her.

"I'm so glad you've come," she says, looking down. "Thank you. Please sit. Would you like something to eat? Maybe a cup of tea?"

I shake my head. "Where's John?"

"I prefer to speak to you alone, if that's all right." She gestures to my chair.

I sit with my coat still buttoned to the top.

Dana takes the chair opposite. "Are you all right? Do you want to take a shower while you're here, or maybe change clothes?"

I look down at myself. I guess the clone meant what he said. Dark clouds of dust and splotches of dirt mar my pants and coat. I slept in a cemetery—I *fell* at the cemetery and rolled around on the ground.

"I'm fine," I say, wondering simultaneously when I last washed my face.

"Oh, okay. Maybe you want to take your coat off?"

"What do you want, Dana?" I say.

She raises her eyes in a shy manner. "What you saw must have come as a shock, and I'm very sorry about that."

I glare at her for the twenty years I thought I knew who she was. Then I say, "I'm getting used to shocks, to tell you the truth," and look away in disgust.

"I didn't want to deceive you," she says, cupping her chin in her hand, elbow propped upon the table. "I shouldn't have. I'm sorry." Her shame shows in the way her eyes reach out to me, then seek out the tabletop. She sighs heavily like a depressed person. Is it an act? Is it genuine? Dana and John have always been so even. I thought it was because they were mature human beings, responsible adults. Parents. They never became overly excited or upset. Always seemed to be in control. But maybe that was because that's all they're capable of.

Whatever the reason, Dana could be acting now, and I'm not going to fall for it.

"You tried to make me think I was mentally ill for saying they took Evander to Jupiter, that they cloned him. But you knew that's exactly what happened. You knew I was right, and you purposely made it harder for me."

"I didn't *want* to do any of that. I hated doing that—"

"And yet somehow you managed."

She'll get no sympathy from me.

She closes her eyes as if withstanding the agony that comes from years of guilt. "Yes, well," she says with trembling lips, "we all have a part to play, and being your mother was mine. It still is."

"You've never been my mother." The words slice the air like knives thrown across the table. "And don't say that other stuff about roles and parts to play. I know all about Jovians and their group effort to trick me."

"I know you do," she says reaching out with her hand and placing it on top of mine. She waits until I meet her eyes again before saying, "Many times I told them I was against what the family was doing, what the family had decided."

I pull my hand back, leaving hers with nothing to grasp. "And yet you went along with it," I say.

"You can't understand. Believe me, I don't blame you for how you feel."

"Thank you for that," I say, my words steeped in sarcasm.

"Evander will be back soon, and the family thought it best

if you went to Peru for a short time so he could get settled without distraction. He has a lot on his—"

"I know why you wanted me to go to Peru. Just like Edmund hoped I would choose to stay in Russia. What I want to know is, did you really spend all those years traveling around the world helping people, or was that just for the benefit of fooling me and Helena?"

"That was the truth. John and I *are* humanitarians—"

"Except you're not human."

She clasps her hands and rests them on her lap. "No, we're not human."

I sense some embarrassment on her part. As if this admission isn't something she ever wanted to make.

Again, too bad. She deserves whatever mental anguish she's experiencing—if it's possible for her to experience such a thing.

"You know how desperate I am to see Evander, and yet you were going to take me away from here? Because the Jovians care for no one but themselves. You care only for your mission. Your plan to save the earth by permanently altering the human race."

Her sad expression dissolves, and she scrunches her brow as if perplexed by what I've said. "That's not what we want," she says softly.

"I don't care what you want," I shout. "I just want my kid back. And there's nothing you can possibly say to change my mind about how I feel about you and the family right now."

I stand, the wood chair scraping against the tile floor as it pushes out behind me.

Dana reaches with her hand again, grasping the air between us. "But we're not all the same. Please, you know we're not."

I'm a few feet away now and feeling safer with more space between us. She's right. Some of the Jovians have raised my hair. She did not, and that's why I didn't know she was one of them. "You've played the same games they play."

When she swipes at her cheeks, I realize she must have begun to cry, and I stifle the instinct to comfort her. "I know what I've done," she says, in an angry tone that I think she's directing at herself, "and I'm sorry. I only wish I could go back and do things differently, but I thought it would work out. I thought I'd be able to help you. I really just wanted to help you."

Can this be the truth?

I creep back to the table and lower into the chair, eyeing her skeptically. I've never seen Dana cry. She clears her throat and then takes a moment to reclaim a calm demeanor. It doesn't seem like an act.

"I'm not like Caroline and Edmund," she says, pausing to dab at her nose with a paper napkin. "We're not all the same. John and I, we both thought it would be better for you to have parents like us, parents who possess patience and warmth, understanding . . . rather than someone like Caroline or Miranda or even James."

It occurs to me that I should tell her I realize she would say anything to get me to accept her lies, but I can't. Because I can see that she's desperate to get through to me. She could have turned her back on me the minute I discovered her true form. She didn't have to reach out to me. It would have been easier to walk away and never speak to me again. But here she is, bearing her soul.

"You have to believe me when I tell you I love you as if you were my own child. I always have." Her voice breaks and mouth bends into a frown.

Watching this emotional display weakens the stronghold inside of me, the foundation of my anger cracks—and that frightens me. I want to believe that she's truly regretful, but if

I do, I'll be vulnerable again. Easier to assume she's a fraud, to remain angry and on the attack.

"Was any of it real?" I say, firmly. "Lying and pretending the way you did? That's not being a mother. That's not love."

"I wasn't pretending with you. I was your mother. I *am* your mother. I was the best mother they would let me be."

"So your feelings for me were real, like a real mother for her child?"

"Yes," she says, begging with her eyes. "Of course they were."

"I don't know," I say, suspicion simmering beneath my skin. The Jovians have fooled me too many times. I can't accept this. I shouldn't accept this.

Only this is Dana. I want to trust that she loved me as much as I loved her.

I think back to my teenage years. The way she and John included me in every conversation, how they shared with me all they learned on their trips, how they helped me get through arguments with my friends—they tried very hard to include Helena in their lives as well, but she pushed them away. They truly were good parents.

I take in a noisy breath. "I just don't know."

She sniffles and looks up with red-rimmed eyes as if she just came up with the answer to the problem. "What about you? Did you feel that I loved you—that I cared for you and took care of you the way a real mother would?"

I know the answer, but I'm reluctant to give it. Instead, I say, "I *thought* I did—"

Her brow rises with hope. "And you loved me back?"

A swollen stream of pain and longing comes barreling up my throat. I can't talk. I can't get air. I shouldn't have come. But I can't hide the truth. "I trusted you," I say, my voice barely a whisper. "I did love you. You were my mom."

Whatever threads of control I've been holding on to let

go. I've lost it, and now I can't breathe. I'm sobbing in great gulping breaths the same way I did when I was a little girl.

Dana limps over, gently bumps foreheads with me, and drapes an arm over my shoulder. She's warm and smells like shampoo. I don't swat her away, and she drapes the other arm around me as well, holding me like she did when I was sixteen and upset about something ridiculous.

She says, "If what you say is true, then you can be sure it was real."

I'm on the back of the clone's motorcycle again, moving in the direction of my old house, the one Andrew and I renovated together, the one Edmund told me to go to, to wait for Evander. After our reconciliation, Dana asked if I would like to stay with her and John, but I can't. Not after all that's happened. I'm physically and mentally drained, and I can't stop thinking about Evander and how I want him back. If Edmund wants me to stay in my old house, I'm going to do it. Plan C, as Fran called it. I should have listened to him—and I wish I knew where he was.

As soon as I get off this bike, I'm going to call him.

When we arrive at the house, I expect the clone to drop me off and leave, but he parks at the end of the front path.

Before either of us has made a move, I say, "What are you doing? You're not coming in."

"Think again," he says without pause.

I lift the shield of my helmet. "Why?"

"This is where I live."

"No, it isn't. I was here the other day. It was empty. Edmund told me I could stay here."

He removes his helmet and dismounts. I'm forced to lean back at a severe angle so his boot doesn't imprint my face. He walks up the shoveled path as he reaches into his jacket pocket.

I hear the chime of keys.

He opens the door, then glances over his shoulder.

I leap off the bike and hurry into the foyer before he can lock me out.

In the living room, there's furniture and homey things like books and vases and even paintings on the walls. In the kitchen, too. And the foyer. Candles on tables, a spice rack on the counter.

This isn't the same house I saw the other day. Someone has set it up. They knew I was coming—or they did it for him, this clone who has been living in my house.

He throws his keys into a clay tray on the sideboard in the entry and tells me he'll be out back. "On the deck," he says.

I want to tell him not to bother trying to act like my husband, but now is not the time to be belligerent. "Where should I put my stuff?"

"I don't care," he says as he steps out the sliding glass door.

I drop my backpack on the floor and dial Fran's number as I head into the kitchen, where I pull open the fridge. While the phone rings, I take inventory: The vegetable bin offers lettuce, carrots, celery, onions, and more. Plastic zip-locked bags of deli meat, sliced cheeses, and a container of olives fill the other drawer. In the door, a jar of mayo, a bottle of maple syrup, a full slab of butter, milk, orange juice. The middle shelf holds a six-pack of beer. As Fran's voicemail message plays, I reach in and grab one. I don't love beer, but the thought of staying under the same roof as the clone makes me want one.

Of course they wouldn't let me live here alone. The clone is my babysitter.

At the tone, I say, "Fran, where are you? Call me. I need to know you're okay."

I retrieve my backpack and head in the direction of my old bedroom, stopping to check out the room that once was my office. There's a twin bed in there now, neatly made, beside a night table with a glass of water and a frame without a picture inside. A dresser backs up against the opposite wall. No socks or pants or underwear on the floor like you'd expect from a young single male. The room smells of carpet shampoo and displays zero personality.

The perfect habitat for a clone.

I continue to the bedroom at the end of the hall, set up as I remember: a queen-size bed to the right when I walk in, night tables to either side, a cordless phone and a box of tissues on one of them. Also, a four-drawer dresser, row of windows with blinds, and curtains in French blue.

I drink the rest of the beer in one long swallow, the bubbles burning my throat, then place the empty bottle beside the tissues. I drop my backpack at the foot of the night table, and dive on top of the mattress, bone tired. Then I jump back up remembering I need to lock the door.

I'll consider how I'm going to get the clone out of my house tomorrow.

20

In the morning, I'm grateful to have my breakfast alone: a bagel thick with cream cheese. The scent of "everything," my favorite flavor, traveled all the way to my bedroom, which proves just how potent they are. As I eat, I worry the clone will come around the corner. The door to his room is closed, but I doubt he's in there. Jovians don't sleep late. They may not sleep at all. I already know he was up early getting bagels.

I sit at the table in front of the sliding glass door and stare at the deck, remembering the sight of Andrew stargazing with the telescope and saying things like, "Venus is blazing tonight, honey, so I guess love is in the air." He was always making me laugh. *If only I could backstroke my arms in windmill circles through space and time to get back to him.* But that's a ridiculous thought considering he's ten years in the past at this point, and the press of time continues to push me deeper into the future.

I've finished eating, so I bring my napkin to the garbage, my plate to the sink. I continue to the front door, looking out to see if the motorcycle balances on its kickstand out there. It does, so the clone must be here somewhere.

The sliding glass door opens with a swoosh, and I spin around.

He walks in with the phone to his ear. "No, we didn't," he says. "She slept in hers, and I slept in mine."

I give him a killer stare and cock my head to the side.

"Oh, I'll try, but you know how stubborn she is," he says, passing me a wink. "All right. Will do. Bye, Caroline."

I cross my arms over my chest, feeling naked though I'm fully dressed in the same clothes I wore yesterday and slept in last night. "Did you just say what I think you said?"

He stops a few feet away in his black jeans and a gray T-shirt, and leers at me as if he can see straight into my vulnerable place. "Don't worry. I won't make you do anything."

I draw in a brusque breath as heat rises to my cheeks, wishing my hatred for him would manifest as a dagger laced with poison. "Get out of my house," I say.

He rushes toward me, invading my personal space. His breath spills over me, and I shuffle backward, stopped by the front door.

He doesn't touch me.

"It's *my* house," he says, loudly. "I'll stay as long as I like."

This confrontation has taken my cool, collected mindset and knocked it on its ass, but I won't let him know I'm afraid. "You're an idiot if you think I'll ever sleep with you."

"Don't tell me you haven't considered it." He taps my chin before backing up a step, still too close for comfort. "I can understand why you would, given I look like I do. Sorry if what I said to Caroline offends you," he says, though I see no apology in his eyes. "I really don't want to sleep with you, but I will if they tell me to. And, news flash, they've told me to."

"You're an idiot," I say.

"I'm also a clone, as you so sweetly pointed out. The

Jovians ask me to do things, and I do them. Sort of like a robot would, only I'm flesh and blood . . . like you."

I'm afraid to pass him, so I stay where I am. "If you say so," I say.

His eyes linger on my face long enough to make me uncomfortable.

"You're pretty in your own wacky-mom sort of way, you know?" He reaches out to touch my cheek, and I slap his hand.

His face widens with surprise for a moment before he regains that all-too-familiar unaffectedness in his eyes. "What would be the harm? I know you're lonely. What's it been, like, ten years since you've had sex?"

That's about as much as I can take right now, so I turn with the intention of getting out of there as fast as I can. As I unlock the bolt and twist the knob, he reaches over my head and presses his hand into the door, thudding it closed.

I spin around with what I hope is a wild look in my eyes. "You do whatever they ask, like a loyal puppy."

He shows no sign of embarrassment. "Yes, I do."

"Well," I scramble for something to say, "why not try thinking for yourself? Use your brain, you know? You don't have to do everything they tell you to do."

He walks over to the sideboard and takes his keys from the tray. "You mean, the way you do?"

I don't do whatever the Jovians tell me to do, so this makes no sense.

"Maybe you just don't realize it," he adds.

It's true that this is the Jovian house Edmund wanted me to live in. And I'm here, waiting for Evander to come, like he wanted me to. But my place with them is written in the stars —out of my control—Uncle Jimmy told me so.

"From the constipated look on your face, I can see that you agree," he says. "You're right where they want you to be."

He's smarter than I assumed, and that makes him dangerous not only because he's someone to be reckoned with but because he has earned some respect. As he steps toward me again, I worry that I've misjudged him. He was supposed to be a driver, and now he's watching over me and closing doors when I want to go out.

"We could be in this together, you know," he says, in a sweet tone. "You don't have to be alone anymore."

I wish he'd leave. I hate him, and I'm lonely, and I'm ready to fight and wanting to take his offer of companionship all at the same time. It's a tangled ball of desperation that makes me sweat.

"I want to help you," he says, sounding sincere.

It would be easy to give in, to accept his offer.

"I wish that were true," I say, "but you're just a person pretending to be another person."

"Suit yourself." He pulls the door open but then hesitates. "Hey, listen, if it's too much, you don't have to call me Andrew. My friends call me Drew."

"You have friends?" My attempt at a joke accompanies an even lamer sound of amusement, one that comes from a dismal place inside of me. "That is hard to believe. . . . "

"I'm going to meet some now, as a matter of fact. Is it just that you don't like me, or maybe you're seeing Fran?"

I answer with a frown.

"That's a no?"

"Why don't you ask him yourself? The Jovians have him as far as I know."

"You two have been spending a lot of time together," he says. "He's probably falling in love with you. Or you with him."

"Don't be juvenile," I say.

"So you're not in love with Fran. That's good. If you want me, you can have me. I'm available, as they say."

Obviously the Jovians have not become any more knowledgeable about human emotion than when I left Kirksberg ten years ago. "You could *never* take my husband's place."

He steps toward the door, then turns and gazes over his shoulder at me with some kind of pensive, steely-eyed look —probably thinks he's sexy. "You'll be here when I get back?"

I glare at him. He knows I have nowhere to go.

"That's what I thought," he says.

Several hours later, the clone returns with dinner: Chinese food.

We sit like a couple; me on one side of the kitchen table, him on the other.

I've taken the pint of lo mein and made it my own. Meanwhile, he uses the chopsticks to deliver kang pao to his mouth, dropping food on the table and floor as he does so.

We haven't said much besides "hello" since he walked in, and the silence grows as stiff as a backache.

"I know you hate me," he says, "but I'm trying to help you."

"I don't need your help," I say in a dull manner.

"Andrew wouldn't want you to be alone. You can pretend I'm him if you want."

This makes me sneer at my noodles. He has the Jovians' lack of social graces, I'll give him that. "Can you not talk, please?"

Three seconds later, he says, "What *do* you want?"

"Isn't it obvious? I want my child back. Tell Caroline that's all I want. I don't need a new husband, thank you."

"I don't think getting your child back is going to be possible."

My eyes blink an angry staccato. I wish he'd shut up.

I say, "Edmund said he would bring Evander—"

He shakes his head. "I mean because he's not a child anymore."

Unfortunately I have to agree. Pretending Evander is a child no longer works, as much as I wish it were so.

"He's not even the person you knew in Russia. Not anymore."

Now he's just trying to scare me.

"You realize I saw him only four, five weeks ago." I'm chewing my lo mein as if I have no worries at all.

"Have you ever been to Jupiter?"

I stare at him, Jovian style, because going to Jupiter is something I know nothing about. My daydreams took me there in my mind, but it's not a trip I want to make in my body.

"It has a way of changing a person," he says. "You'll see soon enough."

What he said should probably bother me, but all I can think is, *He just said I'm going to see Evander soon enough.*

"So let's say the two of you are reunited, like you want." He sets his chopsticks on the table beside the container of Kang Pau. "Then what? Will you run again? To Russia, or maybe someplace else? A crowded city like Sydney or Bangkok. I mean, assuming you can convince him to run with you."

This is none of his business, and *who cares?* Evander and I will figure it out. "Do you think I would tell you my plan?"

He shrugs like a snarly teenager. "No one else to tell."

I continue to twirl the noodles in my container. Noodles are more important than he is.

"Come on, Sveta, tell me. What's the plan?"

"The plan is to survive."

"There are many ways to do that."

"I have to protect my child," I say. "I would die for him. I doubt clones can understand that, never having had parents."

He remains utterly still, thinking, maybe, but not giving anything away. It's the same impenetrable armor all Jovians wear. "You're right," he says. "I'm barely human, as you pointed out, but that doesn't change the fact that you need to accept Evander for who he is and move on. It's time for your son to claim his place in this world. That's what he's been doing. He's going to rule this nation one day."

"Ha! So I've heard."

"You don't believe it?"

"I don't think he'll want to. I know him a lot better than the Jovians do."

"Why wouldn't he want to? The opportunity is there, and he's a natural leader. He's built for this. He has everything a leader needs: likeability, charisma, intelligence."

I think of all the young girls who used to bat their lashes at him in Russia. How they would congregate around him, give him their phone numbers, ask him to call them. And then I remember Nadia, the one who got us into all of this trouble.

"You speak as if you've met him," I say.

"Yeah, I did. Real nice guy."

"Does he know you're a—"

"Clone of his father. Yes."

My heartbeat quickens. *Poor Evander. Seeing a duplicate of his father had to be so strange and disturbing.*

"What did he think about that?" I say. "About you?"

"Your son is a marvelous specimen as far as humans go. He has a keen universal instinct. By far the brightest human I've ever encountered. He took it all in stride."

I eye him with suspicion because this smells of insult.

"Even if the Jovians weren't involved," he adds, "it would be hard for you to keep Evander down."

"I'm not trying to keep him down," I say with venom. "Only a Jovian would equate being a concerned parent with keeping a child down."

I cross the kitchen and toss the carton of lo mein into the garbage. Then, instead of going back to the table, I continue through the living area toward my room. I've heard about as much as I can take for one night.

"Are you coming back," he calls out. "I thought we'd watch a movie together."

I have no words for him.

The following morning, after I've eaten a carton of yogurt and I'm ready for a shower, the clone shows up in the doorway of his bedroom as I pass through the hall.

"How did you sleep," he asks. The usual coy grin has taken a back seat to a more mature, less-cocky aura.

"Fine," I say, determined not to speak to him.

"Wait. I want to apologize."

Of course he does. He won't quit until he's tried every angle.

"I'm sorry for my rudeness. I realize I've been juvenile and obnoxious. Then again I'm just a clone. I'm not important. I know that."

It feels like he's playing to what he believes are my assumptions.

The problem is I don't like to hear anyone speak badly of themselves. Then again, I don't have much empathy for him. He's sneaky. Just another babysitter keeping me under the Jovians' collective thumb.

"It's fine," I say, as I reach the door to my room. "Don't worry about it."

"Wait, wait a second. Come here." He waves me closer with his hand.

I stare at him, thinking, *Absolutely not.*

"Just come here for a second and stand in front of me."

I shake my head. "I need to shower." I turn away because I don't want to look at him.

In the meantime, he comes to me and reaches for my hand.

I try to step back, but he says, "Ah, ah, one second," grabbing my other hand and tugging me closer.

His face hovers inches from mine.

I try not to breathe because when I do, I smell Andrew.

He chuckles and says, "You're so tense. Are you afraid of me?"

"No," I say as I try but fail to twist out of his grip.

"What is it? You don't like my face?"

The words "shut up" leap from my mouth.

His blue-green eyes are killing me.

I drop my chin and concentrate on my feet. My shoulders hover around my earlobes as panic swells in my chest. The fake Andrew up close is not something I can withstand, and I'm cringing and pulling back on the inside, slipping into quicksand. All he has to do is smile right now, and I'll lose this battle for self-control.

"Svetlana," he says, sounding exactly like my Andrew once did.

I raise my head, and what I see causes an internal startle. When he puts on the right expression, it's exact. An identical twin. And right now he's looking at me like Andrew did that first day we met, with concern that's practically palpable.

"You've been alone for too long," he says softly.

He lets go of my wrists and rests his hands on my waist as if someone has turned the music on and we're about to slow dance. "Is this okay?"

I can't answer. My body has been reminded of what it feels like for Andrew to touch me. To be surrounded by his clean cotton scent, his gentle warmth and embrace. *But this isn't Andrew. This is the clone.*

Even so, I can't get myself to tell him to stop or leave me alone. How many times have I longed to replicate this experience: the contentment and comfort of my husband alive again? When Andrew died, I hugged my pillow and breathed in the scent of him for months. And now I'm standing in the hallway of our former home with a man who resembles him to a perfect degree. The voice in my head that reminds me he isn't real, that he isn't something I want, moves farther and farther away until it's just air passing through the vent, no syllables of distinction, no words to grab hold of. Just background noise.

I let out a long breath that massages some of my reluctance away, and he says, "You don't have to be alone anymore."

Then he takes my face in his hands and looks down on me with loving eyes before pressing his lips to my own.

I'd forgotten the taste of him, and my defenses disintegrate. It's like welcoming my husband home after he's been away for years. My body becomes a pulsing rush of red that wants more.

He raises his head and smiles into my face just like Andrew used to—and then he walks away.

21

That night, after I've washed and put on a tank top and underwear for pajamas, I prop up my pillows and attempt to read a book, but my mind keeps telling me Andrew is just beyond the closed door, in the room down the hall. I've been thinking about him all day—the real Andrew, not the Drew Andrew. The same longing I endured years ago, during the aftermath of his death, has been resurrected.

I wish you could come back to me, or I could find my way back to you.

There's a tap on the door, and my pulse quickens with anticipation. It could be Andrew, my brain thinks, and then, sure enough, Andrew appears. He steps into my bedroom.

Real Andrew or fake? Fake or real? I've done a good job of confusing myself.

"Just saying goodnight," he says with a humble little grin that seems to profess his love.

"Goodnight," I say, but my eyes linger—and I suppose they deliver another message.

Actually, I know they do.

I have given him an invitation I had not meant to send. Perhaps it was out of my control. Or maybe I sent it on purpose, but it was meant for someone else.

He slow-steps deeper into the room. "Have you been thinking about me, by any chance?" Leaning over the bed, he straightens the blanket that rises to my chest, hovering for a second before our eyes meet again.

To my surprise, he bends down and kisses me.

My brain tells me this isn't the real thing, only an imitation. The problem is, it (my brain) doesn't care. *I* don't care. I'll take the replica. Because it's been a long time since I've held Andrew, and I'll take him any way I can. I'm tired, and worn out, and the part of me that does all of the fighting and resisting must have slipped out for a drink because she can't be found. I admit that I wouldn't mind being kissed right now. Being held right now. Feeling less lonely right now.

Is there anything wrong with that?

It's better than wallowing in grief because my husband is dead and my son is on another planet.

The clone straightens up and takes a step backward. "I guess I'll see you in the morning."

I lay there and breathe. My internal voice tells him not to go, then tells me there's no way I'll be able to sleep knowing he's only footsteps away. I'm heartbroken and have been for years. I've been thinking of nothing but Andrew all day. And though my brain knows the clone is not the real thing, my body has no problem forgetting it.

I breathe in and when I let that breath go, a whisper escapes: "You can stay," it says, and alarms sound within my body.

My mouth has betrayed me.

His response is subtle. For a moment, he doesn't move at all. He probably doesn't want to appear too eager, too celebratory. It would be a shame to scare me off when he's on the cusp of getting what he wants. He must tread carefully lest he do something to extinguish my desire.

He says, "I thought so," and removes his shirt.

He gets in beside me, puts his arms around me, and pulls me close. When I stare into his eyes, I see Andrew's eyes. Andrew's face. The warmth our bodies generate lulls me into a blissful relaxed state. And then he touches his lips to mine, and I'm transported back to a time where life was happy and simple and never lonely. We kiss for a while before he pulls my tank top over my head and whispers my name. I'm falling into a heavenly cloud, deep in my memory of Andrew, into the past, when I was surrounded by love and security. Happiness.

We gently roll so that I'm on top of him, our bodies two halves, the smooth feel of arms and legs and everything else. Our warm bed and the heavy blankets shroud us from the rest of the world. Andrew's hands glide down my back and squeeze my waist, then venture into places he hasn't touched in years. His breathing and my own quicken, and my body begins to come alive in ways I'd forgotten were possible. He says, "I love you so much," and I'm about to say I love him, too, when something buzzes inside my head. Something that jars my eyes open.

I stop kissing him. Pause in a moment of stillness. *Did I just feel something, or didn't I?*

"What happened?" Andrew whispers and then kisses me again.

A dull ache at the top of my head oozes downward, and my ears fill with a familiar sound. The sound of Russia. The buzz of Jovians peering into my private thoughts.

A picture of the supreme being comes to mind: young cousin David, wherever he is, the center of Jovian oneness. *David wanted me to have more children.* I pull up, roll to the side. *David knows what I'm doing.* Suddenly I'm awash in a full-body blush of embarrassment.

My heart begins to bang on my chest so hard that it hurts. *What am I doing?*

Andrew reaches for me once again, pulls me close, and kisses me. "There's nothing to worry about. I'm here now. I'm with you."

"No." I push against his chest as a flash of panic writhes through me like a frightened animal desperate to get out.

He tries to kiss me again but I'm still pushing so he can't quite reach. "It's okay," he whispers. "Come here."

But it's too late. Now when I look at him, all I see is Drew. The spell is broken. I'm caught in a wave of self-disgust that has tossed me onto hard ground.

I have to get out of this bed.

I'm looking for my clothes. I don't want to have this conversation naked. I use my toes to retrieve my underwear and find the tank top under the pillow. As I put my clothes back on, I feel Drew's eyes on me.

"But you were doing it," he says somewhat gruffly, more like himself than my husband. "You were *enjoying* it. Why can't you just let it happen?"

"You're not Andrew," I say, sitting up. "I was confused."

He grabs his forehead and grumbles something I don't catch. "Does it even matter?" he says harshly.

"I wish you were him," I say. "I really wish you were."

"Well, I'm as close as you're ever going to get. I have his DNA. We're made of the same things. The exact same things."

"You're not the same," I say.

"Can't you just go with it?"

I throw the covers off of me and swing my legs over the side. The cold air shakes away the warmth we'd generated. The buzz in my head settles back, retreats.

"No," I say and I grab my pillow and head out of the room.

The doorbell rings.

I gasp as I sit up and rub my face. Light filters through the blinds. I'm in Drew's room, his bed. Alone. The prior night barges into my mind: the smooth skin-to-skin contact, gentle touch, entangled bodies. *I feel sick.*

The bell rings again.

Could Drew have gone out and forgotten his key? I should leave him out in the cold. I hope he's freezing and there's a blizzard, and that he's forgotten his coat.

I get up and search for something to put on but can't find anything because there's nothing of mine here. I'm in my underwear and flimsy tank top. See-through. I suppose it doesn't make a difference considering he saw all of this and more last night.

I rush down the hall with my arms crossed over my braless chest. Before I make it there, I recoil as Drew comes running from the kitchen, swooping into the foyer as if we're in a race to the front door.

"I'll get it. Go back to bed," he says with a swipe of his arm through the air.

But I'm already there, looking through the window. Seeing Fran. *Wait. Is it?* I see two hands. Can't be Fran.

I turn the bolt and pull the door open.

"What the hell?" Fran's deep voice quells my confusion. "You're here? With *him?*"

I turn and look at Drew as if I don't know who Fran could be talking about.

"No," I say, stupidly. "I can explain."

"No need," he says. "I've been trying to call you."

My phone. It's in the master bedroom. With my clothes.

"Where have you been? *You* disappeared!" I shout.

His shoulders droop a little. "I know I did. I'm sorry." Then he stares Drew down with the kind of FBI contemptuousness that no doubt once caused criminals to crack.

Instead of showing signs of being scared or worried, though, Drew wears a smirk, and I swear he's entertained by every awful aspect of this mortifying situation.

"I don't know who this joker is, but he's not Andrew, that's pretty obvious."

"It's not what you think. I just . . . " Words stumble away, tripping over folds in my brain.

I really regret my decision to not put a bra on. Or literally anything else.

Drew extends his hand. "It's nice to meet you, Fran."

With a subtle shake of his head, Fran says, "Not happening, bro."

Then he points at me. "This is exactly what you *didn't* want. You're in their house. Living with *this* guy. When did this happen?"

"Caroline let me leave Starbright. I couldn't find you, so I was trying to get away. I wanted to go to the Jovian mansion and hide out there, but then Drew followed me on his motorcycle. What was I supposed to do? I was exhausted and hungry. He gave me a ride."

This admittance embarrasses me to a soul-crushing extent. *How weak am I?*

The clone shrugs and says, "It's not her fault. I'm pretty irresistible."

"Oh, I know whose fault it is," Fran says in a deep octave. "And I'm not sure what to do about it yet, but you better believe —"

"Before you get yourself all worked up," Drew says, talking over him, "you should know it was consensual."

"Shut up, Drew!" My shoulders hunch up to my ears, and I shift my gaze to the floor. "Nothing happened. *Nothing!*"

"It wasn't nothing," he says, grinning.

"You weren't even there last night," I say, seething.

"That's funny because I woke up in your bed."

"Enough!" Fran's voice is like a clap of thunder that stops us from saying more. He looks up at the ceiling and swipes his hand across his forehead. "Svetlana, are you okay?"

"I'm fine. I'm only staying here until Evander gets back," I say. "I couldn't stay at Dana and John's anymore, not after they betrayed me. I'm here because of Evander. That's all."

Fran tilts his head in the direction of the living room. "Can we talk somewhere he's not? And maybe, uh, you could put some clothes on?"

Drew heads toward the sliding glass door, saying, "I'll be on the deck if you need me."

"No one needs you," Fran says.

I run to my room and put on a clean shirt and pair of leggings.

When I rejoin Fran in the living room, he looks up and says, "That's better. I mean, we're close but we're not that close." He smiles. His first since he walked through the door.

I say, "Please erase it from your memory."

"Well, I don't know if we need to go that far, but . . . "

He grins that big-softie grin that he saves for every once in a blue moon.

Before he can say anything more, I shout, "Fran, you have two arms!"

"Yup. And two hands too." He raises the new hand, opens and closes it a couple of times, eyes it with admiration.

"How did this happen?"

"Your in-laws," he says, shaking his head in awe. "They know things we humans have no idea about."

"And yet they're still pretty stupid when it comes to understanding us in general. They didn't hurt you, did they?"

"No. I mean, actually I have no damn idea. All I remember is that you and I made it into the lobby, you took off, I stayed behind to block them, you know, to give you a chance to get away."

"That's why I didn't want you to come!"

"Wait. I'm not finished. Suddenly Miranda's husband, Leo, appeared right beside me. I mean, he definitely didn't take the stairs down from the balcony. He literally materialized beside me. I told him he wouldn't get past me, and that was it. The last thing I remember."

"What did he do to you?"

"No clue. I woke up in a room with medical equipment and laboratory stuff. That gave me a minor meltdown, but nothing hurt, so it's not like he had smashed me in the head or knocked me out, and I wasn't groggy like I'd been drugged. Still, I was convinced they wanted to experiment on me—but I wasn't tied down in any way. I checked the door, and it was locked, and then I noticed a second door in the back of the room and ran for it. As soon as I reached for the knob, David came through—"

My mind skips back to the day in the park, when Fran and another FBI agent stood in front of me and Evander, shielding us from the hovering sphere of glowing energy David had become. "Did David want revenge?" I say.

"I assumed whatever was going to happen wouldn't be pretty. But he came in, in human form, and spoke to me without animosity. He told me they knew how to fix my arm, and asked if I wanted them to. I thought he meant they could give me a robotic limb, like the ones you talked about. I told him if they had an extra one of those lying around, I'd be happy to take it. I wasn't too worried because that type of prosthetic wouldn't require much in the way of surgery. But he said that wasn't what he meant."

"And?"

"I asked him what it entailed, and he said it was similar to a stem cell procedure."

"And it only took a day?"

"I guess it was a couple of days—I set out looking for you as soon as I left Starbright—and yeah, that's damn hard to believe. I asked him why he was doing it, and he said it was in his best interest to make life better for me. Better for *all* humans. He said he knew how to fix my arm, and fixing my arm would be helpful for me, so he wanted to do it."

I sit there, allowing the words to sink in. "He said that? I never would have expected him to say something like that to you."

"Well, I sure as hell didn't remind him that I'd aimed my gun at him that day at the UFO Festival. Though we both know bullets wouldn't have had an effect. The weird thing was, after talking to David, I wasn't afraid. I believed him when he said he wanted to help me."

"Did David do the procedure himself?"

"I have no idea who did it or how. Honestly, I don't want to know. I woke up, and my arm was there, just like it used to be."

"That's incredible." I laugh and grab his arm and give it a hug, then smile into Fran's face.

"I know," he says, brimming with cheerfulness. He hugs me close, squeezing me for a second before letting me go. Then says, "Which brings me to you."

I ease back into the couch.

"I want to ask you a question—and that's all it is, so don't get mad—just something for you to consider."

"Okay," I say.

"Promise you won't get the wrong idea."

I slump a little. "What is it?"

"Do you think it's possible the Jovians' intentions are good?"

"You mean, for Earth, or—"

He nods. "Earth and also," he hesitates, "the people they know. Like you."

I try not to take that the wrong way, though his words feel like a betrayal. "You know they've done some pretty awful things to me."

"Yeah, I know, but hear me out. All I mean is maybe they go about offering their help in the wrong way."

"Like forcing it on me? Like drugging me when I gave birth?"

"Which was terrible, I completely agree. But didn't you tell me that Caroline said that's how she gave birth?"

"Yes, she said that."

"And you're sure drugs were involved?"

"I felt really weird when I woke up, so—"

"But what if that's how they do it on Jupiter? What if that's the norm for Jovians? Not being conscious for the birth, I mean. Maybe they didn't consider that you'd want to be conscious, that being unconscious wouldn't be something you appreciated."

I'm blinking in the wake of his suggestion. I'd always assumed they had disregarded me and whatever I wanted.

A little crack of light has entered my brain. I know they don't understand me, but maybe *I* don't understand them. Maybe it goes both ways.

"Let me ask you this: Was Caroline surprised to find that you were angry with her? That day in the tower, when she brought Evander to you—"

"She was *always* surprised when I was angry."

I close my eyes as a painful realization comes to mind:

"Do you think sending Drew to look after me might be their way of helping, too?"

"I hate the idea of you being with him, but I gotta admit, it could be."

"I've told Caroline I wanted my husband back. I've said those exact words to her!"

"I'm sure you have."

I cover my mouth and whisper through my hand. "They probably think I want a replacement for Andrew." I pause to consider what this could mean. "They might think that if I have a new Andrew, I'll be happy again. They don't understand that Andrew can't be replaced."

And then my thoughts move yet a step further. "Oh my God, do you think they cloned Andrew just for me?"

"Whoa," he says, rubbing the scruff of his chin, "I don't know about that. Drew is at least twenty-five years old so that wouldn't add up, unless . . . "

"What?"

"I'm just wondering. Nah, never mind. It's stupid."

"Tell me."

"Maybe they did something to make him grow faster? I mean, judging from your son, it seems plausible. But, I don't know, I doubt they cloned him just for you."

I take a breath. "I hope you're right."

A moment passes as my brain recuperates from spinning out. I don't want to admit that the Jovians may have good intentions when it comes to me, but it's a possibility. At least some of the time. Still, I can't help but think they're dangerous in some ways. Even if their intentions are good, they're changing the world, changing the human species. What "improvements" will they make, and what will happen to the rest of us, the ones who are not improved?

Fran's inspecting his arm, twisting it this way and that. "I really do like my new arm."

"Yeah, me too."

"And you answered the door in your underwear," he says under his breath, "so I'm guessing you like the clone at least a little bit."

I groan, knowing I'll never live the moment down. "I just wanted him to be the real thing. I thought it might be good enough for pretending. I thought I could live with it."

"And now?"

Confessing to Fran feels like one step away from confessing to my husband. "Once you admit to yourself that something's not real, pretending doesn't work anymore."

"Good. You want to get out of here?"

I stand, checking over my shoulder to see where Drew is. He's no longer on the deck, but I didn't hear him come in. "Do you think he'll try to stop us?"

Fran doesn't even bother to glance over his shoulder. "He'd be stupid to try," he says with all of the authority of six-foot-tall FBI agent who just grew back a missing limb.

"I'll get my backpack." As I jog down the hall to my bedroom, my phone pings. It's a text message from Dana.

22

Fran stays in the car as I take the steps to the back door, entering a space redolent with the aroma of roast chicken, buttery noodles and . . . sugar cookies. Feelings-of-home food. My American home, anyway. I go straight to the fridge as if I still live there.

Dana wobbles in on crutches and says hello. If it weren't for the crutches, I might not have remembered what I saw in the bathroom.

"Looks uncomfortable," I say, gazing at her over my shoulder. "What did you do to it exactly?"

She sighs like a person who's annoyed with herself. "I fell out of the apple tree. I was trying to test a new weather gauge the team put together."

"The team?" I grab a bottle of juice and close the door.

"One of Starbright's, of course. They're always inventing new instruments, and this one detects severe weather for, you know, air travel. The weather forecast called for hail, which doesn't happen too often around here, so I set it up, and the branch I was on cracked and dropped out from underneath me."

I squinch my face and whisper *ouch*. "Didn't your parents ever tell you not to climb trees? You're not a bird, you know. Or can you fly?"

I'm only half joking.

She looks up. "Ha ha," she says.

"Can't David just fix it for you? He replaced Fran's arm, I'm sure he could do wonders with a broken leg."

"I'm very happy for Fran. And I suppose David could fix my leg, and he will if it doesn't heal on its own. I should be back to myself in a couple of days," she says looking down upon her broken limb with an air of disdain. "I'm embarrassed, to tell you the truth. I feel so darn clumsy."

"Where's John?"

He steps into the kitchen as if on cue, his laptop in hand. "Hey, honey. It's good to see you two back on speaking terms."

"Uh-huh," I say, still a little leery about the whole thing.

He places the computer on the kitchen table. "Before we sit, Dana, you'll be happy to know I purchased the flights. We're leaving at 10 p.m. out of Philadelphia."

"Wonderful," she says. "Thank you."

"Peru?" I say. "You're really going? I thought that was just a—"

"The trip has been delayed," Dana says, "but, yes, we're still going."

I open the fridge again, take out a glass container of macaroni and cheese leftovers. Mom's homemade recipe, the kind of comfortable food (what I call it) I love, and just what I need at this moment. "Mind if I eat this? It looks so good."

Dana's eyes light up and her lips curl into a half smile. "Help yourself."

I put it in the microwave, and hit the Reheat button. "Does John know the Jovians fixed Fran's arm?"

"I heard," John says, taking his seat at the table. "That's great."

Of course he knows. They all know.

The microwave stops with a string of beeps. I pull out the food, steamy and wafting creamy goodness. "So, what did you want to tell me?" I say as I take my place at the kitchen table.

Dana leans her crutches against the table and carefully lowers into her chair. "I'm just wondering," she says, "have you read the file yet?"

"The one I found in the basement of Starbright?"

I'd forgotten all about it.

Dana raises her brows and says, "Yes."

"I haven't. But I did have a question for you about a letter I found from Miss Sonja. It said you chose me."

"Oh," she says, "yes, that's true."

"You wanted to adopt me, specifically? And Miss Sonja said you could because you were taking Helena as well. I just wondered why you chose me. How was it you even knew I existed?"

"It's in your best interest to read the file," John says in one of his serious-dad tones.

"Can't you just tell me?"

Dana shakes her head. "It's complicated and—just better if you read the file."

"Fine." I roll my eyes. "I really don't care about the file unless there's something about Evander in there. I've already learned enough mind-blowing history for one week."

"That's understandable," John says with his usual manner of reassurance.

I continue to eat the macaroni and cheese. Then pause to say, "Have you two seen the spaceship?"

"Which one?" Dana asks.

"The one that crashed-landed—"

"Oh, yes, of course," she says. "Why?"

"Uncle Jimmy came to me in a dream. He said there's something on board that ship for me."

Dana trades glances with John. "I can't imagine what that might be," she says.

I continue to eat, until I realize they're both staring at me. I put my fork down in preparation for whatever is coming next.

"Listen." Dana pats the tabletop. "Now that we're here together, and we're all calm, I want to say something important."

"All right," I say, though her words cause internal dread.

"John and I had hoped that one day you would come to love the family. Not just us, but the Jovians. You're the only human in the family, I'm sure you realize that."

"Yes, that's pretty clear."

"For years now, the Jovians have tolerated what they consider somewhat unusual behavior on your part." She checks in with me for a second before continuing. "Simply because they don't understand you the way John and I do. But the truth is, they don't know what to do with you anymore. Maybe they never did."

That's the kind of statement that hits like a smack to the back of my head. "They don't have to do *anything* with me. They can leave me alone, let me live my life."

"Yes, I know that's what you want." She adjusts her position in the chair, leaning forward. "And I get it, I truly do, but that's not what I mean."

"What do you mean?"

She blinks in a contemplative way. She's so human it's uncanny. "There are some questions you need to ask yourself. For starters, what is it that you want?"

My shoulders rise on their own accord. "It's pretty simple, actually. I want the same things I've wanted all along.

An ordinary life with my child, without Jovians breathing down my neck, dictating our every move."

"I understand," she says. "Is there anything else?"

I go blank. *What is Dana trying to get me to say?* It's not like I'm going to ask for a car or a house or money. I can make those things happen on my own. If the Jovians leave me alone, I'll happily take care of myself and Evander for the rest of our lives. "I want a life filled with children and apple pie and trips to the bookstore. Maybe a part-time job, if that's not too much to ask. I mean, that's what I've always wanted: the life I had with Andrew." I laugh in that ironic way I have learned to laugh.

Dana looks at me with dire seriousness. "That's what I thought, but I wanted to make sure. Okay."

"Okay?"

"I'll tell Caroline."

"Caroline already thinks she gave me the answer by sending me a clone of Andrew. If you see her, you can tell her it's not going to work. No one can take the place of my husband."

"I know," Dana says, "and this is exactly the kind of information that will help her understand you better."

"Please don't ask me to work on my relationship with Caroline because I won't."

"I wouldn't ask you to do that."

"So Fran was right? They want to help me? Is that what all of this is about? I thought Caroline was trying to trick me into—"

"She does want to help." Dana sits back. "We all do, believe it or not."

Dana seems beaten tonight. Weighed down. Or maybe she's just tired and her leg is causing her pain.

"Thank you," I say. "But what's the matter? Are you in pain?"

"Me? Oh," she says, with downcast eyes, "I'm fine. But we do have one more thing to show you, and you may not like what you see. Just, please, promise you won't panic."

I don't think she meant to throw a grenade, but there's no way to brace oneself when a Jovian tells you not to panic, so I say nothing and hope not to detonate when she shows me whatever it is she needs to show me.

"How bad is it going to be?" I say, addressing John this time.

He opens the laptop computer. "It's not bad. We'll let you be the judge."

Tapping a few keys, he brings up a web page and turns the computer around to face me.

A news clip begins to play.

It's a city street, looks like Philadelphia. Broad Street, or one of the other historic sections. A dense crowd of people walk down the middle of the road like they would for a protest, only none of them look angry. Four or five who are dressed in business suits lead the group. A Black woman I've seen before—she's a politician—along with a couple of other ladies, a tallish man in the center of them all, and an Asian man on the opposite side. All around them groups of people hold signs and banners, cheering and waving.

What does this have to do with me?

The camera zooms in on the tall man who's front and center, and I realize it's my son. It's Evander, though in much older form. He's wearing a suit and has a closely cropped businessman haircut. He looks like an adult, a man in his thirties. Which would make him my age, maybe older.

How can this be?

The crowd begins to chant, "Peterman! Peterman! Peterman!" The camera pans to the left and right to show the depth of the adoring fans, the sidewalk brimming with human beings. "Peterman for Senator. Peterman for a fair America!"

"My son is a politician?" I say.

I remember Uncle Jimmy's words, how he said the new Jovian-humans would move into leadership positions. How they would "become Earth's presidents and prime ministers."

"He's going to be the senator of Pennsylvania," Dana says, and I feel her attention on me, as she waits for my response.

"How do you know he'll win?"

"He'll win," she says.

John seconds it with a "Yes, he will."

The Jovians are going forward with their plan to influence human thinking, to dispense a nonviolent philosophy, to create a more caring race that thinks outside of their egocentric world, one that considers the rest of the universe. But in what other ways will they be different? If they're smarter and stronger and more likable, those advantages could be used in other ways—ways that will dominate the species. And what might that mean? If the strong survive, what will happen to the weaker race? What will happen to the unimproved humans?

Uncle Jimmy's "Don't let them do it" haunts me. Could I have stopped them? He also told me it was "written in the stars." So which is it?

"They're doing it," I whisper. "They're going ahead with their plan."

Dana pauses the clip. "Yes, they are."

"How long has he been back?" I say. "On Earth, I mean."

"I'm not sure. They had one of his brothers handling the early part of the campaign."

"And by *brothers* you mean the clones. But how can that be? The ones I've seen look like twenty-year-old Evander."

"They haven't all been to Jupiter," John says, "but a group of them went last year."

I'm confused. "Going to Jupiter has made Evander age faster?"

"Yes," he says, "and that's normal."

"And some of the clones had traveled before he did, so they can play the role of Evander Peterman, the politician, when necessary?"

"Yes," Dana says. "When necessary."

"But this is the real Evander in this video? You're sure?"

"It's your son." Dana's chin twitches as if she's holding back a cry. Her eyes fill, though tears don't fall.

I don't know what to say. I believe Dana speaks the truth, and yet I can't get myself to accept it. This man on the screen is not the son who left me in Russia. He's a grown-up. Evander had a short childhood as it was, but this is unbelievable. I turn back to the video. Un-pause it. The Peterman chant continues. The crowd bumps down the middle of the avenue, following their leader, hundreds of followers, probably five hundred or more, strong. Evander smiles and waves, as charismatic as ever. The people react to him with shouts and cheers as if he were a human God. My son brims with confidence and excitement, and what I can only assume is happiness.

He looks happy.

"Listen," Dana says, resting her hand on my arm and guiding my focus away from the screen. "From what I know and what I see, it seems to me you're going to have to choose."

She has approached with careful words, probably because she wants to avoid setting off the land mine she knows rests at the center of my chest. Still, what she says has the opposite effect. Rather than calming me, easing me into awareness, she has put me on guard.

"They want to push me out of the way," I say, with bile in my voice. "They have always wanted me out of the way."

Her eyes tell me I'm wrong. "You have choices," she says.

"And what are they?" My breathing is erratic. I have that trapped feeling I so often get when faced with issues that surround the Jovian family.

"You can stay here, in Kirksberg, if you want to, with the family, and you can visit with Evander whenever you like …" She pauses as if to gauge my response.

I shake my head, because that is inconceivable. I won't stay with the family. "What else? What are the other options?"

"You can go somewhere else." She sits back in her chair. "Anywhere."

"They are letting me go?"

"You've always been free to go."

And then it hits me. "You mean without Evander."

"You can still visit him, but he'll always be surrounded by family."

"You're telling me I won't have a say in my son's life."

"He has great respect for you. What you think, your wishes and values, will always weigh into his decision making. I have no doubt about that."

"They probably want me to go back to Russia."

"I don't know that they have a preference," she says.

I rub my forehead and then press my knuckles into my lips. I'm losing him. That's all I can think: *I'm losing him.*

"I can't live without Evander," I say. "I want to go somewhere else with him. He and I will come back here to visit, maybe once in a while, but I can tell you right now, we will *not* stay in Kirksberg. I'm his mother, and I still make the decisions."

I know how ridiculous this sounds considering what I've just seen in the video, but I say it anyway. Because screw them: I *am* his mother. I always will be, no matter how old he is.

Both Dana and John appear to be thinking of next moves. John tilts his head and makes a humming sound as if preparing a suggestion. Instead of speaking, though, he bites a fingernail, which is very human of him. The silence makes me angry.

Is there nothing I can do?

"Of course you're his mother," Dana says, "but I have to ask, what about what Evander wants? From what I see in this video clip, he seems to be on board with the family plan."

I hold back my anger as her words bounce off a wall I've erected in my brain. A few words can't topple the stronghold that's grown over a decade of motherhood, a decade in which I have prepared myself for the day the family would attempt to steal my son. "They could be making him do it," I say in the hope that delivering the words with calm makes it a sane suggestion, a viable possibility. "He and I are very close. He will want what I want."

Dana brings her hands together and weaves her fingers in front of her, resting them on the table and staring at them as if they hold a crystal ball.

I reach out and cover her hands with one of my own. "Is there anything else I should know? Please tell me."

She meets my eyes, and with an abundance of tranquility, says, "If what you say is true, if Evander will want what you want, then you have nothing to despair."

Like that, the world brightens. My mother says there is nothing to despair. And while some lingering worry persists like flashes of heat lightning in the stormy atmosphere of my mind, the majority of clouds clear, allowing me to breathe freely again.

"Everything will be all right," my mother says. "Do you trust me?"

I do. Before I knew she was Jovian, I trusted her for years.

And now, in spite of that affiliation, I know she wants what's best for me. "Yes," I tell her.

"Have you finished eating?"

I show her the empty bowl.

"Good. Then it's time for you to go to Starbright. Evander is there. He's waiting for you."

"Oh my . . . " An overenthusiastic screech rises from deep within me as I leap to my feet.

"Come, give us a hug," Dana's chin quivers as she reaches out for John with one hand and for me with the other. I'm so excited to see Evander that I don't know if I can stand still long enough to get them both in an embrace. I open my arms, and the three of us make a circle. Me, my mother, my father. I don't care anymore that they're Jovian. Dana and John have been good to me. They're my parents, and I love them.

For a fleeting second it feels like we're saying goodbye. Like I'm going on a trip and won't see them for a long time. But I'm not.

I'm going to see Evander, and I can't wait.

23

I burst from the house, my coat half on, half off. Through the passenger-side window, Fran's eyes grow large.

"Are they after you?" his voice booms as I open the car door. He must have turned the car around and backed in after he'd dropped me off because it's facing the street. It's idling, too, his hand on the gear shift, the other grasping the wheel, ready to take off at warp speed.

"Evander's back. He's home. Evander is here, Fran!"

"In Kirksberg?"

"At Starbright," I say, glowing like a new star.

His skepticism steels his face. "Hold up. Did Dana tell you this?"

"Yes, but—"

"Can you trust her? I mean, are you sure you can trust her?"

I didn't doubt her when she told me, though come to think of it, she just told me what I've wanted to hear for weeks.

"She wasn't lying," I say with confidence.

"Okay, okay let's think this through," he says. "We have to assume it could be a trap."

"Not this time. I don't think so."

Could it be? I was so sure I could trust Dana and John just a second ago.

"No, it's *not* a trap," I say.

His brown eyes scan my face.

"They showed me a video of Evander in Philadelphia. He's running for senator."

"Okay," he says. "You're sure it was him?"

"I'm sure. Please, let's go."

As he turns onto the road, my knees are bobbing up and down, and I can't stop rubbing my hands together. My heart tells me time is as slippery as sand and will find a way through the spaces in between my fingers if I'm not careful—or that something will get in between me and this opportunity to see my son. The good moments in life pass so quickly while the moments of sadness and longing move like boulders pushed uphill.

I'm going to see Evander!

I close my eyes and will myself to breathe more slowly, afraid I'm teetering toward hyperventilation. Evander is a grown man. He's running for senator. The news clip playing in my mind tugs at my worry center. What if this is what he wants? What if they're not making him do it? But, no, it will be okay. Dana says I have nothing to despair.

"I'm coming in with you," Fran says.

"Oh, no, not this time. If there's any chance this isn't—"

"Then I can help you get out of it."

"No, Fran. You've gone above and beyond already. Whatever happens, I'm ready for it. Dana is going to tell Caroline what I want. You were right, she wants to help me."

"You're sure of that?"

"I am."

"Keep your phone in your hand," he says. I look up and realize we're here, passing the security gate, sliding down the modest hill into the parking lot.

I feel for my phone in my coat pocket. "I've got it."

"Text me when you get inside. I'll be right here with the car running. If anything at all seems off—"

"It's going to be fine. Evander is here."

There are things you just know. Things that are built into your DNA.

Still, I hesitate before I go. I'm so excited to see my son, and I want Fran to feel the same happiness. "You have to call Lisa and Max."

He veers back a little as if I've thrown something sticky at him.

"Just tell them you still love them."

"I want to," he says, and as he gazes out the windshield, I can see the doubt creep into his eyes, the fear that keeps him from getting what he wants.

"They still love you. Action is the cure for fear, remember? You told me that."

He deflates, frustrated with me for saying so, I suppose, but then he perks back up, the anger dissipating. "I do want to call them."

"Do it," I say. "Please."

"Yeah, okay." Then he puts his stern FBI face back on. "Be sure to keep that phone in your hand until Evander shows up."

"I will," I say, and I stretch myself across the car seat and grab him in a hug. He's so wide, like a small billboard; it's hard to get a sturdy hold on him. Either way, the hug doesn't feel big enough, so I back up a bit, smile and rub my nose into his. "You're a good man, Fran Vasquez. I've always been a huge fan."

He rolls his eyes and shakes his head, so overwhelmed

that apparently he can't speak. He taps the steering wheel a few times. "You better go."

I move back into the passenger seat.

"Good luck," he says, reminding me that none of this is said and done, none of it is over until I get to see my son.

"Thank you. Call Lisa now." I open the car door while I wait for his response.

"I will."

"Now, please."

"Right now?" he says loudly.

"Press the button, or I'm not leaving."

He grumbles as he grabs the phone, then hesitates as he stares at the screen. But he does it. He presses the button.

The entrance to Starbright opens as I approach, though I don't recall it being an automatic door. I'm inching along now before I pass through so I can see inside. The lobby seems to be empty.

"Evander?" I say, as I take in the vast space with polished floors, the unmanned receptionist desk and spiral staircase that stretches upward.

And then I see David observing me from the balcony.

The door isn't automatic. David has opened the door for me.

"Hello, Svetlana," he says. "It's nice to see you."

"Hi, David." I attempt to greet him in an ordinary way, though I can't stop envisioning his true form. It occurs to me that I'm not holding my phone like Fran told me to. A feeling of electricity prickles across my scalp and raises my hair the way it always used to when I looked a Jovian in the eye.

"But it's not that way anymore, is it?" he says, reading my mind.

My tongue sticks to the roof of my dry mouth. Maybe I

should tell him how nice it was for him to have fixed Fran's arm.

Caroline's voice appears from behind: "You're here. Wonderful."

She and Miranda have come through the doors that lead to the fake office and the spaceship in the basement.

I back up a step. I'd thought I wouldn't have to deal with the others today. I imagined Evander would be right here when I arrived. Are they trying to . . . *oh my God!* Did Dana lie to me?

"I'm supposed to meet Evander," I say, fighting my flight reflex.

"We'll bring you to him now," Caroline says, as if I'm a guest and she's a host who doesn't hold grudges.

"Why didn't he come to get me himself?"

Caroline stops. Stares. Tilts her head. "We're happy to escort you."

"He's in a private place," Miranda says, "where you can say goodbye."

My ears prick, and I fumble for my phone in the deep well of my coat pocket. I'm so keyed up that I pull it out and inadvertently toss it onto the stone floor.

It slides up to Miranda's feet, and she bends over and lifts it, face up, before I can reach it. "You've broken the screen," she says.

I can't text Fran. I can't text Fran even if I need to.

I take a step backward. "What do you mean 'say goodbye'?"

Next thing I know David appears beside Caroline. I didn't see him come down from the balcony. I didn't hear the tap of his feet upon the floor as he crossed the lobby. And yet there he is, real as day, looking like my husband, though his eyes are sharp instead of kind.

He says, "We are your family, and we will never hurt you."

The words cause my eyes to drop closed, my body to tremble as drastically as it did that day in the park when David became the supreme being and said the same thing. So they fixed Fran's arm, and now they're going to *what*—take me prisoner?

Have Dana and John, and maybe even Fran betrayed me?

The three Jovians remain still. Like AI robots listening for their wake words, they're waiting for my response. "I, uh," I scratch my head and consider running. The entrance is only a few steps away. If I can make it outside, Fran will see—

"Mom."

"Evander," I shout, though I don't mean to. I turn to find him in a corridor on the opposite side of the room. But is it really him? It could be one of his so-called brothers.

As he approaches, he smiles with his whole face. He's older, that much is apparent. He has the jawline of a grown man, the stubble, the sturdy angles and solid construction of an adult. He looks just as he did in the video John showed me. I start toward him, my urgency boiling inside. When I reach him, the words clog up my throat. I crack to pieces. I've missed so many years with him. Time has become fleeting and slick, a plane of glass I'm afraid I'll break if I so much as move. I feel as if I have crossed an entire country to get to Evander, as if I have climbed a mountain and found him standing at the pinnacle.

"How are you?" he says, his kind eyes reaching for me.

I want to tell him that I'm a different person from the one he left in Russia, that part of me has become old and worn, ragged and weak due to a newly broken foundation. My past has been rebuilt with mottled shades of truth. Truths I haven't yet had time to piece together. Some I'm not sure I can accept.

I've fought my way to this moment, back to my son. And

now that I'm here, now that we're together, I don't know what to do, what to say.

Where do we go from here?

The answer to that, apparently, is to a room down the hall, a room with two chairs and nothing else. As soon as we enter this room, I become saturated with the feel-good chemicals that flood my body with relief. The other Jovians have remained behind. We have privacy, as Miranda so callously pointed out.

And now Evander and I are standing two feet apart, and it's difficult for me to accept that I'm the mother of this grown man with serious hair and businessman slacks and a sweater that looks like cashmere. This man who resembles me more than he ever did before. When I'm close enough to hug him, I do so with abandon.

He feels like the person I remember. The kid back in Russia, patient and yet eager for his independence. As much as he's changed physically, I know it's my Evander and not a clone.

We're still in a hug when he says, "It's so good to see you." The sound of his voice is like honey in my ear, and the love inside of me swells like too-ripe fruit, so sweet it's painful.

When we pull apart, I wipe my eyes.

"You never cry," he says.

"Sometimes I do."

"You knew I'd be back. Edmund told you. You must be getting soft in your old age."

I laugh a little. "You went all the way to Jupiter and left me alone with the family."

"It was an unfortunate necessity." We share a look before

his cheerfulness withers and his eyes seek out the floor. "Can you forgive me?"

"They took you. It wasn't your fault. What were you supposed to do?"

"You told me they would come, and you were right, not that I ever doubted you."

"And they cloned you, too. Years ago, but you already know that."

"Yes." His placid expression remains unchanged. "It was also—"

"An unfortunate necessity?" I say, crossing my arms over my chest. "Of course it was."

"Mom?"

"And now you are *this* person," I say in my motherly tone, the one I used when I was the adult, and he, still a child. "You're an adult with an enormous amount of responsibility. Are you all right with this?"

"It's nothing I can't handle."

"I know that's true." I turn away as my face gives in to the disappointment I feel. "You're a wonderful child."

Instead of joining me in the laugh I'd hoped for, he takes my hands and smiles bittersweetly. "Listen, you know I would never lie to you. And I know you don't trust the family and what they're doing, but what they're doing is right and good." He pauses there, then says, "It's for the good of all existence."

I realize that I'm shaking my head, not because I don't agree but because I'm only human with a mind that opens only so far, and I know this is one of those things I must take his word for.

"What they're doing has to be done," he says.

I don't want to believe him, but I have no choice. It's Evander. I do trust him. He's no longer a child who needs protecting—even if I could protect him—which I realize now was never a possibility.

"It's necessary," I say. "I get it."

"Earth is not just a beautiful planet where humans happened to sprout out of the ground. It's a stopping point. A resting place in the universe. And more than that, a place of rejuvenation. It can't die."

Goose bumps grow out of the skin on my arms. "You can stop it from dying? Stop the global warming and the war and the drought and fires."

"All of those things."

A strange mixture of pride and surreality spreads through me. "I'm so glad to know I produced the human being who has this ability," I say with a humorous air.

He laughs the same coy way he used to in Russia.

"You always did so well in your homeschool courses," I add, and once again, we laugh together, and I feel as if our souls connect, or maybe *reconnect* is a better word.

"I have to show you something," he says in a lighthearted manner.

"Fine," I say. "As long as it's not more clones."

We walk together down the corridor, into a part of the building I've never visited.

Evander glances at an eye recognition panel in front of the next door we come to.

"Are you taking me to the telescope?"

A blunt click occurs before the door pops opens. "Did Dad ever show you the planetarium?"

"I didn't know there was one."

I step into a globe of a space. It's like being inside an immense egg, white and smooth, domed with a small cluster of lounge chairs at its center. He gestures to one for me and sits in the one beside it. Then he reaches for something on the floor, a gadget of some kind that fits in the palm of his hand. Maybe a remote control.

"I want to take you on a short tour through the universe," he says.

"I didn't know we'd be traveling today. Is there a seatbelt I should put on?"

He smiles, his eyes twinkling. "You've always had a great sense of humor."

"*Spasibo*," I say.

The lights dim and the night sky spreads wide overhead. The moon's silvery old-man face makes an entrance followed by what appears to be the North star, the ceiling like a map of the many constellations—Ursa Major and her Big Dipper, Cassiopeia and her obvious *W*, the Great Square of Pegasus. Soon after that, Evander shifts our perspective so that Orion's brilliant belt and its surrounding star garden of origination swoop into sight.

This tour is not much different from the trips through the universe that I've taken in my mind. Streaming toward us like a vibrant river, a cascading rush of glittering light comes into view, and Evander says, "*galaxias kyklos*, also known as The Milky Way." Shooting stars flit this way and that like sparks loosed from a crackling fire.

"Are we right in the middle?" I ask.

"Yes, we are. Lively, isn't it?"

His face wears the same look of wonder Andrew's used to.

A comet flames past, its fiery tail singeing the darkness with a bright trail. Evander takes us in close to Mars for a moment, then flies full speed ahead, lingering when we arrive at the massive body of Jupiter.

"The gas giant," he says. "Perhaps the most impressive planet in all the solar system."

"I'm sure that's what the Jovians like to think," I mutter as if I'm angry. "How was your trip, by the way?"

"Great," he says as he homes in on one of Jupiter's moons and says, "Callisto." We continue past, and it's only a moment before a star I know quite well comes into view. It shines with a gentle brightness that feels both powerful and pure, an illumination of Andrew's kind and gentle soul. When I realize I've been staring for some time, I pull myself away and find Evander watching me.

"You're still in love with my father," he says.

"I miss him terribly. But obviously he has a, um, completely new kind of existence."

"Yes," he says, smiling as if charmed by my fumbling words. "In this universe, he's a star. A star that brings you comfort."

He clicks the remote, and the lights go back up. I turn to him, and he lifts something from the chair beside the one he sits in. "It's important that you see this."

It's my file. The one I rolled up and stuffed in my coat pocket, rumpled now and worn around the edges. I'm tired of seeing it: first Caroline pushed it on me, then Dana, and now Evander.

"I've seen it," I tell him, "and I already know. My American parents are Jovian. They chose me from the orphanage."

"Yes, but there's more. You haven't read the whole thing."

"I didn't have time. I've been busy searching for my son." I make a face that says "you're a pain in the butt, but I still love you," or, at least that's what I mean for it to say.

"I understand. Maybe you would like to take a look now. When we were in Russia, you told me you didn't know much about your birth parents."

"I have vague memories. I know they were KGB. They went out one day and never returned. They were killed. We've spoken about this."

He opens the file. "Their names are Maria and Oleg Petrov."

The sounds of the names attach like little pins that prick my insides. Somehow they ring familiar.

"I didn't know the names of my parents," I say. "I don't remember if I called them Mama and Papa or something else, and Sonja wouldn't share their given names. But Maria and Oleg somehow sounds right."

"Do you want to see pictures?"

"You found photos of them?"

"They're in the file. They've been in the file. All you had to do was open it."

I lean closer to him. He splays the folder across his lap, then shuffles through a few pages and holds out three well-preserved photographs. I reach for them, suddenly eager to see.

The first is my mother. With her long brown hair and blue eyes, she looks a lot like me. Or, I should say I resemble her. Not clone perfect, but the familial connection is clear. My father is pictured in front of a wrought iron fence wearing a full-length winter coat and holding a rolled newspaper. There's a church with many onion domes in the background. He's thin with a gleam of mischievousness in his eye. A third photo shows them together. My mother holds a swaddled baby. Me, I guess.

"They're travelers," Evander says, interrupting my thoughts.

"They *are* travelers? Present tense?"

"They are."

"My birth parents."

"Yes."

"Are alive."

"Yes. They travel to various locations in the galaxy."

He points to the ceiling above us, which only moments before illuminated pictures of outer space.

"You mean, like lightyears away?"

"Sometimes," he says.

"Like Ida Moore," I say because nothing else, no other thought or word comes to the surface. "So, she isn't unstable."

"Ida? Not at all. She's a brilliant intellectual. One of the smartest human beings I've ever met. She's been a friend to the Jovians for many years now."

I feel as if I've just fallen down mentally. I need a second to grasp all of this, to make sense of it.

"So, my parents left me alone to—"

"Travel," he says. "Yes. They didn't intend to have you."

Caroline said the same thing.

"You weren't convinced when Caroline told you," he says, and I realize he may have just read my mind.

"I thought she was trying to hurt me."

"She wasn't, but she didn't do a good job of conveying the information. Your parents met the family before you were born. As Caroline tried to tell you, they didn't plan to have children. They had already agreed to become travelers before Maria was pregnant. Caroline was genuine when she told you no one, none of the Jovians, has ever meant to hurt you. And you know I would never purposely hurt you."

So Fran was right.

"The problem as I see it, outside of basic communication skills, is that the Jovians don't understand humans the way you and I understand them—because they're a very different species, one that's not built on 'being nice' versus having a position of animosity or holding grudges or judging others. They don't understand 'being nice' because they never mean to harm. It's a foreign concept for them. Does that make sense?"

This new perspective pushes a button that begins a chain reaction: my understanding falls into place like fainting dominoes. "I think so," I say, but I still find all of this hard to believe. "My human parents gave me up? They didn't die, they weren't KGB?"

"They *were* KGB, but they didn't die. They left you so they could travel the universe."

"They didn't want a child, so they gave me to the orphanage?"

"Not right away. They loved you. Giving you up wasn't an easy decision. Your mother was very conflicted. Both of your parents were, actually, but especially Maria."

His explanation doesn't make it better. "Somehow she was persuaded," I say.

"Maria and Oleg agreed that what has to be done—what the Jovians must do—is necessary."

The word *necessary* plunges into my arms like a baby flung from the roof of a building. I've caught it, and my world comes together like metal filings drawn to a magnet. Uncle Jimmy's *It was written in the stars* flashes through my mind.

I've never been at the helm of my ship.

"So they left me with Ms. Sonja. Why not give me to Dana and John right away?"

"Your mother wanted you to stay in Russia. The Jovians don't know why. I personally think she worried the family wasn't up to the task of raising a young human. Maria planned to come back from her first excursion and raise you herself."

"But she didn't."

"No, her travels were extended, no fault of her own."

"For *years?*" I say. "Her travels were extended—"

"That's correct."

"So Dana and John came to get me and raised me in Jovian sight."

"The Jovians had made a promise," he says, giving weight to the words. "If Maria and Oleg didn't return by the time you aged out of the orphanage, they would step in."

It makes sense. My life with the bright light of truth shined upon it. But something still bothers me. I have a sinking feeling, and now I realize why. "What about me and your father? Was that planned as well?"

Evander places his hand on my arm as if to slow the cascade of my fearful thoughts. "That's what is so wonderful about all of this: it wasn't. Fate of a different sort brought you two together."

"What do you mean?"

"I mean that Andrew meeting you was just Andrew going out for ice cream."

Can this be true? We met the way young people meet? Simply because they happen to be at the same place at the same time. Two unsuspecting souls coming together, grabbing hold, and deciding never to let go?

"Caroline might have set it up if it hadn't happened the way it did, but she didn't have the chance," Evander says. "My father insisted they allow him to attend not only college but grad school. Soon after he returned to Kirksberg, he entered your ice cream shop on his own accord, and what happened after that was a whole different kind of fate."

I'm so relieved I want to cry.

"And you know I wouldn't lie to you," he says.

"I believe you," I say, softly.

I sense his pride in being the one to tell me.

"What upsets me is that he didn't even know about his family," I say. "They raised him without telling him who they were."

"That was purposefully done. My grandfather, who

you've always called Uncle Jimmy," he says, as if I didn't know, "insisted that whatever child came from his work in the lab must be as human as possible. And the only way that could happen would be to conceal the truth about the family line. The child would have to go out there and make friends and partake in life like any other human child would."

"They also knew he wouldn't live long," I add.

"Only months after he was born, they became aware that it wasn't likely he'd live past ten or twelve."

"And David couldn't fix him?"

"I can see why you might think that, but no. David couldn't fix him."

"And he lived to thirty."

"When he reached the age of twenty, the family encouraged him to meet someone. They thought, and hoped, he would fall in love while he was still very young, but my father took his time. I guess he was waiting for the right person to come along."

"And that person was me," I say.

It occurs to me that whether we were set up or not makes no difference because our love, regardless, was real.

Evander shifts in his chair, leaning closer to me. "When my father died, you wanted to travel back in time, is that right?"

"Oh, well . . ." I pull back, slightly embarrassed. "Yes, that's true, but it's not something I actually believed was possible. I never told anyone."

"Right, but thanks to David you don't actually have to tell anyone in order for others to know," he says. "As you are well aware, the Jovians share a collective consciousness. David was always impressed by how astute your thoughts were."

I remember when David paid me a compliment using that word. It was the night Uncle Jimmy left for Mintaka for good.

"But I'm no longer connected to the family," I say.

"We thought that was for the best, as I'm sure you agree."

He just said "we" like he's part of them. My son is part Jovian, part of the collective consciousness he speaks of, and I should have known that would happen, but his "we" still surprises and bothers me. It's like the Jovians have claimed a piece of him, taken part of him from me. This is a new Evander, I realize. Not one I know completely. He's changed in ways I'm not familiar with. He's different not only because he's older but because the boy I knew no longer exists.

And this makes me a little afraid of him.

Then again, no matter how he's changed and what he's gone through and witnessed and knows, he's still my son. He's still loyal to me. He's proven his loyalty by showing up today, by taking me away privately and telling me everything I need and want to know.

I can still trust him.

"Tell me about wanting to go back in time," he says.

"It seems kind of silly when you say out loud."

"It's not," he says with the firmness that comes with adulthood.

"Okay." I ease back in the chair and take a breath. "When your father died, I felt he was still very close to me, that if I reached back somehow, with my mind, I'd be able to grab onto him and pull myself into the place where he still lived. Then we could—" I stop. I can't say it. It sounds too desperate.

"Go ahead," he says.

"Still be together."

He sits back. "I get that. And it's so interesting that you say it."

"My mind kept thinking of these things even though I knew it couldn't be done. It was a very strong urge."

"But it *can* be done. Your instincts were right. It's possible for you to travel back in time," he says, "though not the way you imagine."

This isn't what I expected to hear, and my heart does one of those anxious butterfly flutters. I sense that he's about to make an offer of some kind.

"Time is an illusion," he says. "The difference between the past, present, and future is only a stubbornly persistent misperception."

"I think I've read that before. Is it something Einstein said?"

"Yes," he says. "You know Uncle Jimmy knew Einstein quite well?"

"Why am I not surprised?" I shake my head in an incredulous way.

He continues: "Time is subject to the individual. Time and space are intertwined. It moves slower as gravity increases."

"Is that why you're older now? Because you were moving very fast on your travels to—"

"I'm older now because it suits the plan. More important, what I want you to know is that I have traveled very far and very fast, and you can do something similar—and doing so will get you back to my father."

I've slipped into a surreal state. The kind where I tell myself I can't be hearing correctly. I must be dreaming. Is Evander really here? Am I?

"Stay with me, Mom. I know it's overwhelming, but try to focus. We don't have much time."

I'm scared. I don't know why. This should be wonderful news. Exciting, exhilarating news. But if I accept it, if I buy into it, will I end up disappointed? If it doesn't happen, will I go mad? Maybe I already am! Then again, if it does happen, if it works and I travel back to Andrew, will things be just like they used to be? Will we love each other the way we loved each other ten years ago? Will I be the same Svetlana and he be the same Andrew? Or will I wish I remained here, in my original life, where I simply longed for what I once had?

"You can travel back to my father," Evander says, "to a different version of your world."

"One where he won't die when he's thirty?"

"Yes, that's correct."

He just said I can go to a place where Andrew won't die. *A different version of my world.* It's like I've been sailing down the street and have crashed into a massive rock that popped up without warning. I've been thrown overboard, and now I'm holding my breath to keep from drowning.

When I finally let go of my breath, the air rushes out, and I've forgotten what to do next. I'm gripping the chair's armrests, holding on for dear life, my eyes blinking like I can't wake from an outrageous dream. I can't think. I can't breathe. I've slipped out of my own mind. . . .

Evander places his hand on my back. It's warm and very real, like an anchor that stops my slide away from reality, stops the fear and conjecture that have made a swirling mess of my brain. In a moment, I regain a sense of calm.

"You will leave this world, and you will have a new life, a different life."

I sit up. "A life without Jovians?"

"Yes."

It sounds wonderful, until something occurs to me: If I live in a world without Jovians, where will Evander be?

"And what about you? Will I have you?" I say.

He tells me no with his eyes, and I wish I hadn't asked.

"I'll be *here,*" he says, reaching for my hand.

I grab hold and squeeze tight.

"I have much to do. If the family is successful, what we've done will affect the universe throughout time. Earth is where everything came together just right. We can't let it slip away.

We have to try. And I'm an important piece of the puzzle. I have a part to play."

The Jovian phrase ripples through my mind.

"But I can't leave without you," I say.

"Of course you can."

I open my mouth to protest, but he stops me.

"Staying here is the right thing for me," he says, "and you have to do what's right for you. You deserve happiness. If I can make that happen for you, I'll be happy as well."

Then he lets my hand go. "It's best if you leave. Trust me. This world will not always be a good place for your kind."

My eyes grow large. "My kind?"

He rubs his chin. A sad preoccupation dulls the light in his eyes.

"You mean human beings, don't you? Ordinary ones?"

His nod is almost imperceptible. "I'll take care of them as best I can, no matter what happens," he says. "You have my word."

I'm afraid if I try to speak, I'll lose it. "I know you will, but what if—"

"You're a wonderful mother, an exceptional human being. You've raised me well, and now I have work to do, the work I was born to do. We don't have time for what-ifs."

My heart is breaking because I know he's right. I have to leave. And he has a job I can't even fathom in front of him.

There's nothing to say. I need to get back to Andrew, and I also know that I will be heartbroken for the rest of my life.

Caroline wasn't lying to me. Edmund wasn't lying to me. Miranda wasn't lying to me.

I know this now because Evander wouldn't lie to me.

24

As we cross the Starbright lobby, I suffer a terrible case of déjà vu. All of this has happened before, I'm sure, and in this way my intuition tells me that life truly is a circle without beginning, middle, or end, and one way or another, it continues to spin as the universe furls and unfurls again.

Evander leads me down the stairs to the long corridor that takes us to the fake office with the vintage-style desk and empty filing cabinet. The window remains open to the warehouse that holds the spaceship from the 1960s. Beside it, there's a door, which was covered with paneling the last time I was here.

He must be taking me to see the spaceship that will one day return me to my life with Andrew.

"Uncle Jimmy said there's something on the spaceship for me," I say. "He must have meant a seat that will take me home."

Evander smiles. "Yes, but he didn't mean the original ship."

He opens the door, and I step into the cold blue light of

the warehouse. An eerie vibration fills my ears, and a strange buzz of energy swirls around me, tickling my skin as it seeps into my body. It's a gentle, lapping buzz, not at all worrisome, one that pushes away my concern and eases me into a state of calm.

"Everything that you can see outside of the observation booth on the opposite wall is the inside of the ship."

I take a slow turn around. The original ship I saw here just a few days ago is gone. What I thought was a warehouse is a surprisingly rounded space. Smooth walls, high ceiling, some kind of construction or mechanism resting in its middle. It's a vast, mostly empty space. "Does everyone at Starbright know this is here?"

"Few humans know about it. Most Jovians do."

Some light across the way catches my eye. It's a glassed-in area with people inside. The observation booth Evander mentioned. I recognize Caroline in her finery speaking to David, who stands beside Dana and John. Someone large stands beside John. Fran? I wave, and he waves back. Dana blows a kiss and John raises one hand. And then a woman enters the room. She's small but stately looking in heels and slacks. A taupe-colored sweater. Something about her seems familiar.

"Is that Nadia?"

Evander raises his head. I sense a touch of sheepishness in his response when he says. "My wife. Yes."

I laugh as I close my eyes and shake my head because this is so much more than I would have expected from my young son. "I'm happy for you," I say, remembering how coyly he acted back in Russia the day I retrieved him from the park, the day he met Nadia. "So I was right. You did fall in love with her."

"I did. You know me very well."

"I do," I say. And then, "I see Caroline in the observation

booth, so they know you're showing me the spaceship? Fran and I are allowed to see their secrets?"

"They want the best for you, Mom. They never meant to harm you. If they knew what it meant to forgive, they would ask for forgiveness."

The low hydraulic whine of an engine powering up vibrates below our feet.

"It's beginning," he tells me.

The center of the room starts to move. It's like a huge gearwheel set in the floor, slowly picking up speed as it spins. Metallic clicking sounds erupt as a giant module rises from this gear in a slow, smooth movement like the monstrous bud of a sunflower pushing up from the ground. It hovers for a moment like a carnival ride before its petals begin to unfurl, opening one by one in continuous, liquid motion. Each of maybe one hundred petals backbends into a horizontal position, and then glides and snaps into place where it hovers just above the floor.

After a moment, the entire flower head has fully bloomed.

"It's beautiful," I say.

"Each capsule in the circle is a life pod. Let me show you."

He takes my hand and leads me to the nearest petal. "This is how we travel," he says.

Long and wide enough for a reclined adult, the pod comes to rounded points at both the top and bottom, and bulges in the middle like the shape of a cat's eye. The inside appears to be soft and padded both on the bottom and partway along the sides. Tubes and wires run along its sleek metal sides. Smooth silver buttons and glowing lights are sprinkled here and there, for no apparent rhyme or reason.

The sound of doors opening around the room startles me, drawing my attention to the perimeter of the ship. From each door a person wearing a white jumpsuit emerges, and the air becomes lively with the tap of footsteps, the shift of material. Women. Men. People of every ethnicity approach the pods in front of them. Young adults, and the middle-aged. One of them is quite old from what I see of their tiny steps and bent-forward stance.

An old woman. *Ida Moore?*

"These people are travelers?" I whisper.

Evander follows my gaze to Ida. "Yes."

"They're going somewhere today?"

"They are."

I scan the area. "Are my parents here?"

"They're already out there, traveling. Have been for a long time."

The travelers don't speak to one another. The way in which they step into the pods tells me they've prepared for this moment. There's no hesitation, no questions asked, no reluctance. They step in, sit down, lie back. Even Ida, who takes longer to reach her pod and then struggles to enter it without falling backward, gets in and lies down without pause. I watch as a metal cover rises from the bottom of each capsule, moving at consistent speed until it closes over the traveler's head, one after the next, until they're all encased.

"And you are going as well," Evander says. He rests his hands on the empty pod in front of us. "This one is yours. It will take care of you the same way an egg cares for an embryo. Nutrition, warmth, comfort, vitals, all will be monitored until you reach your destination."

"I don't understand," I say. "I'm leaving now? But I'm not ready."

He puts a hand on my shoulder and somehow his confidence enters my veins, relaxes the tense muscles in my back and neck. He looks into my eyes. "I would never lie to you. Everything will be fine. There is nothing you need to do. No need to prepare. You've raised me well. I will make you proud, I promise. All you have to do is get in."

I gaze at the pod. The strength of Evander's touch and the ship's strange atmosphere work their calming magic on me, but an undercurrent of worry remains. What will happen to the ordinary humans? I could have stopped the Jovians from making the clones.

"You couldn't have," he tells me. "There was nothing you could have done."

My son has just read my mind; this time I'm sure.

"All you have to do is get in," he says.

But the tubes and wires, the sleek interior of the capsule, still frighten me.

"I don't know if I want to," I say.

"Andrew will be there when you wake up."

Andrew. Yes. Andrew will be there. "I want to be with him," I say. "I have no doubt about that. But I'm scared." Tears blur my vision. I rub my eyes.

"You'll be fine."

"You've traveled like this before?"

"Yes."

"You're sure it will take me to Andrew."

"Just like backstroking through time," he says, with a lightness that's entirely convincing. "You'll get in and sit down. You'll lie back. The pod will manifest, and you'll sleep until you get there."

I have a thousand questions and at least that many worries, but they pass over me like a stream of air passing over a moving vehicle.

"How long will it take?" I say.

"It doesn't matter. It will feel like a night's restful sleep during which you dream of the stars."

"If I asked you to come with me, if I told you I couldn't let you do what you're going to do, would you come?"

As he considers his answer, the placid expression on his face remains. "What you think and feel and know mean more to me than what anyone else in the world thinks and feels and knows. But that's not what you want, Mom. I know you trust me to do the right thing, and I will."

I do trust him. He's my Evander. My child. My son.

"Will you be all right without me?" I say.

"I'm no longer a ten-year-old," he says with a wry smile. "I assure you I can handle it."

He hugs me, and I don't want him to let go. But he does, and he kisses my cheek. "You'll always be my family, and I'll always love you."

I hug him again.

He holds my hand as I climb into the pod.

I sit. I lie back. I don't cry.

Evander stays right there, just outside, just in front of me. His expression is steadfast. This is the way it must be. Our eyes lock in a mutual gaze. Our mother-and-son bond has never been as strong as it is today.

The cover begins to move, first over my feet and then my calves, rising and enclosing, now my chest and then my neck. The last thing I see before it covers my head are Evander's eyes. His beautiful blue-green eyes just like his father's.

And then the lights go out.

25

I'm screaming with such ferocity that I'm worried one of my lungs may burst. But no. The scream ends, and I'm still breathing. Panting. Sweating up and down the sides of my face. Legs trembling as I am let down from . . . *What the hell is happening to me?*

I'm squeezing the life out of a cordless telephone in my hand.

On a carpeted floor, beside a bed.

My bedroom? In Ashbury Falls?

I feel sick to my stomach. . . .

My stomach . . . is a mountain.

Oh God, no. *The baby is coming.*

Evander is coming!

I look at the phone. I can't press the button for Miranda. No way will I call her. I'll give birth by myself right here on the floor before—

Someone calls my name. Whoever it is, is down the hall. A man. It sounded like—footsteps rush into the room. I raise my head and twist to see.

"It's you," I say in between breaths.

At that, Andrew stops short. "What happened? Why are you on the floor? I was only gone for a minute. You already had another one? Holy mackerel, what is that five? How fast are they coming?"

I reach for him like a turtle flipped on her back.

"You're here," I say with a disbelieving squint.

I made it. I made it back to him.

He kneels beside me, takes the phone from my hand. "Of course I'm here. Can you sit up?"

As he reaches for me, I grab him with both hands and breathe him in. His scent makes me dizzy with pleasure—clean cotton sheets, laundry soap, maleness—just the way I recall. Then I remember how forty pounds of pregnancy weight in my middle makes it hard to sit upright.

"Hold me," I say as I gaze into his roundy face and happy-go-lucky eyes. I need to know he's real. I feel as if I'm in shock. And why wouldn't I be? "Hold me, Andrew."

He does his best to wrap his arms around me. I don't care if we sit here on this bedroom floor all day. I close my eyes and say, "This is *amazing*."

"Yeah, I'm sure it does feel amazing when the contraction ends," he says.

My skin tingles in response to his touch. "I love you so much."

He stops and eyes me again. "I love you, too. And this is a nice conversation that we're having, but I think we need to get to the hospital. Can you stand?"

"No, I mean, I *really* love you," I insist.

Andrew supports me on one side, getting under my shoulder and arm, preparing to hoist me to a stand. I suck in my breath and brace myself for movement. My leg muscles feel warm and pliable as if I just ran a mile as fast as I can. I study his face up close. He glances back at me with an unsure expression. "I really love you, too," he says. "Are you a little dizzy or maybe lightheaded?"

I comb my fingers through his light-brown hair and note the muscular young-man body. "How old are you?" I glide my fingers across his jawline.

His eyes widen. "Wow, that last contraction must have been a doozy." His complexion pales. "Maybe you're not getting enough oxygen. Are you breathing okay?"

"I don't know. You might have to give me mouth-to-mouth." I feel giddy happy. "You look to be about twenty-eight."

"Thank you, but you know I'm thirty-one." He pauses as his face sags with worry. "Don't you?"

A year older than the year he died. *Good. That's good.*

"Then I am twenty-six," I say even though I gave birth to Evander when I was twenty-five.

Evander said it would be a different version of my world.

Andrew guides me and my pregnant body to the edge of the bed. I don't remember being this big, but I guess I was.

"I'm serious now," he says, dutiful husband that he is, "are you dizzy?"

"A little, yes." I cradle my belly, which sits like a small igloo over the foundation of my stomach.

"I'm going to grab your bag just hang on." While gripping my shoulder with one hand, he reaches for my backpack on the floor a few feet away with the other. He has to let go of me for a second. "Got it," he says, then secures me again. "We better get going or I'm afraid your daughter may be born in the car."

"Daughter?" I belt out my surprise.

Andrew freezes before he passes me a look of steely-eyed concern.

"Are you serious?" he says. "You've had, like, ten ultrasounds."

I don't know what to say.

"I'm sorry. For a second I forgot . . . what was happening," I mutter because I can't think of anything better.

Andrew breaks into laughter.

I join him. Laughing with Andrew is like having a drink of water after a ten-year drought.

At the same time, the fact that I'm having a girl reminds me that Evander won't be here. Because this is a different version of my world.

Andrew takes my hand. "We'll call her Evan, just like you want to."

"Okay, yes, Evan. I'm happy it's a girl."

I try to sound convincing, but I can't stop the pain from reaching my voice.

"Try not to have her until we get to the hospital, okay?"

He takes my arm and drapes it across his shoulders. "On three, two, one."

I stand. It's easy with Andrew leveraging me up. Without thinking, I say, "Thank God I don't have to call Miranda."

"Who's that? The doula's backup?"

He doesn't know Miranda. There's no Miranda here. Hopefully there are no Jovians at all. Evander said there wouldn't be. "She's just a, uh, friend," I say.

"An imaginary one, maybe." Andrew presses forward with his arm clutching my waist. "I want you monitored by professionals."

We move through the bedroom like a four-legged creature, oddly balanced and struggling every step of the way. He has my backpack in his left hand. Soon the foyer's tiled floor passes under our feet, and when I look up, I can see into the living room. There's no picture of L'Origine on the wall. The eat-in kitchen has a chandelier of stained glass fruits. "Kirksberg," I say under my breath.

"*Kecks*-burg," Andrew says, correcting me as he drops the backpack by the front door. "Is that what you said?"

"Kecksburg, yes." The word feels strange in my mouth because this is a different version of my world.

"I thought you might have mispronounced it. Doesn't matter, I brought the car around. The AC's on full blast, so it should be nice and chilly in there."

I rest my head on his shoulder and breathe him in, his scent rippling in lovely waves over the crown of my head. "My parents will come?"

He opens the front door. I see the rising sun peeking up from the horizon. The sky is a mix of starry night and light peach morning as if the artist who painted it couldn't decide whether she wanted to capture day or night.

"Maria and Oleg flew in from Russia two days ago. You spoke to your mother on the phone last night. Please tell me you remember."

He's talking about my *real* parents. If there are no Jovians, my parents would not be travelers, and if they're not travelers, that means they're what? Spies? Or maybe former spies. Then again, they could just be regular people.

Because this is a different version of my world. Different parents, different town, different child. A world that's safe for *my kind.*

My young husband's brows rise with concern. "They insisted they stay at a hotel. Nod if this sounds familiar."

"Yes, definitely," I say.

"I'll call them and let them know what's happening just as soon as we get to the hospital."

We baby-step our way to the car. Andrew's phone dings, and he pulls it from his pocket, glances at the screen. "James is on his way."

My heart leaps. "Uncle Jimmy?" I say. Not Edmund or

Caroline, but James, the most human Jovian of all. Or, maybe, as I often suspected, he wasn't actually Jovian.

Andrew deflates a little as if tired, losing patience. "My dad."

"Oh, I know," I say, scrambling for an explanation. "The uncle thing is a private joke between us. I never told you?"

He bends to open the car door. "You're full of surprises today." Then he shuffles me around so I drop gently into the seat. "Maybe you did say something about that a while back. Doesn't matter."

Now that I'm in the passenger seat, he squats in front of me and holds one of my hands. "Look, I've taken care of everything, just like we planned. There's nothing to worry about."

"I'm not worried," I say. "I'm just happy you're here."

I touch his face, as my insides swell with gratitude. I do everything in my power not to cry as the pain from my old life rises up and curdles my insides.

"Hey, hey, it's all right," he says, when he sees my distress. "Of course I'm here."

"And you're coming to the hospital?"

"You can't exactly drive yourself. Especially from this side of the car."

My lips quiver into a smile. "It's going to be wonderful, isn't it?"

"I sure hope so."

"I never stopped loving you."

"That is—" His face falls in a moment of confusion. "Good to know. And I have never stopped loving you, if that's what you need to hear right now."

I reach for him and draw him in as best I can with the baby in between us. "We'll raise our children here," I whisper in his ear as I gaze at the house.

"Yes, starting with this one."

"And we'll grow old together."

"That's the plan."

"How many children?"

"As many as you want. As many as we can handle."

"And we'll be happy."

"Yes. But right now we really need to get going."

He nudges me out of our embrace, and I look at him with all the love in my heart bubbling through my veins.

"I thought women were supposed to get cranky when they give birth," he says.

I shake my head. "I'm filled with love for you."

He leans in and kisses my lips. The kind of kiss only Andrew could give, the kind that snaps us right back into place in the universe, our bodies on Earth and our souls in the ether, entwined forever. It's a kiss like no other, like we never parted.

"I'll be by your side the whole time," he says. "We'll do the breathing and the relaxation, and you can squeeze the blood out of my hand and curse and do whatever you have to do. I can take it."

"I'm not afraid," I say.

"Neither am I."

He stands, retrieves my backpack by the front entrance and throws it in the back seat, then carefully closes my door and runs to the other side. He climbs in behind the wheel and pulls his seatbelt across his chest. Then he takes a deep breath. "This is it," he says. "When we get back home, we'll be parents."

"A family," I say, reaching out to hold his hand.

"You better believe it."

He puts the car into drive, and we speed headfirst onto the road. The bright golden rays of the morning light reach out to touch us as we dive into the start of our new life.

ACKNOWLEDGMENTS

I wouldn't change my writing life for anything. But writing and publishing a book can be difficult, to say the least, and I am so grateful to my family and friends for their endless support of my creative ventures.

Joe, Sienna, Dad, Mom, and Jen, your enthusiasm makes it all worthwhile! I want to thank my husband for his help with marketing and my daughter for showing me the ropes on social media.

Thank you to my editor, Tricia LaRochelle. I'm forever appreciative of not only your expertise but your friendship.

To my beta readers—Abigail Burke, Debra Dynes, Katherine Bartis, and John Remington—I admire you for your honesty and good advice, and I absolutely would not have a book without your help.

Thank you, Ron Skelton and Lisa Hopwood, for your sharp eyes.

To the indie community, thank you for your support, advice, reviews, and many laughs. I'm so glad to be a part of the Bookstagram universe.

Most of all, thank you to the readers of my books. I love hearing from you!

And, to the writers of every book I've ever read and loved, thank you for the years of inspiration.

ABOUT THE AUTHOR

Kim Catanzarite remembers looking at the moon through a telescope as a little girl growing up in Ridgewood, New Jersey, and becoming spellbound by the enormity and brightness of the sky. Today, she enjoys watching *Ancient Aliens* and readily admits that she wants to believe. She lives in South Jersey with her husband and daughter.